One Last Night

Lauren Ford lives in Australia with her husband, two children and one overly excitable Sheepadoodle. She has a background in film distribution, acquisitions and script development. When she isn't writing, she can be found reading anything involving romance, patting unsuspecting animals or continuing her quest for the perfect gluten-free bacon and egg roll.

Also by Lauren Ford

Liv Is Not A Loser
One Last Night

One ♥
♥ Last
Night

LAUREN FORD

🔟 CANELO

First published in the United Kingdom in 2025 by

Canelo, an imprint of
Canelo Digital Publishing Limited,
20 Vauxhall Bridge Road,
London SW1V 2SA
United Kingdom

A Penguin Random House Company

The authorised representative in the EEA is Dorling Kindersley Verlag
GmbH. Arnulfstr. 124, 80636 Munich, Germany

A CIP catalogue record for this book is available from the British Library.

Print ISBN 978 1 80436 245 7
Ebook ISBN 978 1 80436 244 0

Cover design by Emily Courdelle

Printed and bound in Great Britain by Clays Ltd, Elcograf S.p.A.

Look for more great books at
www.canelo.co
www.dk.com

I

For my fellow people pleasers. Take the day off.

Chapter One

I've been waiting all day for this moment.

I place my lunch on the bench and drop my shoulders to release the tension they've been carrying all day. The Moreton Bay bug in front of me has been coated in batter and deep-fried to perfection. The crustacean sits on a bed of lettuce in a soft brioche roll and topped with Harrison James's famous secret mayonnaise recipe. The combination is crispy, salty, with a hint of sweetness, and hands-down my favourite thing to eat in the world.

It will be the last one I ever eat, so I take a moment to savour and grieve my loss. No more lightly battered seafood for me. Or for anyone after tonight. At least not from this restaurant. Our chef, Harrison, could bottle and sell this mayonnaise, but in the six years he's worked for our family's seafood restaurant The Shark Biscuit, he's never given away his secret ingredient. Is it a pinch of shichimi? Kaffir lime leaves? Crushed weaver ants? Over the years, I've tried to find out in ways I'm not proud of, but in my defence, I need to know. It's whittled its way into my brain and torments me.

Tonight, I give up. I only want to savour this moment.

The sun throws an orange hue over the calm ocean. A few people are fishing on the end of the jetty, and a couple sit dangling their feet over the edge eating hot chips wrapped in paper. I know, because I served them earlier.

They kiss between eating their chips, and the girl snuggles into her boyfriend's side as they look over the tranquil water.

My ash blonde hair flows in the breeze, so I take one of the many hair ties from my wrist and throw it into a messy bun. I won't allow any distractions as I bite into my roll. My eyes close. A groan of appreciation slips out as I wipe a drop of mayonnaise from the side of my mouth.

'I know I'm good, but I didn't realise I was *that* good.'

To my left, Harrison James leans against a paling from the jetty with a cocky grin as he gestures to my lunch. I have no rebuttal because he knows how good his food is – stupidly good – but I'll never admit that out loud.

His hair is usually shaved short, but he's started to grow it out. The sign that after tonight he won't be working in a kitchen. That thought makes my appetite vanish. I drop my beautiful seafood roll and wipe my hands on a napkin. I thought I'd walked far enough away from the restaurant that I could steal a few moments of peace, but I should have picked a bench much further up the water's edge.

I choose to look at the ocean and not Harrison when I reply. 'You ruined my moment.'

'Considering I created your moment, that's unkind.'

I'm not giving him any compliments. He already heard the groan, so that should be sufficient.

'I'm on my lunch break, Harrison.'

'It's three o'clock. Lunch has been and gone.'

'I didn't get a chance to eat. Today has been mental.'

It felt like every person who's ever visited the restaurant returned this week for one final meal. My dad has been overwhelmed with pride and sadness. He didn't expect this level of support and outcry when he announced the restaurant was closing after forty-three years of service. I'm not surprised. I knew what this place means to the locals. Locals who eat the same thing every time and sit in the same spot in the restaurant. They even know the other customers. Dad built a community with his food. It was the vision he and Mum had for this restaurant when they opened it. Mum would have loved chatting with all the customers this week. After tonight, it will all disappear, and it's my fault. My fingers instinctively find the gold locket hanging from my chain, and I swing it back and forth, trying to calm my thoughts. *Forgive me, Mum.*

'Have they gone?' I peek at Harrison for a split second so I can read his face. He'll know who I'm referring to – the couple who were crying all over Dad. They had their wedding reception at the restaurant and came here nearly every week for take-away. People love Harrison's bug rolls. His seared scallops are a close second.

'Yes. I packaged them up some extra calamari and walked them out. Made sure they left.'

I couldn't handle any more hugs or tears today so I'd taken my bug roll and escaped. I didn't realise Harrison had noticed.

'You're hiding a lot today,' says Harrison.

'Just tired.' *And emotionally drained.*

'Your dad needs to go home and rest before tonight.' *I know.*

'He won't.'

'You need to make him.'

'When have I ever got him to do anything?' My tone is more resigned than sharp, but Harrison still scoffs.

'I'll try and talk to him, but I need you to come inside.'

'I will. Give me five minutes.' My bug roll is now cold, and it's depressing as hell that my last ever bite of this meal has been ruined.

Harrison comes to stand next to the park bench and gazes out to the ocean. 'Storm's coming.'

'It's a beautiful clear sky.' I gesture to the sky with a full arm extension to let him know he's wrong.

'Storm's coming.'

'You need to present new information for the conversation to progress.'

'A storm is *definitely* coming.' Harrison drops his chin and stares down at me. The sun hits his hair and reveals a copper tinge that's usually hidden when it's shorter. It makes his blue eyes stand out, so I look away. I can't handle Harrison or his intense eyes right now.

'Do you always have to be so negative?'

'I'm a realist. And a storm *is* coming. The warnings just came out.' I'd left my phone back at the restaurant because I wanted to concentrate on the view and my food – no doom scrolling. I needed some zero-interactions-with-humans time to recharge before all the required talking and conversing with customers tonight. Most are lovely, but it still drains me.

'It will blow over. They always do.' I'm tired of this day and this conversation.

'We should close early. That would get your dad to go home at least.'

I glare up at him because I can't believe he's serious. 'On our last night? You want to tell my dad that news?'

Harrison runs his hands over his face in frustration. His forearms are out on display. I focus on the rolled cuffs of his black long-sleeved T-shirt instead. They're mocking me because after thousands of requests, he still refuses to wear white in the kitchen. It's a standard uniform for chefs. But not Harrison James. He wears whatever bloody colour he

4

wants, and it drives me batty. Although, his decision to wear black might be appropriate for our last night.

'No, I don't. But we need to get sandbags at least.' Harrison raises his hands in surrender. 'Just as a precaution.'

'I'll support the sandbags. But don't mention the storm to Dad. I don't want to worry him.'

Harrison takes a few steps away but then swivels back.

'Are you okay?' It's no more than a whisper. He's not looking in my direction, so I turn to see if someone has appeared behind me. I lift a finger and point it at my chest.

'Me? Am *I* okay?'

Harrison gives me his full attention, and his eyes zero in on me before he answers.

'Yes, you. The only other person here. I'm not talking to myself,' Harrison snaps at me, and the world feels normal again.

'Why would I not be okay?'

Harrison folds his arms over his chest and gives me the steely look I'm used to seeing. It's typically well into a shift before I'm gifted with Harrison's version of stink-eye.

'Because I thought you might be having some feelings about your family's restaurant shutting down tonight. But maybe it isn't affecting you at all.' Harrison drops his hands and takes a step closer. Invading my personal space, I have to look up to keep my eyes on him. 'Or are you keeping your head in the sand about this as well as the storm?'

Harrison and I trade glares as the silence lingers. It's a game of chicken. Who'll arc up the most? Who'll stay calm? Tonight, I'm going with calm.

'I'm fine. Thank you for your concern.' I plaster a purposely fake smile on my face, but Harrison doesn't take the bait. His jaw ticks back and forth like he's arranging the words in his mouth and deciding which ones he'll allow out.

He shakes his head only slightly before he abruptly turns. He throws over his shoulder, 'I'm okay too, Agnes. Thanks for checking.'

Well played. He gets to walk away, leaving me feeling guilty, but how was I to know we're suddenly checking in with each other about our feelings? He can't change the rules on our final night together without giving me a heads-up. Seven hours to go. Seven hours and I'm free of this restaurant. Free of all the guilt I'm carrying and free of Harrison James.

A cool breeze hits my face as a dark cloud appears in the distance.

Shit. A storm *is* coming.

—

The restaurant is quiet now the lunch customers have left, and we have a few hours before the rush of dinner service. Customers are still placing orders at the take-away counter, but most of the restaurant is quiet. I walk around the tables, checking the place settings and straightening chairs. Neither job needs attending, but I like it when the restaurant is quiet.

I take a moment to try and pull a memory of Mum in the restaurant. I picture her wavy hair up in a clip as she'd carefully place the cutlery on the tables, just as I learnt to do after she passed. She's been gone so long now that I can't work out if I remember her smiling as she looked out onto the ocean or if I've created the memory in my head. Either way, I relish feeling close to her, even for a few minutes.

I can hear the rhythmic tapping of a knife slicing through food coming from the kitchen. That sound has been a constant since my childhood and I wonder if I'll miss it tomorrow, knowing I'll never hear it the same way again. It doesn't have the same sharpness when Dad cooks at home. The stainless-steel countertops throw a sound that won't be repeated again for me.

There's also a relief that releases a lightness over my entire body that I won't hear that noise again. I've hidden that emotion. Never told a soul. The sound continues, and I realise while it's calming, it also hits my head in a way that makes me want to run. How can a sound make me feel so conflicted?

I walk onto the deck and hear the hardwood beams creak under my feet. The deck extension has aged rapidly over the past few years, and the skillion roof has visible water damage. Most people don't notice since the view over the ocean is magnificent and holds their attention. I take a moment to admire the view and try to experience it as our customers would, but it's useless. I feel the same way I have for years about this place; a gnawing need to escape.

I pull down a few of the shutters since the wind has picked up. The shutters need replacing and won't keep the rain out if it starts pouring. We'll have to move people to the inside tables – future Agnes's problem. I tilt the shutters to stop the breeze and hope the rain doesn't start until after dinner service.

As I come back inside, Scout Bray leans against the bar at the side of the restaurant, wiping down the counter as she studies me. She claimed the bar area after her first two shifts when she secretly admitted that she hated seafood and loved cocktails, so her time was best spent behind the bar.

'Are you crying yet?' asks Scout as I join her at the bar.

'No.'

'That's a shame.' Scout grins, so I know she's joking.

'You'd prefer I was crying?'

She leans in and pretends to whisper, 'I'm not meant to tell you, but there's a kitty going.'

'About me crying?'

'Everyone has to guess at what time you'll cry tonight.'

'Delightful. What time did you put down?'

'I wouldn't partake in something so awful.' Scout continues to clean the same spot on the counter as she gives me a cheeky smirk. Her razor-straight hair is the prettiest rose gold colour and sits perfectly in line with her jaw. It was brighter a few weeks ago but has faded to a lighter hue. It will probably be another colour next week. I know the pattern now. The brightest shade until it fades away, and I miss the vibrant colour but fall in love with the softer shade until she turns up with the next colour. Never the same shade twice. We should have started a kitty about her next hair colour. I could have won that.

'If you tell me, I could help you out.' That makes her eyebrows jump up her forehead.

'You're secretly evil, Aggie, you know that.' A devilish smile creeps across Scout's face, and that expression is one of my favourite things about her.

'What's the kitty now?'

'Seven dollars,' says Scout and gives me a pitiful shrug.

'My tears are only worth seven dollars?!' I throw my hands in the air to show my disbelief. We had a kitty once to guess how many oysters we could secretly hide in our apprentice chef Noah's pockets before he noticed, and it got up to eighty-nine dollars.

'Everyone's kind of broke, and not everyone's found new jobs, so...'

Scout doesn't need to finish that sentence for it to bring the reality of the night back into focus. I should be crying all night for what I'm doing to these people. No one would be worried if I had taken over the business. I can clearly remember the night Dad presented me with the keys to the restaurant. It was symbolic because I already had multiple keys to every door. Dad was gifting me The Shark Biscuit. It was the hardest thing I've ever done and the closest I've come to being honest with Dad about this place, but I slowly pushed the keys back across the table. If I had said yes, the doors would have stayed open, and business would have continued as usual. I avoid Scout's eyeline so she can't read the devastation on my face.

'What if I don't cry at all?' The truth is I will hold off as long as I can and cry in the shower or on my pillow when I get home.

'Harrison wins.' No way. I can't let that happen. It irks me that Harrison knew precisely how I'd react tonight. I don't care about the measly seven dollars. I don't want him to know he's right.

'Well, he won't. I'm sure the tears will come later tonight.'

'About eight-fifteen would be perfect.' Scout winks at me before she disappears into the kitchen.

—

I find Dad sitting in the kitchen amongst the chaos of the staff. He's not prepping or checking over everyone's

9

shoulder as usual; instead, he's simply watching the staff work. Dad looks like someone sitting on the beach, watching each wave roll in. His eyes move to observe Harrison directing orders as he usually does. Dad hasn't noticed me yet, so I walk over and wrap my arms around him from behind. I should be helping, and I will do so in a minute. Right now, I need to hug Dad because I know tonight is hard for him.

The kitchen hasn't changed much since Mum and Dad opened the restaurant over four decades ago. Things have been upgraded and replaced, but it's still the mum and pop small kitchen set-up it's always been. Harrison requested we upgrade the fryers when he started, but that was probably more from a health and safety aspect. Dad believed in quality food, a limited menu and friendly staff. It's how it's always been done at The Shark Biscuit.

I never thought Harrison would take the position here once Dad gave him a tour of the kitchen. I thought it would be too small, too casual and certainly not fancy enough for the reputation Harrison's cooking had in the industry.

It's an assembly line kitchen set-up that has Harrison in the centre. He's across every meal, every move the staff make, and nothing gets past him. Nothing gets past me either, which is the only thing we have in common.

'You don't want to make chilli prawns for old times' sake?'

Dad hugs my arms and holds them over his chest.

'Not tonight. I'm just taking it all in. It's amazing to watch. Harrison has done a brilliant job.'

'You taught him everything he knows.'

Dad shakes his head. 'Not even close.'

I lean in further to whisper, 'Dad, you're not going to like me saying this, but you need to go home and rest for a few hours.'

'I'm okay, love. I can rest tomorrow.' He pats my arm in an attempt to end the conversation.

The side door of the kitchen flies open and bangs against the wall. Everyone in the kitchen jumps at the loud thud. The stopper needed replacing months ago, but no one got around to it. When I eventually remembered, it was no longer important since we were shutting down.

Harrison's eyes scowl in Noah's direction, but he's oblivious to Harrison's annoyance. He bounces over to Harrison's side but sees Dad and me first and waves.

Noah's well over six feet tall and probably weighs less than my right leg. He's a tall, lean, human version of a golden retriever. I was shocked when Harrison agreed to hire him as an apprentice. While Noah spends all day smiling while he cuts endless onions, Harrison rarely smiles. I wasn't sure he had teeth until he sneezed one day. They're an odd pairing, but somehow it works between them.

I wave back to Noah because he's a friendly kid. I say kid because he's only in his early twenties, and he makes me feel old every time we talk. Dad and Harrison have been helping him get another job after tonight, which eases the acid reflux of guilt swirling in my oesophagus.

'I could only get twenty sandbags.' Noah's voice is loud as he talks to Harrison. They're the same height, but Harrison is more than double his size. Noah has never seemed intimidated by Harrison, which is why I've always had a soft spot for the friendly fella.

'We're going to need more,' says Harrison.

'All gone at the three depots I tried.'

Harrison scans the room, and I know he's looking for me. His eyes always take on a special glint when Harrison James is about to annoy, taunt, frustrate or simply ask me a question. He finds me in the corner and cocks his head to the side as a gesture for me to join them.

'I'll be right back, Dad.' I slip past the staff prepping and stand beside Noah, so he's between Harrison and me.

'We need more sandbags,' says Harrison as he crosses his arms. His black sleeves are pushed past his elbows now, which is a sign that Harrison's stressed.

'I'll check online to see if I can find any, but we're up high enough. I'm sure it will be fine.'

'Agnes.'

'*Harrison.*' I try to match his tone but make it sound more annoying.

'The back isn't up high, and the bathroom floods nearly every time it rains.'

'We'll survive the storm. We always do.' I turn my focus to Noah. 'Thank you for grabbing those bags. I know that's not part of your job.'

'Happy to help. Maybe we could shovel sand from the beach up here.' You can tell Noah loves his suggestion and bless his cotton socks.

Harrison shakes his head before replying. 'That would only wash away.' Harrison says it slowly, like he's not sure Noah will understand him. 'The bag part is crucial.'

'Of course.' Noah chuckles as his bad idea washes off him like unbagged sand. 'We can mop it out like last time.'

'Hopefully, the storm blows over.'

'It's not going to blow over.' Harrison snips at me, and I'm not fighting with him about this. Weather people are wrong all the time.

Noah is nonplussed by Harrison's snippiness as he takes out his phone and taps away. 'I'll post a snap and see if anyone knows where to get more.'

Harrison likes this suggestion, and Noah gets a rare sighting of one or maybe two of Harrison's teeth as his lip moves ever so slightly upwards. 'Good idea. You can duck out any time if you hear of where to go.'

'We need him here. I can get them.'

'Noah can get them. This is my space and my call. Yours is out there.' Harrison gestures to the dining room, and I'm wondering if I could fire him on the last day. I should wait until after he's cooked tonight and then fire him. Dad won't back me up, but it would be a fun parting gift.

'I can see the evil plans ticking away in your head. You basically have a whiteboard on your forehead.'

'You're wrong. I was thinking about sleeping in tomorrow morning. Nothing about you.'

'I. Don't. Believe. You.'

'I don't need you to believe me.' My grin is fake, and I try to make it sinister.

Noah pops his head between us. 'Do you guys still need me here or should I get going on entrées?'

Harrison and I both snap our attention to Noah. His question is innocent, but it's enough for Harrison and me to lay down our guns.

'You can go, but let me know about the snappy thing,' says Harrison as he waves Noah off.

'Snapchat, old man.'

'You giving lessons on being cool, Agnes? We're both in our thirties.'

'I'm only just, thank you very much. Unlike you – you're nearly halfway to forty. Do you know how old—'

'You both ready to do the thing?' I hadn't heard Dad walk over until he slapped Harrison on the back. I get a gentle arm squeeze with his other hand. Harrison and I both let our conversation float away. It was no doubt as useless as most of our discussions.

'Ready when you are,' says Harrison as he peels his eyes off me to answer Dad. 'Noah's got some sandbags. We'll need more, though.'

Dad circles his wrist to flick Harrison's comment away. 'Pfft, you won't need them. Those meteorology people always get it wrong.'

'Like father, like daughter,' Harrison mumbles, but I hear him clearly. He turns to address Dad, who missed his last comment. 'I'd like to be prepared still. Noah can pick you up when he goes out again to get more, so you can have a few drinks tonight.' Harrison's eyes flick to me, and I can somehow read his thoughts. This is how we're going to get Dad to rest.

'Are you two conspiring together?' Dad throws his thumb in my direction. 'This one's trying to get me to go home too. Has there been a ceasefire I didn't know about?'

'Why stop on the last night of the battle?' Harrison and Dad laugh after his remark. After a beat, I join in, but I make sure it's my most evil laugh. Harrison knows it, too.

'I want to be here in time to have a drink with the Whalleys,' says Dad, which means he's softening to the idea.

'We'll take care of them and you'll be back with plenty of time for a drink,' I say and Harrison nods in agreement.

'Okay, you two win. Let's do the thing with the staff, and I'll duck home. I want to be back early, though.'

Harrison and I both agree, and I try to hide my relief.

'Take a seat, Dad, and I'll gather everyone.'

I'm thankful we convinced Dad to take a break. He'd be in too much pain tomorrow if he stayed all day and night. Harrison discreetly dips his chin in my direction to acknowledge our little win and that he's happy with the outcome, too. The way Harrison cares for Dad is his one redeeming feature. His only one.

Chapter Two

Over the last week, Dad has made sure he's spent time with each staff member to say goodbye and check if they've found employment elsewhere. Each conversation lasted longer than he intended, but that's Dad's favourite thing – having a chat. I worry about who he'll chat with next week when the doors of The Shark Biscuit have closed permanently. He needs to rest his body, not his mind. Another reason the guilt has permanently wedged itself under my rib cage and gives me a sharp poke in the side when I worry about what the future holds for Dad.

I haven't asked Harrison where he's going; I couldn't bring myself to ask. I figured I would hear in passing, but I've heard nothing about his plans after tonight. The thought crosses my mind that he might move away. He would have job offers, no doubt. A big restaurant in the city would snap him up in a crab's claw, but it doesn't seem like Harrison's style. I can't imagine him not being the boss and wearing the chef's whites I've never managed to get him to wear.

'We're a fish restaurant. No formalities required.' Harrison barked at me when I formally requested he wear his whites.

'Do fish not deserve the same respect as beef?'

'It's not about respect, it's about level of comfort. Fish are more approachable.'

'That makes no sense.'

'To me it does, and I don't like wearing white when I cook.'

That was the end of that conversation, but we continued fighting about it for six years. Dad never got involved. As long as the customers were delighted with Harrison's food, Dad was happy to let him wear whatever he wanted. Personally, I think he did it just to annoy me. If I'd suggested he wear anything but white he'd be in it every day. I could have let it go, but Harrison and I never let anything go. It's more important to win. Or to annoy the other person. I always win at annoying Harrison James.

'Everyone's ready now,' I say, and Dad gives me the saddest smile that I know took all his effort. His eyes crinkle at the sides in a more permanent way these days. He would be exhausted and in pain but try to cover it with his fake grin. It doesn't fool me. He's devastated that tonight is the last night. He's cranky at getting old and frustrated his body is falling apart, but he still sits there with that half-lopsided smile shining up at me. That expression is why I don't regret the last six years, but it will haunt me after tonight.

Dad stands gingerly as he can't straighten fully anymore. His shoulders slouch forward, with the curve of his back hunched over. He wasn't meant to get this illness. I suppose no one ever is, but he didn't have any warning signs. Dad simply missed a step leaving the restaurant one night and slid awkwardly down the back stairs. The pain was constant for months afterwards. After tests were run, he was diagnosed with osteoporosis. We got second opinions because it didn't feel like a condition suited to him. Second opinions gathered the same result. The doctor said it could have been caused by his excessive smoking, something he quit when I was born, or obesity, which came after I was born. Dad instantly disliked the doctor for both assessments, but the diagnosis did not change.

Dad was always large in stature and solid in frame, but he's considerably shorter now. I can look him in the eye these days when we stand next to each other. I can clearly see his face when he's in pain and trying to hide it. Like right now.

'Let's make it quick. You've already said a lot of your goodbyes.'

Dad nods, relenting. I know he's in real pain when he gives in.

'I'll miss it all, Aggie,' says Dad, taking a long, slow look around the kitchen. Gut punch. That hurt. I avoid looking at him because I'll cry, and Scout won't win her seven dollars. Dad loops his arm over my shoulders and pulls me into his side. He kisses the side of my head when I don't look up at him. 'We'll miss it, but it's time to say goodbye.'

Now it's my turn to nod and hope that's enough of an answer. The truth is I won't miss it. I'm the only one who feels that way, so I'll keep that to myself.

Dad moseys to the front of the kitchen where all the employees working tonight have gathered. We planned a smaller staff for our final night, but we're booked out. It's mostly our regulars who are coming to say goodbye to The Shark Biscuit.

I find a spot next to Scout near the doorway, and she secretly tries to pass me a tissue, but I bat it away.

'Not until eight-fifteen,' I say.

'I'll give you a two-minute warning or pinch you really hard.'

'I'm sure that's against the rules.'

'It's the last night, who cares about rules.' I don't think Scout has ever cared about rules. I hide my laugh behind my hand as Dad addresses the group.

'I'll keep it short because you're probably sick of hearing my voice by now.' Dad rearranges his feet, shuffling to the side a little. On the other side of the kitchen, Harrison leans against the bench. He must notice Dad's uneasy on his feet because he takes a step forward but then stalls when Dad recovers. I'm not sure anyone else would have noticed, but it seems he's watching Dad as closely as I am.

Harrison glances across the room and his eyes scrutinise my face like they're looking for something, but I'm not sure what that could be. He shakes his head a fraction before turning back to listen to Dad.

'You've all been an integral part of the success of this place. I appreciate all your hard work, your professionalism when you were tired or the customers were rude, and the way you always worked as a team.'

Dad shifts again. He's been on his feet all day, and I don't think he has much left in him.

'I know most of you know this, but I'm telling you again because I'm the boss, and I'm old, so indulge me. The Shark Biscuit was my late wife Beatrice's – Birdie to those who knew her well – idea. It was only us at the start. We learnt as we went but Birdie was smart. Beautiful and smart, just like her daughter.'

A few of the staff turn and regard me with affection. Some of their stares linger, and I know now that they're looking for tears. I rub my tongue on the top of my mouth because I read somewhere that it stops you from crying. All it's doing is making my tongue sore, but at least I'm not sobbing in front of everyone. All tears will be held back. None have been given permission to be released.

'I knew Birdie could make this place a success. She was better with the customers than me, so I stayed in the back cooking. It wasn't until Aggie arrived that we hired our first employee and look at it now.' Dad lifts his hands and genuinely seems in awe of the business he and Mum built.

He loves telling this story. I know it off by heart, but that's okay. I love hearing it. He doesn't talk about Mum often because I think it makes him too sad.

'Aggie, could you please come here.' Dad points to me across the group and gestures for me to come forward like I've been selected from the crowd at a game show. I keep my head down as I weave through the employees. Dad wraps one arm around me and pulls me tight against his side.

'I want to thank my daughter, who you all know, but this place wouldn't have stayed open all these years without her help. She was practically raised amongst the walls of this restaurant.' Not practically, I was. 'It's in her blood, and it's been a gift to work with her. It wasn't the same when she went off to university, but it wasn't long until she came back to us.' That's not an accurate retelling of what happened, but I'd never interrupt Dad. 'Thank you for loving this place as much as I've loved it and always caring for everyone who's stepped foot into the restaurant. That's what my little Aggie does, she takes care of people.' Dad tugs me closer, and I wrap my arms around him for a hug.

I whisper into his ear, 'I love you, Dad.' He kisses me on the side of my head before addressing the group again. He keeps me tight against his side. I think it might be helping him stay standing.

'And to Harrison. Come up here, too.' Dad waves his free hand to Harrison. He ducks his head as he comes to stand next to Dad.

'Six years ago, when my health went to shit, this one here,' Dad pats Harrison on the back and leaves his hand to rest there, 'helped us keep the business open. We didn't think we could, but he walked through that door and made this kitchen his own.'

Harrison glances back at Dad, his expression neutral. Then, slowly, a smile finds its way to the surface of Harrison's face. It must have been buried deep, but it fought its way out.

'Thank you to these two for giving The Shark Biscuit a second life. I couldn't have done any of this without you both. They're a bloody great team.' Dad pats and hugs us both again.

I angle my head towards Dad so my eye roll is only visible to Harrison. He snorts a half-laugh half-scoff, and I understand its meaning perfectly.

'The only thing I couldn't get these two to do was agree on anything. Like a bull and a mule these two. At least it was entertaining.' Dad lets out a loud chuckle, and the employees all join in. I catch Harrison sneering across the group. He doesn't seem to appreciate everyone laughing at this any more than I do.

'All right.' Dad brings the group's focus back to him. 'Let's enjoy our last night. To The Shark Biscuit!' Dad raises his hand and pretends to hold a drink to cheer as everyone repeats, '*To The Shark Biscuit.*'

Dad takes a step away but stumbles just as Harrison grabs his arm. Harrison turns it into a handshake and claps Dad on the arm with his other hand. He guides him over to the bench so Dad can lean on it, and no one in the room is aware of Dad's mishap.

'While you're all here, I wanted to give you a small gift.' I pull a basket from the counter and pass it to Noah. 'Everyone take one and pass it on.'

Noah holds up the silver keychain in his fingers. It's a surfboard with a shark bite taken out. It has the words *Shark Biscuit* engraved on the back.

'It's only a small token, but I hope you remember us and how much we loved having you work here with us. This place is very special to a lot of people, especially my family, so thank you for all your hard work. We appreciate it, and we're sorry it's coming to an end, but we're glad we could have one more night with you all.'

Still no tears, but it's only because I'm numb now. The dinner rush will start soon, and then it'll finally be done. No more Shark Biscuit, and I can't wait. Six hours to go.

–

The staff disperse as a few customers arrive for an early dinner. Most have young children and will be gone in forty-five minutes.

Dad lingers in the kitchen, still talking to Harrison, but waves to me as he opens the side door. They shake hands, and Harrison moves closer to say something. Dad pulls back and looks over to me. He has a contemplative expression on his face. I'm not sure what they could be discussing, but it's sent Dad's mind into overdrive. Dad mumbles something to Harrison, shakes his hand again and leaves.

Harrison gazes out the door. I'm unsure if he's watching Dad or deep in thought. He folds his fingers around the back of his head and then lets them drop in what seems to be frustration. Maybe they were talking about the weather again? I'm not sure, but from the way Harrison stomps back to his area and starts barking orders at Noah, I might leave him alone. On second thoughts, it might be a perfect time to annoy him and find out what they were discussing.

Noah already looks like he needs a break from Harrison's directions, so I position myself between the two of them with my back to Harrison. I hear his gruff exhale, but I ignore him.

'Scout offered to get some sandbags if you're too busy,' I say to Noah, but he's in a trance, slicing bacon, and only peeks at me for a second.

'Happy to do whatever you guys tell me to do.' Noah knows how to walk the tightrope between Harrison and me.

'Don't distract the kid, Agnes, he'll cut off a finger.' I ignore Harrison's voice that has rudely joined our conversation.

'Thanks, I'll let you know.'

'Not a problem. Just let me know when I can pick up Ernie.'

'You're behind, and no more talking.' Noah jumps at the sound of Harrison's voice and scampers off. Harrison didn't yell or raise his voice, but there's an authoritarian edge that gets people to pay attention.

When I can't avoid it any longer, I swing around to face Harrison. I figured his head would be down working, but he's upright with his arms crossed, and I almost bump into him.

'Stop distracting the employees. *Please.*'

'He's my employee, and I was not distracting him.'

23

'This is my area, and you're a distraction.'

'It's the last night, Harrison, why don't you take a breath.' I turn away because Harrison's too intense for me right now.

'Why don't you start acting like it's the last night!' Harrison picks up his favourite knife and starts chopping tomatoes like he's taking revenge out on them.

I lean over and whisper to him because I know the staff enjoy watching our usual sparring matches and I don't want them to overhear.

'What's that supposed to mean?'

'You're like a robot, Agnes.' He spits my name out like it's acid. His head stays down while he cuts the life and breath out of those tomatoes. His skills are impressive, but he doesn't need to know that.

I don't want to discuss tonight, so instead, I ask something I've always wondered. 'You know, you're the only one who calls me by my full name. Why is that?'

'Nice change of subject, but I'll bite.' He puts down the knife and spins towards me. 'Your name is Agnes.'

'I'm aware.'

'What's the problem then? Am I getting in trouble right now for calling you by your name? Maybe your dad was right. You are a mule.'

'I am the bull. I am not a mule.'

'I don't know how that's better, but let's move on from that ridiculous analogy.'

I take a calming breath, and usually, this is when I'd choose to walk away from Harrison and how he loves to twist me in knots, but tonight I'm staying to fight. Tonight, I've got nothing better to do but fight one last time with Harrison James.

'I was trying to say that you're the only one who calls me Agnes. To everyone else, I'm Aggie, but you choose to call me Agnes, and I think you do it on purpose.'

Harrison leans in and having his cerulean eyes so close makes me nervous.

'For the first time in a long while, you might be right. It *is* on purpose.' Harrison leans in even further and it makes my pulse race. He's gaining the upper hand and I don't like it. He mock whispers, 'When I want to get your attention, I use your name. Groundbreaking.'

'You could call me Aggie.'

He leans back and shakes his head. 'No.'

'Why? Everyone else does.'

'I don't care what everyone else does. You should know that by now.'

'You love riling me up. I think it's your secret guilty pleasure.'

'Not secret and not guilty. Just my pleasure.'

I throw my hands in the air and slap one on the counter. A young waiter notices, and now I think I might actually be the mule. I involuntarily raise my voice as I step into Harrison's personal space. 'You are infuriating, you know that, right?'

Harrison taps on the sign above his workspace. It's black with white writing, and all it says is: No Yelling.

It was sometime last year when he turned up to work with the sign. No explanation. There was no staff meeting to explain, but yelling was banned in the kitchen. I'm not a yeller, nor is Dad, so it's never been an issue, but it quickly became known with the staff that no raised voices would be tolerated in Harrison James's kitchen.

He leaves his hand on the sign and smirks in a way that enrages me. I hate it when he taps his sign. It makes me want to take up yelling as a sport.

I take a moment to compose myself. My back is turned away from the kitchen, so the staff can't hear me.

'When have I ever yelled at you or anyone ever?'

Harrison contemplates the question before breathing out, 'Never.' At least he's honest.

'And yet you continually tap your little sign the second I get even remotely worked up.' I whack the stupid sign to bring home the point. The kitchen staff definitely saw me do that.

'Just reminding you.' Harrison winks, making me want to pull every single eyelash from his insanely pretty eyes.

'You are the most infuriating person I have ever met. Tonight might be the night I finally let it all out and yell at you.' I cross my arms, feeling very smug about my empty threat.

'No, you won't.' Harrison resumes chopping tomatoes but with less vigour now. The steam from his engine is tapering out.

'And how do you know that?'

'Because I know you.' He says it matter-of-factly, and I don't know how to respond. 'Think of it this way: only one last night, and you'll never see me tap that sign again.' It should make me feel relieved, but something about the finite nature of his statement gives me that pain under my ribs again. 'I have to get a few more in before the night is out.'

'I might rip the sign down and sauté it with your scallops.'

'That would never work. That's why you're not a chef. Listen, it's been great chatting, but I have a restaurant full of people to cook for, and you have to,' Harrison flicks his wrist in a circle towards me, 'do whatever it is you do.'

He's a little shit because he knows what I do. I run this damn restaurant, and there'd be no food or people for him to cook for without me. Harrison grins widely, and it's as fraudulent as a crumbed crab stick. He shoos me away with another flick of his wrist, which might be more annoying than tapping his sign. Deep breaths. One. Two. Three.

I finish my third breath, and I realise Harrison is watching me. He often watches me take my calming breaths, which is ironic since he's the one who causes them.

'Why are you staring?' I ask.

'Does that work?'

'Breathing? Yep, it works. Do it daily.'

Harrison rolls his eyes. 'I mean the I'm-going-to-excise-every-demon-from-my-body breathing you always do around me. Does it work?'

'Every time.' I plaster a wide, teeth-baring smile and walk proudly away.

The stronger person walks away. The weaker person watches as I swish my hips for effect. In the fury of sparring with Harrison, I forgot to ask what he and Dad were discussing. I'm sure he wouldn't have told me anyway.

I take two steps away before I forget why I came into the kitchen in the first place. I twist around and throw Harrison's keepsake on the counter. It's a brilliant power move.

'Happy last night at The Shark Biscuit.'

Harrison studies the keychain on the counter as he wipes his hands on a towel. He picks up the keychain and flips it over in his fingers.

He examines it with an unsettling intensity. His mood has changed from the playful, infuriating Harrison to the quiet, withdrawn Harrison in seconds.

He tucks the key chain in his pocket and doesn't look at me when he replies. 'Happy last night, Agnes.'

Five and a half hours to go.

Chapter Three

The first wave of dinner customers arrive at the same time the rain decides to grace us with its presence. It's only lightly raining, but it's the kind of steady rain that won't pass over in an hour. I'm waiting for Harrison to give me an *I told you so* about the storm, but he's said nothing so far. Perhaps he's waiting to see how bad the storm is before he gloats. In my defence, weather people are forever wrong, and it's the last thing I wanted to deal with today.

I check off our booking system as the door flies open. Mr Whalley holds open the door as he shakes his umbrella outside before placing it carefully next to the door. He's wearing the clothing of a golfer: dress shorts with a belt and a polo shirt tucked in. It's his usual outfit, matched with socks and leather shoes. I'm guessing he was in sports shoes and swapped them out for his dinner reservation tonight. He continues to hold the door open until Mrs Whalley prances in with a raincoat over her head. The rain hasn't touched her short, perfectly styled hair. She passes the raincoat to her husband as she notices me and gifts me with the warmest smile that makes her eyes sparkle. Her make-up is impeccable with beautiful red lips. I guess she's in her seventies but has always seemed much younger.

'Aggie, we made it.' She approaches me with open arms, and I greet her with a hug. Mr Whalley waves when I glance over her shoulder; he's not the hugger in the relationship. He's kind, though. My favourite customers – Dad's, too – and they've only ever been Mr and Mrs Whalley to all the staff. I'm sure they'd be fine with us calling them by their first names – Dot and Scott – but there's also something special about them being Mr and Mrs Whalley. They're a beautiful package deal.

'What a terrible night for this weather,' says Mrs Whalley as we step apart. 'Is your dad disappointed? I was hoping we'd have a clear view of the ocean for our last meal.' *Me too.*

'He's at home resting but will be back soon.'

'That's a good idea.'

'You know Dad, he'll make the best of this situation. He's only interested in talking to everyone anyway.'

The affection Mrs Whalley has for Dad fills her face. 'That is absolutely your dad. You must be sad it's all ending too?'

Her enquiry is kind-natured, but I'm going to try to side-step that question.

'We're all sad, but it's time. Let me show you to your table.'

Mr and Mrs Whalley are our VIPs tonight, so I sit them at the best table on the deck area. It's covered, so they aren't getting wet yet. If the angle of the rain shifts or the ferocity picks up, that might change. For now, they're in their favourite spot.

'I'll be right back. Harrison wanted to come and say hello, so I'll grab him.'

'Only if he's not busy,' says Mr Whalley, but he knows Harrison will make time for our most loyal customers.

Scout's in her element, mixing cocktails as I slip through the restaurant. I swing open the door to the kitchen, lean in and search for Harrison. He's deep in conversation with the kitchen staff, but he looks up when notices me watching. I mouth *The Whalleys*, and he ducks his head to say something to the staff before walking over to me.

'After you.' I gesture for him to walk first as I hold the door open for him.

'How kind of you, *Agnes*.' Harrison emphasises my name to be a smart-arse, but I don't acknowledge his terrible attempt to annoy me. We walk through the restaurant, which is nearly half-full now.

My fingers curve around my gold locket and move it back and forth on my chain. I hold it firmly in my hand as I continue to jostle it left and right. Harrison's eyes follow the movement.

'You've worn that every day I've known you. Do you ever take it off?' I thought he would have had a dig about the storm, so his question catches me off-guard.

'No.'

'Even to shower?' Harrison whispers out the side of his mouth.

'You asking about my shower habits seems a little intrusive even for you.' I smile at a customer who notices us walking past.

Harrison scoffs at my comeback. 'I figure I have one night to ask all the lingering questions about Agnes Keegan before the night is over. Like, why does she wear the same damn locket every single day?'

'You know it would be so easy for me to never tell you.' I glance at Harrison quickly as he gives me a side-eye.

'Then I'll assume it's a police tracking device or you're in some kind of cult.'

We're almost at the Whalleys' table, so I throw Harrison a bone. 'It was my mum's. Mine now.' That small amount of information should tell him how important it is to me. He's lucky I shared that much with him. Harrison dips his chin as his gaze lingers on the locket.

'Any other questions before this place closes and I disappear from your life?'

For some reason, that gets him to stop in his tracks. I go over the words I said because I'm not sure what made him halt. Harrison studies me intently, and it makes me peer down at my clothes. I would assume I have a mayo stain down my shirt that no one wants to mention, but I'm clean.

'What just happened?' My voice is soft when I ask.

'Nothing.' Harrison walks ahead without a glance back. He's so damn infuriating. Even the back of him walking away is annoying me.

We step out onto the deck and Harrison greets the Whalleys with affection, which very few customers receive. Harrison is always professional and polite, but I can tell he genuinely likes these two.

'Thank you for coming in even with the storm.' Harrison's eyes flick to mine when he says storm, but I look away.

'We wouldn't be anywhere else.' Mrs Whalley taps Harrison's hand gently, and he doesn't pull away. This couple might be his favourite people in the world. 'I hope Ernie can make it in. We'd love to have one last drink with him.'

'One of the young ones is going to get him a little later,' says Harrison. I would like to mock him for using the term *young ones*, but it's not an appropriate time.

'And what's next for you, Chef? Where can we find you come next week?' asks Mr Whalley. Finally, the information I've been wanting and I don't have to ask.

Harrison hesitates for a second as it seems he doesn't know how to reply.

'That's still up in the air.'

'Weighing up all your offers,' says Mrs Whalley and Harrison only responds with a half-head nod. The focus turns to me as she asks, 'And you, Agnes? Where are you off to?'

I step forward, my arm brushing against Harrison, but he doesn't move. 'I'll start applying for jobs once everything is finished up here.'

'Back to accounting?' asks Mr Whalley. They're incredibly kind people because back to accounting is a positive way to spin it. I have a degree in accounting and a résumé filled with restaurant experience. I'll be starting at the bottom, but I long for the days when I can sit my backside in a chair and stare at boring spreadsheets for eight hours. I won't need to greet or have small talk with any customers and that relief swirls again in my belly. I don't know how I'm so different to both my parents, but I've come to accept my body doesn't enjoy over-exposure to people.

'Yes, hopefully, but I'll help Dad first. I'm still hoping someone will want to buy it.'

I feel Harrison's arm tense beside me and he takes a small step away.

'He had no bites?' asks Mr Whalley, and I shake my head. 'With this view, it's absurd.'

My reply is cut off when Harrison says, 'I have to get back, but I have something special prepared for you both tonight if you're happy to go with my recommendations.'

The Whalleys are thrilled with that idea. Any talk of the restaurant closing has been wiped from their minds by the prospect of a signature Harrison James selection.

'Thank you, Harrison.' Mrs Whalley looks to me as she says, 'He's such a kind man.'

I almost let the laugh pop out, but I swallow it instead. That's going to cause an ulcer later in life.

'M'kay, I better go too, but I'll check on you shortly.'

Harrison and I both beam warmly at the Whalleys but wipe it from our faces the second our backs are turned.

'You have them fooled,' I whisper out the side of my mouth.

'You can talk. That BS you were spinning back there.'

'About what?' I'm trying to think about any bullshit I was peddling, but I come up short. The tone of my voice must get Harrison's attention because he slows down, and his eyes bore into mine.

'I thought, at the very least, we were honest with each other.'

'Yes, brutally honest.' I'm waiting for him to explain his obvious annoyance. 'What's going on?' We arrive at the kitchen door, where our paths will go in different directions, but I hang back waiting for his answer.

His piercing eyes scan my face one more time before he ducks his chin and says, 'Nothing, Agnes,' and then retreats to the kitchen. It seems I'm saying all the wrong things to Harrison tonight, and I have no idea why.

Chapter Four

I hang up the phone and cancel another booking in the system. People are cancelling left and right, and I don't blame them. The weather has gotten angry, and I wouldn't want to drive in these conditions. At the rate people are cancelling, we'll be able to close early, as Harrison suggested.

I try to maintain a relaxed, reassuring smile as I swiftly walk through the restaurant and check the conditions on the deck.

I'm a second too late when a gust of wind blasts through the deck, sending napkins and cutlery flying as someone lets out a shriek. It's not the sound you want coming from a guest at your restaurant.

I attempt to raise my voice over the noise of the rain to address all the diners. 'I'm so sorry. I'll move you all to tables inside.'

Within minutes, everyone is comfortable and warm at their new tables. It's not too difficult to find space since half our bookings have been cancelled.

I venture back to the deck to deal with the shutters since they're letting water in like a fresh spring. The first panel was easy to close, but I'm struggling with the next lot against the force of the wind.

A figure leans over me, and with one swift heave, the shutters close. Looking up, I see Harrison examining the shutters to check they're fastened. His muscular arms hover around me, caging me in as his eyes dart down to mine. Our eyes lock for a second until mine hover over his jaw and I wonder what he'd look like with some facial hair, maybe a beard. I flick the thought from my brain because I'm not sure where that came from.

'Some storm we're not having tonight,' he says, giving me an annoyingly sexy smirk and I try not to think of that beard again.

'It will blow over.' I know that's not true, but seeing Harrison's eyes narrow is fun.

'You are literally covered in rain right now. You are impossible.'

He steps back, keeping his arms above me as he retreats. I discreetly flick off the water that's drenched my arms away from Harrison's sight.

'Just a few drops of rain, hey?' I can hear the teasing in his tone.

'Do you have something useful to add to the conversation?'

After a pause, Harrison mumbles, 'What do you want for dinner?'

Huh? I usually grab something after my shift or see what we have too much of and eat that on the run.

My confusion must be visible because Harrison replies, 'It's the last night. I'm doing something nice. What would you like?'

'You're busy. I'll grab something later.'

I start pulling the tables further away from the railing so I don't have to see Harrison glaring at me.

'It's a meal, Agnes. Just tell me what you want.'

'I'm fine. I had a late lunch, remember.'

I see Harrison shaking his head from the corner of my eye, his hands staying on his hips as he drops looks down at his feet. He gives me one more long glare before slipping back inside.

With perfect timing, my stomach growls. Apparently, the bug roll wasn't enough. If I felt comfortable, I would have requested a serving of Harrison's seared scallops, but I couldn't bring myself to ask him for some reason. I take care of myself. Harrison James being pleasant makes me uneasy. I don't want to end our last night fighting, but I don't know how to drop my guard with him; it's been up for so long, and it's all I know when dealing with Harrison. I'm not used to the looks and questions he's giving me tonight. Can't he pretend it's only a regular night like I am?

I sneak into the kitchen to find a towel to wipe the chill of the rain from my arms. Before I finish cleaning up, a plate of scallops gets plonked down in front of me. Harrison walks away without saying a word, so I call out, 'Table number?'

'It's for you,' Harrison throws over his shoulder without looking back. A plate of Harrison's famous seared scallops sits in front of me, just as I'd ordered in my mind. I hate that he knew what I'd like while feeling secretly a little emotional that he knew what I wanted without asking.

Scout's head pops around the corner into the kitchen. 'Ah, Agnes?' She has an alarmed edge to her voice.

I have a mouthful of scallops, so I can't reply. They're too exquisite to rush them, so I answer with my eyebrows.

'You might want to take a peek into the dining room. You have a guest.'

Scout stands behind the door leading out to the dining area, snooping through the round glass window before frantically waving me over. I bring my plate with me to see what or who could be putting sheer panic on Scout's face. My fork is loaded, and I take a glorious bite of my dinner as I glance over her shoulder.

The restaurant looks calm. No one is crying or screaming. The sound of rain is drowning out some of the noise from the guests, but otherwise everything looks in place.

'What's got you in a tizzy?'

'Look at who just arrived.' Scout points her finger at the group standing at the entrance. I bend my neck too far to see who she's pointing to as my mouth drops open.

'No! He's here?' I swallow my dinner too quickly and then have a semi-coughing fit. 'Why would he come tonight?'

'Who's here?' Harrison's voice startles me because I was too focused staring at my ex-boyfriend to hear him approach. 'It's not someone famous is it? I can't deal with that shit tonight.'

'Devin,' I answer without taking my attention off my ex as he scans the restaurant. *Why would he come here on the last night?*

'The spoon-fork guy?' says Harrison as Scout tries to hide her delight at Devin's nickname.

'It's Spork. His last name is Spork,' I say flatly.

'I know, that's what I said. Spoon-fork. I personally prefer Splade. Sounds tougher.' Harrison is enjoying teasing Devin too much. He always has.

'Not now, Harrison.'

'It's not only him.' Scout's head slowly turns to regard me with sympathy.

'Don't say it.' Scout grimaces as I place my plate on the counter and rub the palm of my hand over my forehead to ease the instant headache that has formed. 'His family are here too?' I mumble and then quickly glance up to see Scout give me a sad nod. I return to more forehead rubbing. 'Oh crap, that means his mum is here.'

'And a whole bunch of other people just walked through the door.' That's enough to make me scurry over and peer over Scout's head again.

'That's his sister and her fiancé.' My pulse becomes jittery as I notice more people arriving. 'Oh shit, his nana is here.'

'Why is this a disaster?' Harrison sounds confused by my reaction, and I know he hates being confused. I wave Harrison away, but he doesn't move. 'Tell me why you have the same look on your face when we order too many mussels, and I'll go.'

Scout ignores Harrison and interjects, 'You don't have to see him, you know.'

'That would be rude.' I pick up my plate again to stress-eat the remainder of my meal. A thought pops into my head. 'Did he have a booking? I didn't see his name on the list.' I run through the names for the remaining bookings in my mind, and it hits me. 'Booking for six-thirty under Nelly. That's his grandmother's name.'

'That's dodgy as hell,' says Scout.

I flick my fork in the air and finish my last bite. 'He'll say he wanted it to be a surprise.'

'You already know how to dismiss his *very* clear red flags.' Scout and I have a silent battle with eyebrows, bug eyes and chin flexes. I know she's right, so I drop my shoulders and let her win. She gives me a gentle shoulder rub.

'Scout, you go seat them and get the low-down. Ask Spoon-face discreetly if he wants this to be a surprise for

Agnes,' says Harrison as he takes my empty plate and puts it in the rack for cleaning.

Scout struts out of the kitchen like a woman on a mission. I rub my head again. I know I'll have a migraine soon from the stress of tonight, my dad, the storm, and now Devin turning up.

Harrison fills a glass with water and hands it to me.

'Stop stressing. You'll give yourself a migraine.' I'm too frazzled to argue and follow my instructions. I must be feeling stressed if I'm complying with Harrison's demands.

'What's the problem? So, your boyfriend's here for a meal on our last night. Explain the issue to me so we can all get on with our night.'

The last thing I want to do now is get into this with Harrison, but his eyeballing isn't wavering as he waits for me to answer.

'Don't worry, Harrison,' I say, but his stare deepens, so I answer quickly, 'Because we broke up, and now he's here with his whole family.'

'You broke up? Why did I not know about this?' The shock in Harrison's voice startles me because I didn't think he'd give two hoots about my love life.

'Why would you know about it? We don't talk about this stuff.' I flick my finger back and forth between Harrison and I because we've never discussed our relationships. I've only ever heard whispers in the kitchen about Harrison's love life.

'Did it just happen?'

'Three months ago, nearly four now.'

Harrison's head flies back, and he blinks rapidly like his brain is trying to process the information.

'That's a long time to hide that.'

'I wasn't hiding it.' I square my shoulders as I face Harrison. 'You don't tell me about the women you date.'

'That's because I don't date.'

I scoff because I should have expected that answer. 'My mistake.'

'Not what I meant. I meant—'

My hand waves in dismissal because he's not being helpful right now. 'It doesn't matter any—'

'It's weird,' Harrison interrupts me, and he knows it annoys me. 'I interrupted you, but in fairness, you interrupted me first. Scout is right. It's weird. Did he hurt you?'

My head rears back in shock. 'What?'

'I can tell him to leave.'

Harrison moves towards the doors so I reach out to stop him.

'Calm down, Rocky. No, he didn't hurt me.'

'Did you break up with him?'

'Yes.' I nod without looking at Harrison, nibbling on my nail.

'Do you have any lingering feelings for him? No chance of a backslide?'

'Gross and no.'

Harrison alternates between interrogating me and surveying the dining room. 'Why did you break up?'

'None of your beeswax.'

'Mature,' says Harrison with his nose pinned against the glass of the kitchen door.

'Stop being a nosy parker then.'

'Stop using sayings made for children.'

'We're getting off track here.'

Harrison thinks momentarily before facing me, resting his back against the door.

41

'Maybe it's not weird that he's here because I assume you, in an attempt to always be the good guy, told him you'd stay friends afterwards.'

'That's not even—'

'Am I right?'

'Yes, but that's not a bad thing. We were together for nearly a year. It's the mature thing to do. How many exes are you friends with?'

'None,' Harrison says emphatically.

'My point is well made then.'

'Not at all.' Harrison steps behind me, nudges me towards the glass and looks over my shoulder into the restaurant. He leans in closer for effect. I'm unsure what effect he's going for, but I'm listening. I'm also overcome with Harrison's scent. I think it must be his cologne mixed with the aroma from the kitchen because it's a combination of spices, sand and musk. 'Because I don't normally hide from my friends when they come to see me.'

I tilt my head to look up at Harrison. He *may* have a point, but he doesn't know why we broke up. Harrison's eyes remain locked with mine as he continues, 'It might not be weird he's here, but it is 100 per cent weird he didn't book it under his name. Or call you first. Shifty as shit.'

I break Harrison's unwavering eye contact and step to the side. My cheeks are flushed, so I pat them to cool them down.

'He's friendly.' It's all I've got because I can't ignore him tonight, and I need Harrison not to make things more awkward.

'You need to make it clear you guys are over. *Clear.*' Harrison is forceful with his words. 'Because this shit here seems like a gesture a boyfriend would do.'

I don't respond as I take in his words. The truth is I'm okay seeing Devin. It's his family that makes this awkward, his mother in particular.

Scout flies through the door, interrupting us, and she's puffing. She probably took less than fifty steps, but her adrenaline must be pumping. She's loving the drama.

'Reporting back. His mum wanted it to be a surprise. She made the booking. Something doesn't add up. Devin looks pale.'

'That's just how he looks. Agnes likes the sick-looking fellas.' I don't react to Harrison's joke, but Scout tries to hide her laugh.

'You want me to go out there and talk to him?' Harrison offers, and I'm startled by his suggestion. Harrison is the one acting weird tonight. 'I'm a nice guy. Don't look at me like I just grew a second head.'

'Now that's weird, right? Harrison offering to talk to my ex-boyfriend is what's weird right now,' I say to Scout.

'Not really,' says Scout as she shrugs her shoulder.

'Thank you.' Harrison beams at Scout, who's somehow become his ally in this conversation.

'I'm going to make their drink order. I'll see what intel I can get.'

'Thanks, Scout,' I call as she bounces out the door.

Harrison turns his attention back to me, lowering his head so our faces line up.

'What's the biggest issue with him being here? For you. Not for Spoon-fork loser out there or his family. What's the biggest issue for you?'

Harrison regards me with such an earnest expression that I can't look away.

I lower my voice, so only Harrison and no one else in the kitchen can hear. 'His mum hates me. She was awful when we dated. We fought about it all the time. He always took her side.'

Harrison stands to his full height again. 'I didn't know that.'

'Why do you keep saying that? You've never asked anything about my relationship.'

'Ex-relationship. Just because I didn't ask, you still could have told me.'

'I don't understand this fight, which isn't that unusual, but still. You're making my headache worse.'

'So, the mum hated you. Big deal. Hate her back.'

'Mature.'

Harrison chuckles. 'I'm joking. But seriously, who cares?' Crossing his arms, he leans against the counter. I'm sure he's got one hundred things waiting for him to rush to, but his focus is entirely on this conversation.

'I care. I hate people hating me. Or worse, being overly nice, but it's all fake. And she'll hate me more now that I broke up with him. I hate conflict.'

'You and I disagree all the time,' says Harrison.

'That's different.'

'I don't see how.'

'Right now is how it's different. It's easy to fight with you.'

'Thank you.' Harrison grins, which makes me shake my head. He misunderstood me like usual.

'That wasn't a compliment.'

'Feels like one. Is that why you never worry about hurting my feelings?'

'It's because you don't care about hurting my feelings. It's an even arrangement.'

Scout enters the kitchen, breaking the tension between Harrison and me and returning our focus to the current problem.

'No new intel. His nana is avoiding soda as it upsets her stomach, and his mum isn't happy we don't stock freshly squeezed juice.'

'We're not a bloody juice bar,' says Harrison, echoing my exact thoughts.

Noah darts through the kitchen to Harrison's side. 'Ah, sorry to interrupt. I have a sauce vierge emergency.'

'Of course you do.' Harrison takes two steps away but then turns back. 'Are you okay, or do you want someone to go with you?'

'Oh, fun! What's the drama? Bad customer? Drunk customer? Nude customer again?' Noah is bouncing with the prospect of drama.

'When have we had a nude customer?' I ask because I've never heard that story. I notice Scout striking her hand across her throat to Noah. Harrison and I both shift our eyes to her.

'I'll fill you guys in later. One drama at a time. You say hi to Devin, and I'll hang close by pretending to deal with customers.'

'You should probably deal with the customers, not just pretend,' adds Harrison.

'Pfft. Let's go.'

'Say hi to the *Star Trek* guy.' Noah winks at Harrison and then laughs.

'That's Spock,' says Harrison as he eyes him curiously.

'I know. Funny, right?'

'Let's go.' Harrison gestures with his head, and Noah follows blindly behind. Harrison quietly says, 'We call him Spoon-Fork, not Star Trek.'

'Ah, so close.'

Harrison is obviously training Noah in more than food service – little shit.

Chapter Five

I'm stalling for as long as possible by checking every table and inspecting the deck in case the rain is gushing in again. Basically, I'm doing my job, but I can't delay it any longer, so I glance up, pretend not to notice Devin and then do a double-take that could get me into acting school. He stands and waves as his family yells *Surprise!*

With my hand on my heart, I make sure I look surprised and touched. The hand on my heart is helping with the pounding – not from the surprise, but from the raging weirdness of this situation.

Devin's family all seem genuinely happy they were able to surprise me. His sister, Alma, waves with exuberance as her fiancé, Leroy, glances my way and then resumes eating his free bread. Devin's mother, Barbara Spork, aka the villain that appears in all my nightmares, is eyeing me with a sharp leer over the rim of her glasses. It's the perfect villain pose. My nightmares will enjoy the new imagery tonight. She's probably watching me with that crusty stare because I haven't made my way over yet.

I move seamlessly through the restaurant until Mrs Whalley snags my hand to stop me.

'Everything okay, dear?' She gently rubs the top of the hand. 'You look a little pale?'

I smile to reassure her. She's the loveliest customer, and I must remember to make sure they don't get charged for their dinner tonight.

'Yes, I'm perfectly fine, thank you. Is everything okay with your entrées?'

'Amazing as ever,' says Mr Whalley as he tips his fork to me before loading it with more fried soft-shell crab.

'Thank you, I'll check in on both of you soon.'

Eleven more steps, and I'll be at the table with my ex-boyfriend and his immediate family. Devin greets me slightly away from the table and kisses me on the cheek. He hated kissing in public, so I'm taken aback that he'd greet me that way in front of his family. And more importantly, we broke up – no more kissing required.

'Surprise!' he says again before he puts his hand on the back of his mother's chair. His father, Frank, has barely glanced up, and that's not unusual. He keeps his head down and mouth closed in nearly all social situations. I think he's avoiding any behaviour that would make Barbara unhappy.

'Big surprise. Thank you all for coming.' My smile is wide and my head nods rapidly as I try to acknowledge everyone at the table. I linger on Devin's eighty-five-year-old grandmother because she was always my favourite. Nelly stands carefully and gives me a light hug. She's tiny, and I've missed her. Barbara's mother is nothing like her daughter.

'How have you been?' I ask her before she sits back down.

'Same old. Doing fuck-all.' I laugh as Devin shakes his head.

'Mum!' Barbara scolds her mum for her language, but Nelly couldn't care less.

She waves Barbara away and continues, 'It's true. I rarely do anything fun these days. You should come over and play cards again. I enjoyed that.'

'I'd love to.' I just lied to the sweetest, foul-mouthed old lady, but what else could I say? The truth is that I would love to keep in touch if it wasn't going to be super awkward with Devin and I didn't have to see Barbara.

Devin helps Nelly sit down again and I walk over and hug Alma. She reaches up for her hug and whispers, 'Where have you been, lady?' I pull back, realising she's waiting for an answer. I thought it was a funny comment, but it feels like she's a little miffed we haven't seen each other.

I know it's different in every situation, but I didn't feel that breaking up with Devin and trying to keep his family was appropriate; losing them was part of the break-up.

'I've been busy, sorry. With the restaurant closing and everything.'

Alma bobs her head up and down, releasing some stray hairs from her tight bun. If her mother wasn't here, it would be down and messy, but she knows how to avoid comments on her appearance, so her hair is tight and restrained tonight.

'Of course, I'm so sorry. It must be devastating for you. Let's grab a coffee soon.' She rubs my arm back and forth with an expression that tells me my absence has been forgiven. I will talk to Devin about how he feels about me befriending his sister.

'That would be lovely.' I try to move away, but she grabs my arm and pulls me back. 'Before I forget, did Devin tell you we picked the date for the wedding?'

'Ah…' I search for Devin, who's still standing near his mother. He's not looking my way, but Barbara stares me down like a cop who's found me holding a murder weapon. Alma glances between Devin and me, but he's not helping me. Once again, he's left me to navigate his family alone. Things never change. 'He didn't mention it, sorry.'

'Devin! How could you not tell Agnes?' Alma doesn't wait for Devin's answer as she proceeds to tell me all the wedding plans. I'm waiting patiently for a break to tell her I need to get back to work, but a pause doesn't seem to be coming anytime soon.

'You're needed in the kitchen.' Harrison's sharp voice cuts through any chatter at the table. The urgency in his tone makes it sound like there's been an emergency.

'Everything okay?'

'No.' That's all Harrison says as he politely dips his head to Devin's family and retreats into the kitchen. I don't think the attempt at politeness was for Devin's sake, but because as head chef, he needs to be courteous to all customers. He'd hate for someone to accuse him of being a stand-offish chef, even on our last night.

'I, um, better get back.'

The mission was a success as I've greeted everyone – all but one person. I've left Barbara to last, which may have been a smart decision or one a coward makes. Probably a coward if I'm being honest.

I steel my shoulders and pivot to address Barbara across the dining table. Devin still has his hand resting on the back of her chair. He could have sat down at any time, but he has kept close to his mother. Figures.

'I'm sorry I didn't get a chance to catch up properly. I hope you're well, Barbara.' It's polite and leaves no room for further conversation. Or so I thought.

50

'We haven't seen you in so long. We had to come here tonight to check you're still alive.' There's a chilling edge to her comment, and if this were a gangster movie, I'd be fearful for my life right now.

Devin still won't look at me. I was wrong before… *He* is the coward while he continues to remain quiet. Why in hickory hell would I keep in touch with that woman? I'm guessing Devin didn't tell her she was part of the reason we broke up, or she's playing me like a puppet master, and I'm the floppy old puppet.

'Still alive.' I mutter the words, but I'm unsure what to say next, so I figure it's time to check on Harrison. 'Better go. I'll check in later.'

Everyone waves except Barbara, who returns to sipping her drink without another look my way.

'I need to tell you all about the hen's night before I go tonight,' Alma quickly says. 'Margo was hoping you'd help with the menu with all your knowledge.'

Now I'm helping with my ex's sister's hen's night? Next, I'll be a bridesmaid or godmother to their first child, and I'll see Devin more than when we were dating. It's beyond time for me to leave, so I give her a thumbs-up and dart to the kitchen to hide. Maybe there are two cowards here tonight.

There's a clap of thunder as I enter the kitchen. It's appropriate for the direction this night has taken. I wanted to put my head down and count down the hours, but now I have to deal with Devin's family being overly friendly to me. Perhaps Devin didn't give too many details about our break-up and went with the never-true but saving-face mutual break-up reason. I'll back him up if it makes tonight go smoother.

'You're welcome.' Harrison glances up while he checks over an order going out. He sends one back while barking orders at the kitchen staff, not yelling, but in a disciplinarian voice that makes them jump into action.

'For what?' I search the kitchen for the emergency that Harrison had claimed I was needed for urgently.

'For getting you away from that table.'

'I'm not needed in here?' Harrison cocks his eyebrow and gives me a look that conveys, *When have I ever needed you in here?* 'Right.'

'You can say "Thanks Harrison", now.'

'They weren't actually that bad. Everyone was…' I take a moment to re-run the conversation in the mind, 'pleasant. Like they were happy to see me.'

'Why wouldn't they be?'

'Because I dumped Devin?'

'No one holds grudges about that.'

'I thought Barbara would have. She's a grudge-holder from way back.'

Harrison is again presented with the plate and gives it a tick of approval.

'Maybe she's got better things to do than to care about her son's dating life.'

I scoff, and it's a good, loud one because Harrison hasn't met Barbara, so he doesn't know how wrong he truly is with that comment.

I'm on the cusp of sharing details about my relationship with Devin that I never thought I'd tell Harrison, just as Devin pops his head through the kitchen door. He spots Harrison first, which makes him hesitate, and then finds me.

'Sorry to interrupt. Aggie, could I talk to you for a moment?'

'I'll be right out.'

Devin steps back out of the kitchen, and I glance at Harrison as I walk past.

'It's our last night, Agnes,' he says. 'You've got bigger things to focus on than Sliced Meat Boy out there.'

I suppress the snort that tries to escape because Sliced Meat Boy is a new nickname. Harrison must have been waiting a while to use that one.

I find Devin leaning against the front counter. Scout is at the bar serving customers and out of eavesdropping range. She spots me and then does a double-take when she notices Devin. I wave her away, but I know she'll be watching since she's in Harrison's camp regarding her feelings about Devin.

'Hey, how have you been?' That's his opening line.

'Been good. Surprised to see you here tonight.' I'm letting the team down tonight and need to get back to work, so I have limited time for small talk. Devin blows out a breath and fixes his hair. He takes a secret glance at his table, but I catch him. 'No one is watching us.'

'Right.' He continues to fix his short hair that doesn't have any length for styling, let alone fixing.

'What are you doing here, Devin?'

'Nice to see you, too.' I wasn't unkind with my tone, so Devin has no right to have a dig at me.

I let it go because I want to keep the peace and soften my face. 'It's nice to see you. I'm surprised because you weren't on the booking sheet.'

'I know, sorry about that. Mum booked the restaurant. I thought we were going out for Thai, but she changed plans without letting me know.'

'Why would she want to come here?'

'Why not? We love coming here.' Devin is defensive when he replies, and my patience with that is about as thin as a queenfish.

'You know what I mean. It's a little odd to book a table at your son's ex-girlfriend's restaurant.' Devin physically winces when I say ex-girlfriend, and it makes me pause. Is he still hurting over our break-up?

Devin pulls at his collar and then readjusts one of his long sleeves. He won't look me in the eye.

'Devin?' I say slowly as I take a step closer but ensure I'm still hidden by the counter. 'What's going on?' I whisper the last part, hoping it will persuade him to confide in me.

'Here's the thing, Agg.' He pauses and pulls at his collar again.

'There's a thing?'

'A little one.' Devin pinches his fingers together with a slither of a gap between them.

'Okay.'

'I sort of, well, I've been busy at work. I got a promotion, which is why we're out for dinner.'

'That's great. Congratulations.' I have little to no emotion in my voice because he still hasn't got to the point he's clearly avoiding.

'Yeah, it's been mental at work. I've been working around the clock.'

'And?'

'Right, yes. Honestly, I never got a chance to tell my family we broke up. Didn't have the time to get into it.' He finally peers up, and instead of the shame or embarrassment I'm expecting to see in his gaze, I'm met with indignation, that I somehow put him in this position with his family. A moment ago, I was concerned he was still upset about the break-up, but it seems in his world, the break-up didn't happen.

'You never told them?' I pronounce each word carefully so I get crystal clear information in return.

'Nope.' He pops the P sound with his lips, and it's as irritating as Harrison tapping his stupid sign.

'So, they think we're still a couple?'

'Yes.' He nods while not looking at me.

'And that's why your mum booked a table tonight.'

'Yes.' He answers while offering no further information.

'Devin, this is bad.'

His eyes swing to mine finally. 'Mum wanted to be here for your last night, so it's a good thing. I'm glad I could be here with you as well.'

'But they all think we're together?' My arms gesture wildly because this is madness.

'Minor detail of the evening.'

'Minor detail? Or incredibly awkward for them to find out now?'

Devin cranes his neck to recheck his table, because he's got a few minutes before Barbara comes looking for him. His focus returns to me, but he's skittish. He pulls on his long sleeve again before whispering, 'Maybe we just don't tell them?'

My head flies back, which is helpful because I was not enjoying the closeness while furious with him. 'Excuse me?'

'No one needs to know our business.' There's that brazen attitude again. Devin can't decide if he's apologetic or defiant.

'But they think we're together? That we would act like boyfriend and girlfriend. Touching and stuff.'

55

'Not out in public.'

'Right. I forgot.'

'So, not really that different. Just come by again later, so no one's night is ruined. I'll tell them all next week sometime.'

I pause because I do not want to deal with Barbara finding out about the break-up here tonight near me. She's been pleasant in a passive-aggressive, me-wanting-to-spoon-my-brain-out kind of way. Maybe it would be easier to say nothing tonight and let Devin handle it another day.

He must sense my resolve slipping and adds additional points to his argument.

'We'll eat and be out of your hair soon. The storm is getting worse anyway, and Dad will want to get home.'

Feeling resigned to this outcome, I say, 'Okay, just for tonight, but you'll tell them tomorrow.'

'Deal.'

Devin's gaze lingers, and it's got a familiarity in it that makes me pause.

'It's been almost four months. That's a pretty long time. You haven't had one chance to tell them?'

'Seriously, I've been flat out. Hasn't crossed my mind. I don't want things to be weird tonight. I promise I'll tell them soon.'

'Okay. I won't say anything tonight.'

Devin springs forward and kisses me gently on the cheek before rejoining his table. The moment his lips touched my face, my stomach recoiled. It didn't enjoy revisiting being close to Devin.

Scout steps out from behind the bar and over to me.

'What the hell was that about?'

How do I explain this to Scout because I know what she will say — it's ridiculous. And I fully agree. Perhaps I have underestimated my fear of Barbara Spork. For the first time tonight, I'm glad there's a storm, so it means they'll be gone quicker. Surely, they'll only be here for an hour, maybe two at the most.

Three hours and fifteen minutes to go.

Chapter Six

The wind bashes into the shutters on the deck and they fly open as Scout and I rush to secure them for the third time this evening. Rain is pouring down now. This is heavy, fierce, annoying rain. It's the kind that stings when it hits your face and instantly has water gushing down the gutters.

'Give me the TL; DR quickly before we get busy again,' Scout says. We're a distance away from the customers sitting inside, but I still pull her into the corner of the deck to remain hidden and out of the rain.

It pains me to admit this because I know she'll think this is absurd.

'He hasn't told his family we broke up.'

'What!?' Her eyes bug out further than I expected.

'They all think we're still together. His sister asked if I'd help plan her hen's night.'

'So, the entire family are bad with boundaries,' Harrison mumbles. Scout and I spin around, not realising he'd joined us on the deck. He's standing a distance away with his arms folded.

'Ignore him.' Scout waves Harrison away before taking my hand and squeezing it.

'Just hide in the kitchen most of the night. Pretend we're flat out.'

'Half the restaurant is empty.' I gesture to the vacant deck.

'Pretend we have a crisis. Fish crises are the worst.'

'Okay, that works. I'll hide in the kitchen.' Harrison will hate me hanging out in the kitchen all night. 'Surely, they'll only stay an hour or so.'

Scout agrees, and we're both delighted with our plan.

'Or,' Harrison interjects loudly.

Here it comes. 'Or?' I ask.

'Or you don't play along with this ridiculousness and tell them you broke up. Tell his sister you don't want to organise her hen's night because you won't be going. Or probably seeing her again.'

'Devin's going to tell them,' I protest.

'When?'

'Tomorrow. He's been busy and hasn't had a chance.' I don't know why I'm defending Devin, but that's where I've landed tonight.

'Did he have a chance as he was walking in here? When he sat down, waiting for his drink? Or does he have time now while we're making their dinner? He has time, Agnes. He has chosen not to.'

'When he puts it like that, it's a little weird.' Scout is reluctant to look at me when she says this.

I chew on the nail of my pinky finger because it is a little strange. Something doesn't sit right about Devin's reasons, but I can't be as direct as Harrison is suggesting. That's not who I am and that feels harder and more emotionally draining than just trying to get through tonight.

'Have you talked since you broke up?' Scout asks.

'A text message now and then.'

'That's suspiciously vague. What's now and then?' Harrison steps forward and joins our group more fully, which now looks like a secret huddle.

'Now and then is now and then. That's a common phrase.'

'Now and then every week? Now and then every month? Or now and then every day?'

I don't want to answer Harrison because I know it will sound bad. He doesn't understand that I've been trying to detach myself from Devin. I'm trying without much success, but I never feel like I'm in control when it comes to Devin. He always finds a way to twist and spin things; before I know it, he's got his own way, and I feel like I can't say anything. Tonight is a painful wake-up that we're still stuck in the same dynamic that haunted our relationship.

'Every few days. Some days, he texts a lot.'

Scout and Harrison both shake their heads in unison.

'Do you want to get back together with him?' Scout asks.

'No! Not at all.' I try to smooth down my hair, which is getting fuzzier by the minute with the moisture in the air. I try to evade Harrison's intense glare, but it's unavoidable. 'I wanted to soften the blow and I thought the texting would slowly taper off.'

'Just slowly disappear and you don't have to be the bad guy?' Harrison retorts.

'There doesn't have to be a bad guy in break-ups.'

'I agree, but in this one, it's you.'

My mouth drops open in shock because I am *not* the bad guy here. 'How could you say that?' I've been turning myself inside out taking care of Devin's feelings throughout the break-up.

'Because you're not being truthful with him.' Harrison uncrosses his arms and shoves his hands in his pockets. 'I'm going to lay this out for you clearly.'

Harrison turns my body so I can look over the restaurant. He stands behind me, but we're still hidden in the corner of the deck. I'm surrounded by Harrison's musky-beach aroma again and it's strangely growing on me.

'That man believes the window is still a little open. Ajar. You've left it ajar. And every time you reply to his message, and I'm going to assume overuse emojis,' I frown at Harrison but don't say anything because he's correct, 'he thinks he has a chance, and perhaps you guys are only on a break, not a break-up, so he's not going to tell his family because in his cold, utensil heart, he believes you'll get back together.'

Shit. I hate to say it out loud so I'll only think it, but Harrison could be right. 'I was just being nice.'

'And unclear. Time to clear it up.'

'With who? Devin or his family?'

'Him. All of them. Who cares.'

'I care. I don't like people being mad at me.'

'Shocker.' Harrison steps back and the three of us form our huddle again.

'Why don't you just get through dinner and then call him tomorrow to clarify things. Again,' Scout suggests, and I like her idea.

'Yes, I can do that.'

Before I can get the courage to walk inside, Barbara's head pokes out into the deck. She spots us huddled in the corner, corrects her posture and smiles at our group. She would seem like a friendly, polite lady to an outsider, but I know the truth.

'Agnes, would you have time for a photo? We'd like one with the whole family around the table.' She points at Scout. 'Could you come and take it for us?'

'We have a restaurant to run,' says Harrison, but even his direct voice doesn't faze Barbara.

'It will only take a minute. I'm sure the girls don't mind.'

Barbara waves us in and we follow like we're on auto-pilot. I can sense Harrison's unhappiness in the way he strides off in the opposite direction to the kitchen.

'She has a way about her. I was too scared to tell her no,' whispers Scout.

'Tell me about it.'

—

Scout gestures for us to move closer together to fit in the photo. Devin slides in tight to my side. As we wait for Scout to take the photo, Devin raises his arm and places it over my shoulder. My head flicks to him, but he ignores me as he smiles for the photo.

'How's your dad? I haven't seen him tonight,' says Devin as everyone takes their seat. I have to remain standing, which is awkward.

'He'll be back soon. He went home for a rest.'

'Great. I look forward to catching up.'

Devin takes my hand and gives it a gentle stroke. Oh crap. That felt *intimate*. In Devin's mind, that door Harrison was talking about may have opened a little wider. Damn, Harrison. Or damn, Devin.

'Okay. I have to get back to work. Your meals will be out shortly,' I say to the group, pulling my hand away from Devin.

'It's a beautiful restaurant, Agnes. Such a shame. I hope you're dealing with the change coming,' says Barbara before taking a sip of wine.

'Thank you. Yes, it will be certainly different, but Dad can concentrate on his health now.'

'And what will you concentrate on?'

That's a loaded question, and while I know the answer, I don't wish to disclose that information to the Spork family.

'I'm going to take a little time out first. I think I've earned a break.' I'm not telling her any plan of mine. I politely smile and take my leave, but Barbara isn't finished. She leans over and speaks softly, 'Mum hasn't been feeling the best, so when you have your break, I know she'd love a visit or two.'

'Um…' I look to Devin to step in and create a diversion or say something to take the spotlight off me, but he's smiling like this would be a fabulous idea. That metaphorical door has been flung open. 'Sounds good.' What else could I say right now? No biggie – just planning a hen's night and now visiting Devin's ailing grandmother. Totally normal post-break-up behaviour.

'I could take them both out to that sushi place Nana loves,' says Devin, like a child who doesn't want to miss out on praise.

'That would be wonderful, darling.' Barbara pats her son's arm like he's the most precious man ever made. Since she's the one who made him, her appraisal holds little weight.

'Or we could take her to those cooking classes she always talks about?' Devin looks to me to fill in the blanks, but I have no idea what he's referring to, and I hope my vacant stare reflects that.

'You mean the French cooking class?' Barbara claps, and it startles me. 'Oh, she'd love that. Seriously, you two. That would be so lovely of you both. A special memory to share with your nana.' Barbara bobs her head back and forth between Devin and me with giddiness at all the new family plans.

How do I get out of this now? Devin seems to have embedded me deeper into his family. Does he have any intention of telling them about the break-up tomorrow? I'll be the girlfriend who dumped him after the entire family came out to support me tonight. Talk about bad guy. Two thumbs firmly pointing at me.

'I better get back.' I need to get away before I'm signed up for a time-share and funeral savings plan with the Spork family.

'Yes, of course. We're so glad we could all be here for you tonight.' Barbara gestures to the table with a wide arm. 'It's what family do, Agnes. They show up for each other. I know it's just been you and your dad all these years, but you're not alone anymore.'

Devin's eyes are a little misty at Barbara's comment, but to me, it feels like ice water is being poured down my back. She might have good intentions, but I am *not* alone. My dad and I are happy with our little family, and her constant assertion from the time I've known her that we're less than her family makes my blood boil.

'Thank you,' I say through gritted teeth. 'Walk me to the kitchen, Devin?' I exit without waiting for an answer, knowing he'll follow. Each step away from that table brings peace to my entire body. The last four months without Barbara have been fantastic. I miss those days.

Devin and I find our hidden spot next to the front counter, and I check in with Scout as I walk past. There are three more cancellations tonight due to the weather. Maybe this night will be done and dusted in a few short hours.

I reach my corner, spin around, cross my arms and wait for Devin. When he arrives, he's sporting a grin with not a hint of remorse in his demeanour.

'What was that?' I snap, and even Harrison would have flinched from the venom in my tone.

Devin throws his hands up in defence. I notice his eyes flick to his table. He must be checking that no one can see us arguing.

'What was what?'

'Come on, don't make me say it. Organising catch-ups with your nana? Cooking classes?'

Devin shrugs like it's no big deal. 'Nana's health hasn't been too good lately, so I thought it would cheer her up. It will be my shout.' He couldn't possibly think my issue was the cost. Surely, he's playing dumb right now. Once again, I must admit Harrison was right, and it's making me furious.

'Devin, we broke up.' I'm unsure whether to go into more detail, but hopefully, that explains enough.

'And what, so now we can't do something nice together for my nana? I thought you liked hanging out with her?'

'I do. This is not about whether I like your nana or not. She's awesome.'

'Great, then there's no problem.' Yes, there is, and Harrison's voice in the back of my head calls me a bad guy for not closing the door. But how hard do I have to slam that bloody door shut for it to stay closed?

I soften my voice since this seems to be a delicate or tricky concept for Devin to comprehend. 'The problem is that we broke up, so when that happens, you stop doing things like hanging out all the time.'

'But you said you wanted to be friends?'

Yes, I did, and I have many regrets.

'I did, but—'

'We got on really well, and I know you had issues I thought we could have worked through, but regardless of all that, we had fun together.' I had issues? I – being singular – had problems?

'The thing is Devin, that, um—'

'When you're done, I need your help.' Harrison's voice startles me as I didn't realise he was standing behind me.

'You need *my* help?' I poke my thumb in my chest to clarify because Harrison James never needs my help.

'Yes. That's what I said. Are you still working tonight or just doing this?' Harrison gestures to Devin and then me. I notice Devin's posture stiffens as Harrison speaks. He'd rarely talked to Harrison during the time we dated, and now I'm wondering if Devin is intimidated by Harrison. Many people are, I never considered that Devin could be as well. Harrison is always on the annoying rather than scary side for me.

'I'll be with you in two minutes.' Harrison nods, gives Devin a once-over and then walks swiftly away. Devin leers at Harrison until he's well and truly back in the kitchen, and it gives me an idea. It's not one I am proud of, but a circuit breaker I desperately need right now.

'Devin, I didn't want to tell you tonight, but I think it's fair to tell you that I'm seeing someone.'

Hurt crosses his face, and I hate that, but we broke up. A while ago. It shouldn't be this hard.

'Already?' He seems irked that I would start dating again. I clearly don't understand the rules of disengagement, or Devin doesn't, because we're on entirely different pages.

'It's been three months.' Nearly four, but I think it's best not to clarify.

'But you didn't say anything.'

'It's new – very early days. And it's not exactly something you would tell your ex. And I didn't know I'd be seeing you tonight.' And you won't take a hint. And you keep bulldozing me, so I had to make up a lie – all valid reasons.

'So now I'm just the ex.'

Yes.

'No, well, yes, but not the way you put it.' I reach out and touch his arm, but it softens his face, so I carefully remove it again. Touching seems to reopen the door, so no touching moving forward. 'We haven't told anyone. It's very new, so we're keeping it quiet.'

'Who is it?'

'I said we're keeping it quiet.'

'I deserve to know. It's not my friend Pete, is it?' Pete is his friend from university and an absolute twat. Pete would be the last person I would date, so I'm offended that Devin's mind went straight to his loser friend, Pete.

'Absolutely not. Do you think I would date a friend of yours?'

'He's a good-looking guy.' I shrug my shoulders. Devin certainly thinks highly of his 'friend' Pete. 'If it's not Pete, then who?'

I take a step back in an attempt to exit this conversation. I'd take a giant step if I could exit this night and wake up tomorrow morning when this is all over, but my legs aren't that long.

'Listen, it's not worth getting into it now.'

'Just a name, Agg. Who am I going to tell?' Devin is a dog with a bone or a jilted ex-boyfriend with boundary issues.

'Why do you want to know?'

'Why won't you tell me?'

'I have to get back to work. We can talk more later.'

'Is it Bob?' Bob is the name of his co-worker and tennis buddy who is currently dating a lovely woman named Karen. I don't believe she's ever complained about her food while I've been with her.

'Stop naming your friends!' I whisper-yell, hoping it will stop him. Next, he'll probably ask me if I'm dating his dad or maybe his uncle Al, who I had a drink with at his seventieth birthday party.

'Is it?'

'No!' I can't help myself and raise my voice. It's not enough to get the guests' attention, but it's loud enough that Harrison, who is talking with Mr and Mrs Whalley, stands to his full height to survey the situation.

I shake my head so that he won't come back over here. Devin notices it and follows my gaze. He then chuckles, but it's not one that's filled with glee. It's an empty, nasty chuckle.

'That guy? Seriously?' Devin points to Harrison, who's back chatting with the Whalleys. He often checks in after each meal for our loyal customers, but tonight, he's chatting longer than usual.

I drop my chin and stare at Devin directly. 'Yes, that's right. I'm dating Harrison.'

Chapter Seven

I delay it as long as possible by checking over the few bookings left in the system tonight, but I need to talk to Harrison. The thought makes me as queasy as when we found a discarded bag of dirty prawn water. I square my shoulders as I step into the kitchen.

Harrison and Noah are huddled over a meal, perfecting it. Both have a look of pure glee as they finesse with the placement. I walk over quietly to snoop – it's our Cajun spiced fish dish – but they've added chilli plum prawns and sautéed vegetables with a beurre blanc sauce. It looks divine and the sides are not a current item on the menu.

'It looks amazing,' I say as Harrison wipes off the plate before handing it to Noah.

'We thought we'd do something special for the Whalleys tonight.' Noah beams at me as he steps around to carry out the meals.

'They'll love it.'

'We'll see.' Harrison abruptly returns to his area in the kitchen, leaving me standing alone.

'Hello? In a conversation. You can't just walk away.'

Harrison starts cutting something at a speed that is unnatural. 'We were in a conversation?'

I roll my eyes, which I try to avoid because that's all I'd do in Harrison's presence, but this one slips out.

'I was trying to avoid it, but sorry, this can't be helped.' Harrison's gaze flicks my way, but he doesn't move his head. I ditty around on my feet before pushing out, 'So, I have something to tell you.'

'The tone of your voice is scaring me.'

'That's a pretty accurate reaction.' I nod to myself because Harrison still hasn't joined this conversation with eye contact or any physical indication that he's listening. 'I need to tell you something, and I don't want any judgement. Or Harrison-style huffing.'

He places the knife down carefully, wipes his hands and then turns to face me. 'Harrison-style huffing? I haven't heard that one before.'

'I hear it all the time. It's 90 per cent silent but loud enough that I question whether it's a huff or you're simply breathing. It's the gaslighting version of huffing.'

'The perfect amount then?' Harrison's eyes twinkle with mischief, but his mouth barely moves. 'Also, you're being ridiculous, and there's enough of that going on tonight already. What do you need?'

'Firstly, I would walk away from this conversation if I could. I need you to know that.'

That statement is enough to get his full attention. I don't often have Harrison James's attention, so it's an embarrassing shame that I'll lose it in five seconds when I tell him what I've done. 'What predicament have you got yourself in, Agnes?'

'The thing is…'

'This should be good,' Harrison mumbles under his breath.

'You were right. Just the one time.' I cringe to soften the impact of saying those words out loud. It hurts.

'Today?'

'Ever.'

Harrison-style huffing begins.

'Get on with it, what was I right about? The storm?' Harrison reads my face and then clicks his fingers. He chuckles. 'I was right about the ex-boyfriend.' I hate that he can read my face.

'Devin does perhaps believe the window back into our relationship is still, maybe, a little... open.' Harrison nods like this was crystal clear to everyone but me.

'The door is still ajar?'

'Yes, but I've closed it.'

'Great job. Now, I'm going back to work.' Harrison picks up his knife, but I reach out to stop him before he gets lost in chopping. He glances at my hand on his forearm and then at the cooks behind him. I quickly remove the hand again.

'There's a little bit more to it.'

'Of course there is.' Harrison places the knife back down.

'I told him I had started dating someone.'

Harrison takes a moment to reply. He leans forward and bends his head down to my eyeline to ask, 'Agnes?'

I bring my head back so I can maintain some distance. 'Yes?'

Harrison's eyes narrow as if I'm in an interrogation room. 'Are you dating someone?'

'No.' Harrison does the huff-breathing thing, and I point my finger at him so he knows what he's doing.

'If I have this straight, which I assume I probably don't because it's ludicrous...' Harrison glances around the kitchen and lowers his voice when he notices we've attracted some attention. 'You thought it was easier to make up a lie that you will have to make up more lies

71

to back up the first lie, rather than tell him the truth. Is that right?'

'Yes, but I have my reasons. You weren't in the conversation.'

'And I'm glad about that. What else is there then? Do you have a fake boyfriend joining us?'

Suddenly, this all feels very silly, and perhaps I'm better feigning an illness or injury and disappearing tonight. I would any other night, but it's the last night, so I can't escape. I divert my attention and rearrange the mushrooms Harrison has lined up. He knocks my hand away and moves into my personal space again. At least, it blocks me from the rest of the kitchen. I can hide behind the wall of Harrison James as I admit to this embarrassing turn of events. More painfully, I need to ask Harrison for help.

'What did you do, Agnes?'

I have to get the words out of my mouth somehow, or do I...? Harrison doesn't need to know. I could not tell him and hope Devin doesn't say anything to Harrison tonight. Argh!

Before my head explodes, I blurt out, 'You. I'm dating you. But not really. Pretending.'

I keep my attention on the ceiling and then on the floor. Anywhere other than Harrison. Silence. I rub my eyebrow back and forth as a reflex from the awkwardness of the silence. He doesn't say anything, so I keep rambling. 'Just for this evening. Until he leaves. How does that sit with you?'

Harrison still doesn't say anything. I give up and sneak a look as he steps away. Harrison takes a towel and dries his hands slowly.

He rests his hip on the counter and finally speaks. 'Please don't take this the wrong way, but you are a smart and capable human being.'

'Thank you?'

'But—'

'Here we go.'

'This shit is messed up.' Harrison throws the towel onto the counter. 'I want to lay it out for you because you need to hear this back. Currently, you are pretending to date your ex-boyfriend to keep him and his rude family happy, right?'

'Not fake dating, Devin. Just not telling his parents and the rest of his family that we broke up.'

Harrison shakes his head before saying, 'That's the same thing, but said in a more complicated way.'

I nod because I can't deny that.

'And now also pretending to date me. Is that correct?'

I nod again.

'And why are you dating me, Agnes? I assume it's because you didn't want to tell that arse clown to back off, so you created a buffer.' Harrison points to himself. 'Me being the innocent buffer.'

I nod again for the third time, which I hate, but I have nothing else.

'I know you love pleasing people and could never stand for someone to dislike you, but I wonder if there might be an easier solution.' Harrison taps his finger on his chin while he pretends to think. 'I know.' Harrison clicks his fingers. 'Telling the truth.'

'I will. Just not tonight. I can't deal with Devin or his mum tonight.' I drop my head because it's hard to admit that to Harrison.

His voice softens before he asks, 'Is this about us closing? Are you acting out some anxiety by role-playing?'

Harrison trying to analyse me maxes out my comfort level. 'Forget it. I'll find someone else.' I spin around, but Harrison catches me before I can take a step. His hand is on my arm now. We both look up to see the staff watching us again. Harrison quickly removes his hand after turning me back to face him.

'But you already told him. So, you can't find anyone else. It's me. I'm your only option.' I'm a mouse that got trapped taking a massive bite of cheese. Harrison's too happy about my misfortune.

'I clearly didn't think this through. I should have said anyone but you.'

Harrison picks up his knife and starts chopping again. 'But you didn't, so here we are.' He waggles his eyebrows at me, and I know the staff would have seen that. I lean closer so they can't hear my voice.

'Stop enjoying this. Tomorrow, Devin will tell his family and this all goes away. You only have to be my boyfriend for a few hours.'

'Pretend boyfriend.'

'Yes, correct.' I'm glad we are both agreed across that part.

'As your pretend boyfriend, am I meant to know you're also pretend dating Devin?' Harrison wipes his face while breathing out, 'Fuck that was a sentence I didn't need to say right now.'

'You called him Devin. I think that was the first time.' Now, I get to have some enjoyment.

'I'm frazzled.'

'And yes, I wouldn't keep secrets from a boyfriend, fake or otherwise.'

Harrison's eyes roam my face for a moment before returning to his task. 'Okay, Agnes. This is some fun shit you've got yourself into.'

'Just a few hours. That's all.'

Harrison flicks his knife in my direction, dismissing me.

I step away before he says loudly, 'I'm a pretty touchy-feely partner. Just letting you know.'

My eyes dart around the kitchen to see who heard that, and it's clear from the sniggers and averted gazes that everyone heard it.

I drop my chin and level my gaze. 'Hands to yourself, Harrison.'

I hear him chuckle as I storm off. I should have chosen anyone but Harrison James.

Chapter Eight

The one good thing about Devin coming tonight is that I've been distracted from the thing that should be taking up my mind. It's our last night, and I should be spending it with Dad, who hasn't returned yet. Harrison plans to send Noah soon, and I hope the Spork family will have departed by then.

I wipe the bar back and forth with no end in sight as I focus on stressing and overthinking. It's an easy combination to fall into and I might add stress-eating into the mix soon.

'You'll rub off the varnish.' Scout rips the cloth from my hand.

'Sorry. Just keeping busy.'

'Get busy on those tears. I've only got forty-five minutes until I can kiss that money goodbye.' Scout has no idea how easily I could cry at the moment. My feelings about this night are all jumbled up, and now Devin has made it harder for me to be on autopilot, trying to get through until closing. If Dad were here, I could focus on making sure he was happy and enjoying his final night.

I notice Devin watching me out of the corner of my eye, so I slink back further behind the bar area. I'm counting down the minutes until his family finish their meals and leave.

Alma magically appears at the bar and startles both Scout and me. She must have come from the bathroom because I didn't see her leave the table.

'I know you're busy, but can I quickly show you the menu for the hen's?'

Alma's head is down as she scrolls through her phone, trying to find the menu I haven't agreed to look at yet. Scout mouths something to me, but I can't decipher her words. She flicks her head to the side, so I think she's telling me to disappear out the back, or perhaps she has a sore neck. Either way, I take too long studying her because Alma shoves her phone in my face.

She talks at me for ten minutes about sixteen choices for canapés before she finally takes a break, lifts her head and shouts over the restaurant, 'Devin, come here!'

It's like she's at home in her lounge room, and her brother is in the other room. Mrs Whalley is not happy with the disruption and gives Alma a dirty scowl behind her back. I wish I could signal to Mrs Whalley that I agree with her annoyance. Devin didn't hear her, so she braces to call out again. I catch her a second before the words leave her mouth.

'Why don't we go over to the table and see him?' *And stop shouting in my restaurant.*

'Yes, come on.' Alma waves at me to hurry up like it wasn't my idea. Scout mixes a cocktail shaker with hostility, and I wonder if she's pretending it's Alma. Scout doesn't tolerate rude people well.

'Devin, what were you saying again about dessert?'

Alma sits in her seat while I stand uncomfortably beside the table. Devin takes my hand and pulls me onto his seat. He moves over, so we're sharing. At least he didn't pull me into his lap. It's one thing for me not to disclose our break-up; it's another thing entirely to start PDA in the post-touching phase of our relationship.

'You could get macarons from the place on Gordon Parade.' Devin bumps my shoulder as he says, 'You love those little treats.'

We went there once at the start of our relationship and never went back. I have no idea why it's a special memory for Devin.

'Maybe you could all go there when you take your nana out?' Barbara pipes into the conversation, and Devin taps his mum's hand and squeezes it tightly. They remain holding hands as Devin says to his mother, 'That's a great idea. You could come too?'

Barbara beams and I know she was waiting to see if someone would invite her along. It was a test for her children.

I'm still gaping at Devin holding his mother's hand as Barbara says, 'Next week suit, Agnes? You'll have lots of free time. Maybe we'll get to see more of you. I know Devin's been missing you.'

Barbara and Devin share a look, but I don't know what it means.

'Devin's been too busy to miss me. Haven't you?'

Devin suddenly seems uncomfortable and slowly releases his mother's hand.

'I'd miss you no matter how busy I am.' Devin's voice has a melancholy tinge as he reaches up and tucks a loose hair behind my ear. His fingers linger on my cheek, and I know we're being watched. That's the only reason my cheeks have flushed, not because of Devin's closeness. He may not realise that, though.

'That's the boy I raised – such a romantic. You're a lucky girl, Agnes. Do you know how lucky you are?'

I give Barbara a friendly glance to acknowledge her comment, but she is ogling me with wide eyes. 'Do you?' she prompts me again. For anyone else, that would have been a rhetorical question.

'I know how lucky I am, Barbara.' In my head, the luck I'm referring to has nothing to do with Devin but that in a few hours, I'll be comfy in my bed, and this night will be over. Then I'll feel extremely lucky.

Devin's leg is pressed up against mine, and it moves closer. Barbara's questions and Devin's touching are too much. 'I have to work, so I'd better go.' I bend forward to address Alma, 'The macarons sound like a great idea.' *But leave me out of it, please.*

I jump out of the seat and dart backwards, trying to distance myself from all these people. My back hits something solid, and I let out a quiet yelp from the fright.

Strong fingers wrap around my forearms, and I glance back to see Harrison's unwavering focus peering down at me. His anchored gaze captivates me and I hope Devin's family don't notice the subtle shift in my breathing. Harrison makes sure I'm stable before removing his hands. I feel unsettled and unsure if it's from Devin, Barbara or having Harrison staring at me with what seems like tenderness.

'I hope you're all enjoying your meals.' Harrison addresses everyone at the table but doesn't let his gaze near Devin. 'Water has started coming in,' says Harrison quietly to me.

'For real life?'

'Yes, in real life. That's not something I should have to clarify.' Not typically, but tonight, real and fake are getting blurry.

'Sorry, I have to run,' I say, knowing full well that I'm not sorry at all.

'Do you need help?' Devin asks, but Harrison replies before I can, 'No.'

'No, thanks. I'm sure it's nothing major,' I say trying to smooth over Harrison's gruffness and then race to catch up to him. 'You were rude.'

Harrison slows down and flicks a look of disdain in my direction. 'And you are too nice to people who don't deserve it.'

I'm about to launch into my rebuttal, but Noah interrupts us. He waits by the kitchen door and bounces his shoulders up and down like he's excited.

'Sandbagging time!' Noah drops his smile. 'That sounds like a sex move. Is it?'

Harrison throws his thumb in my direction. 'Ask Agnes. She's the one with multiple boyfriends.'

'That's not true! Ignore him, Noah.'

'No judgement, Aggie. I'm sure you'd be a lovely girl-friend, no matter how many fellas you date.'

Noah grins widely at me, and he's so sweet I can't do anything but smile back.

We follow Harrison down the corridor, past the storage room, to the bathroom. The three of us poke our heads in to inspect the damage. Noah takes the three steps down into the room and opens a cubicle door where the water is slowly leaking in. The water should stay contained in this area because the room is sunken. It won't make for a pleasant trip to the bathroom for our customers, though.

'Lucky someone thought of sandbags, isn't it?' says Harrison and I ignore the comment as we walk to the back door.

Once I'm through the door, I wait and hold it open for Noah to pass. He darts outside, and with perfect timing, I let the screen door slam in Harrison's face.

'Oops. Sorry.'

'He's wrong. You're not a lovely girlfriend at all.'

'You'll never know.' I wink at Harrison and traipse over to help Noah.

–

We duck under the wide awnings to avoid the rain, each carrying a few sandbags down the path next to the restaurant. I only carry one because they're stupidly heavy.

'I'll grab the rest.' Noah makes to run back up the path, but Harrison puts out his hand to stop him.

'You go back inside. I don't want you tripping and suing Agnes.'

Noah looks at me with horror. 'I never would.'

'I'd prefer you didn't trip either way. We've got this. Thanks for your help,' says Harrison as Noah reluctantly nods and waits for more instructions. 'You all right to handle things inside for five minutes?'

Noah starts smiling before words form in his brain. 'Absolutely.'

'Right. You're in charge in there until I get back.'

Noah gives us a military salute and rushes inside to run The Shark Biscuit.

'Is he up to it?' I ask.

'Things aren't busy. If you've noticed, we're having some bad weather.'

I'd rather contend with the rain, so I leave Harrison and grab another sandbag from the pile near the side of the restaurant.

'I think we focus on the bathroom and hope it eases before the back gets hit too.'

'Agree.'

Harrison spins around and looks at me like I've grown a second head. 'Agree? That's it?'

'Tonight has been a lot already. I have no energy to fight with you, and I always have energy for that, so I must be maxed out.'

We both grab sandbags and place them carefully against the side wall. More accurately, I pick up a bag and wait to hand it to Harrison, who then places them in the correct position. The water always comes in the bathroom, so this will do little to stop it. At least we can say we tried.

'It's getting late. Dad needs to be here soon, but...'

I don't want to send Noah out in this weather. Harrison can't leave, and neither should I. The last thing I want is Dad to hop into his car and drive himself.

'Let's deal with that problem next.'

I don't know how we'll deal with that problem because the longer we wait, the harder it will be to get Dad here.

Harrison piles the next sandbag in the row. He doesn't look at me as he continues to work but asks, 'So, while you've got no fight in you, and I can take advantage of the situation, tell me, why did you and Spoonie break up?'

I raise my eyebrows at Harrison as I pass him the next sandbag. 'Look at you pretending not to care about gossip. I think you secretly love it. Maybe that's why you love working in the kitchen. You get to hear all the drama and gossip from the staff.'

'You caught me. That's why I cut onions for two years until my eyes bled. All for gossip.'

'Such a drama queen,' I mutter as I lift the next sandbag, but this one doesn't lift as easily as the others. They're starting to fill with water, and my arms have the muscle density of an oyster.

'Here, give that to me before you break something and have no one to sue.' Harrison takes the bag from me like it's filled with air.

'Okay, I'm being useless here, so I'll go.'

'First, tell me why you guys broke up, and then you can go and be useless inside.' Harrison smirks at me, so I know he's joking. I had hoped we'd moved on from my sharing, but Harrison is not letting this go.

'Why do you want to know?'

'I think I have a right to know. I have skin in the game now. Literally.'

'Literally?'

'Yes,' says Harrison, heaving another sandbag against the wall. 'Fine. I think I can guess anyway.'

That sounds like much more fun. 'You get three guesses before I walk inside.'

Harrison stretches his back and dusts off his hands. 'He's a horrible cook, and you couldn't be honest about it.'

'No. You're confusing that with you.'

'We both know that's not true.' Harrison is so confident in his abilities as a chef that he doesn't even take the bait. I can't back that up either. I'm dreaming of another bug roll right now.

'Next guess, he's horrible in bed, and you couldn't be honest about it.'

'No. You're not even trying.'

'I think I'm getting warmer. That one feels like it could be true.'

'You're being unkind.'

'He's horrible at—'

'He's not horrible at anything!'

'He's horrible at break-ups.' *That is true.* 'You'll just have to tell me then.'

'No judgement.' I pin Harrison with a look because if I'm going to share with him, he needs not to give me any shit about it. I'll give him this one chance because he's helping me out. I secretly want to hear his take on it because he's so pragmatic about everything.

'Cross my heart; I'll hold back all judgement towards you. Spoon-face, I make no promises.'

I pick up a sandbag because I hate feeling useless and attempt to hand it over. I only get one step in before Harrison grabs it. 'Why don't you like him? It's not like you've spent much time with him.'

'It's your turn to talk. Stop avoiding the question.'

'Fine, but tell me, and I'll give you all the gossip you're hanging for.'

Harrison gives me a flat stare as he places another bag against the side of the building. 'It's pretty simple. He's an arrogant "nice" guy. He tries to be friendly, but he's just a condescending arsehole. Can't hide the fact that he thinks he's better than us.'

'Who's us?'

'You, me, everyone in this restaurant.'

I can't deny that. He is friendly but genuinely believes he's better than most people. Maybe it's because his mum tells him that most days. 'You might be right,' I say quietly as I lean against the wall.

'I am.' Harrison's confidence is on display again. 'Is that why you broke up with him?'

'Sadly, no. That would have been a better reason.'

Harrison scoffs, but this time, it turns into a chuckle. 'You made up a reason to soften the blow, didn't you?'

I give Harrison a resigned nod because break-ups are complicated and not my specialty. 'What did you tell him?'

I drop my head because I don't want to admit this out loud. I know it's going to sound worse.

'It's bad. Like really bad, but I didn't want to tell him the real reason because I didn't want the blowback.'

Harrison wipes sweat, or it could be rain, from his brow as he takes a moment to catch his breath. 'I have never been more intrigued in my life. First, fake reason.' He puts his hand up to stop me. 'No, tell me the real reason. Real reason first.'

That answer is easy. 'The real reason is his mother.'

'His mother? You can't stand her that much you had to end it?'

'She was in our relationship in a way that felt beyond intrusive, and I couldn't stand it.'

'In what way?'

'We'd have a fight, and he'd leave to tell his mother.'

'He told her about every fight?'

'It gets worse. He'd come back to tell me that Barbara felt he was right and I was wrong. It was like having a fight with two people. Two against one, and I lost every time.'

'That's fucked up. You didn't break up because of his mother. You broke up because he's not a mature adult. That's a great reason for breaking up. Why didn't you just tell him that?'

'We were fighting so much that Barbara started calling me about the fights. I didn't want a phone call from her. I was sick of always being the bad guy. Poor Devin this and poor Devin that. *You don't understand, Aggie.*' I think my Barbara impression is on point.

'So, he's a mummy's boy?'

'A mummy's boy I can handle. I'd even like that. This was like being in a throuple, which I didn't agree to.'

'Gross.'

I agree firmly. 'One hundred per cent.'

'Okay, so you didn't tell him that he and his mum have major issues, and you were freaked out by it. What *did* you tell him?'

'I said we were fighting too much and felt it might be a compatibility issue.' I cover my mouth to say the last part because I know what Harrison's reaction will be. 'Due to our zodiac signs.'

Harrison's mouth drops open. 'No.' The man honestly loves gossip. It's written all over his face. 'Star sign incompatibility?'

'Yep.' I start laughing because it's ridiculous. Harrison joins in and cradles his stomach as he cackles. He wipes his eyes once he's done laughing.

'No wonder he thought your break-up was bullshit.'

'Star sign incompatibility is a real thing.'

'No. It's not.' Harrison points his fingers at me. I'm sure it could be, but it's not worth wasting time fighting about right now. 'It's you trying to dodge the real reason, which is a great one. Perfect for breaking up. Stellar reason for not staying friends too, but here you are.' Harrison clocks me with a glare.

I'm not giving him the satisfaction of agreeing, even though he makes sense. I grumble back, 'We were incompatible. The reason doesn't matter, just the fact. We're not suited. End of story.'

'Tell him that. Exactly that.'

'I will.' Harrison makes a pfft sound, and it's the perfect sound for me to know he doesn't believe me.

'Here's a deal: I'll make you five bug rolls if you tell him. Now you have an incentive.'

'When do I get the rolls?'

Harrison throws the last bag on the pile and then shrugs his shoulders. 'Whenever you request one over the next month, I'll make it. But you must be honest.'

'Stop saying I'm not honest. I'm not a liar.' I stand and pretend to inspect the bag placement, but it's more that I'm feeling uncomfortable. Harrison always calls me out on my shit, but I don't like him picking at this one.

I can feel Harrison tracking my movements as I walk around the bags. The rain remains constant, and I wrap my arms around my middle for warmth.

'I personally don't see the difference between bending the truth and lying.'

'If it's got good intentions, like not hurting someone's feelings, it's different.'

'So well-intentioned lying is acceptable? I'll remember that next time you try and push grilled sardines onto my menu.'

'The joke is on you because, after tonight, I'll never suggest that again.'

That statement changes the mood, and any friendliness between Harrison and me evaporates instantly. A gust of wind flies up and knocks me back. I step awkwardly towards the bags and nearly trip over. Harrison flicks the sand off his hands before offering one out to me. I grab it and he pulls me closer to escape the rain, standing only inches away.

He ducks his chin to talk to me. 'Tell him, Agnes. It's kinder to put the guy out of his misery. I prefer when people are straight with me.' Harrison holds my focus as he stares down. I feel like he's alluding to me not being straight with him, but he's not saying it. He's the one not being straight with me now. I'm about to point this out, but it only takes a second for Harrison to drop my hand, and he's at the back door before I can say anything.

'Harrison?' It's a question because I have no idea what he's talking about.

'I'm going to check the bathroom.' In Harrison language, that means the conversation is over. He steps inside, but I call out again.

'I'll do it. You check on Noah.'

He hesitates at the door and I think he's about to leave. Instead he watches me for a second, and I hope he will revisit the last conversation, but I see the moment he chooses to leave it. The indifference returns to his face.

'You might need to put some towels down so no one slips.'

He doesn't wait for me to reply before he opens and closes the door behind him, leaving me alone with the rain and sandbags. What am I not being straight with him about?

Chapter Nine

After checking in with Scout and the team, I grab the nicest-looking towels because it's bad enough to have towels on the ground so I can at least make them look half-decent.

The water is pooling in the corner, and it's too much to soak up. I'll need to mop it up before it becomes a safety issue.

The storage cupboard is an issue all on its own. A messy, cluttered, unorganised heap that needed sorting through years ago, but no one did. I probably should have done it, but it's an easily forgotten job once the door is shut. The mop is used regularly, but I need a larger bucket. I rearrange some boxes and step over a crate of linens that haven't been used in years. I'm reaching down to grab the bucket when I hear a knock on the storage room door. No one who works here would knock, so that means only one thing: *Devin*. Sigh.

'Aggie?' Devin looks around the dimly lit room and finds me in the back corner.

'Over here.'

'Everything okay?'

'Yes, just need to mop up some water.' I'm waiting for Devin to explain why he's here, but he only looks around the storage cupboard like he's come for a health and safety inspection. 'Are you okay?'

'Um, yeah.' Devin steps into the room and plops himself against a shelf. 'I'm sorry for this mess.'

I wasn't expecting that to come from Devin. I step back over the crates and lean against the door jamb. It's close enough so we can speak quietly but leaves a healthy distance between us. We're hidden in the corridor, so I don't have to worry about Barbara's knowing eyes watching us.

'Sorry for this mess.' I gesture to the horror of the storage cupboard because this night could use some lightness. Devin half smiles, and then there's a heavy silence. 'What's going on, Devin?' I soften my voice, so hopefully he'll talk to me. Not like Harrison, who shut down the second I pushed him for more information, frustrating man.

'I thought you were stressed about the restaurant closing and your dad. I thought maybe you needed a little space. I didn't think the break-up would stick, if I'm honest.' Devin stands and leans on the other side of the door frame. He cocks his head to the side as he addresses me with what feels like a glimpse of the real Devin for the first time tonight – the guy he's like when he's not around his family or his mum. 'I didn't think you'd be dating someone already.'

I take one of my deep calming breaths that are usually reserved for Harrison – one, so I don't blow up at his arrogance, and two, so I can get my lies in order. Not a lie, just a bend in the truth. Oh, *crap*. Harrison cannot be right about my inability to tell the truth. It's only that I don't want to hurt anyone or make them upset. Or disappoint them, especially my dad. It's a kindness. That's how I see it, but Harrison would disagree. The thought that anyone could call me a liar is distressing.

'I didn't plan for it to play out like this, especially not tonight.'

I'm proud of myself for not apologising to him and Devin nods.

'I suppose I wouldn't have known if I hadn't turned up here tonight.'

Devin's only reflection on the night focuses on how he's been affected by turning up unannounced.

He drops his voice and searches my gaze with curiosity. 'Are you happy with him?'

'It's early days.' It's the perfect non-answer, and Devin doesn't realise that 'early days' means in the last hour. And fictional.

'I didn't think you liked him.'

Probably the most insightful Devin's ever been. 'I know. Love. Hate. Cut from the same cloth.' The longer this conversation goes on the harder it is to give vague answers so I can maintain that I'm not a liar.

'Love?'

'Just a saying.'

'Not love. What is it then between you two?'

'It's complicated.' Now *that's* the truth. 'It's too early to say, exactly.'

'I'm here if you ever need to talk.' Devin reaches forward and takes my hand. I don't extend my arm because I wasn't prepared for him to touch me or for it to linger.

'There you are.' Harrison appears behind me and cradles the back of my neck with his hand. With my hair up in a loose bun, it's skin-to-skin contact, and it makes me jump. Devin drops my hand instantly and stands to his full height.

Harrison runs his thumb up and down my neck, and an involuntary shiver runs down my spine. I turn my head slowly to glance at Harrison. He has a devil-infused twinkle in his eye even as he looks at me with a straight face, his thumb still moving back and forth. His strong jaw ticks like he's trying to hide one of his rarely seen precious smiles. He continues talking as if he didn't notice Devin holding my hand.

'Your dad is trying to get hold of you.'

'Okay.' That's all I can muster while he continues to stroke my neck. Harrison doesn't remove his hand when he moves his gaze over to Devin.

Any pleasant mischief is gone from his expression when he speaks. 'Do you think I'm just going to hang back while you hit on my girlfriend?'

No one moves a muscle as the awkwardness crashes over the three of us like we've been dumped by a ten-metre wave. I was unprepared for Harrison to go to the territorial, alpha version of himself. I've only seen it once when a customer got too friendly with Scout one night and Harrison threw his arse out onto the pavement. He had a girlfriend-ish person a while back but I don't remember seeing this version of him when she would drop into the restaurant. She would talk and Harrison would cook and then she'd leave. I don't remember seeing any neck stroking or detangling of ex-boyfriends. I purse my lips to cover my smile. I feel bad for Devin, but I am also grateful to have help getting out of this situation.

'We're only talking, and she was my girlfriend first.' That's the first thing Devin can say, and it's disappointing.

'Gross,' Harrison and I both murmur in unison. I shift my body so I'm blocking Harrison. He only uses it as an opportunity to place his other hand on my hip. Devin notices, and his nose flares. I would like to escape from this situation as, right now, the idea of mopping up dirty water in the bathroom holds considerably more appeal than staying here.

'I better call Dad.'

Harrison nods and then rests his chin on my shoulder as he glares at Devin. 'I think your mum was looking for you.' That's enough to get Devin to exit this situation.

'I'll catch up with you before we go, Aggie.'

Harrison pulls me tighter against his chest to let Devin pass – or to claim his territory. Pretend territory. I can feel the warmth of Harrison's chest against my back and something about it gives me gummy legs, which makes me lean into him further.

Devin disappears around the corner, but Harrison doesn't drop his hand. I peer back at him, and he's still watching the path where Devin left.

'Was that necessary?'

Harrison looks down at me, bringing his face closer than it's ever been. His blue eyes, surrounded by long lashes, paired with the bronze sheen of his cheeks, is all very overwhelming, so I step away before I get caught staring. I'm sure he's used to many compliments about his appearance, especially his eyes. I don't want to accidentally blurt out that they are like iridescent sparkly stars – that would be embarrassing.

Harrison's hand falls from my hip and he tucks both hands into his pockets.

'Yes, and it was fun. I think I might have been a good actor.'

It's my turn to scoff, but he was pretty believable as the surly jealous boyfriend.

'Does Dad really need to speak to me?'

Harrison takes my phone out of his pocket and hands it to me. 'Yes.' Three missed calls from Dad. *Shit.*

'Everyone's been asked to stay off the roads. That non-existent storm is getting worse.'

'Seriously?' We share looks of disappointment because Dad's not returning here tonight. I slump against the shelves and hide my shaking hand as I unlock my phone. I blink rapidly to keep my tears tucked in, but Dad not being here tonight is the cherry on the cake for my hatred of this place. Everything he gave to this restaurant, and now I'm stuck here while Dad's at home alone.

'Okay, I'll call Dad. Thanks for whatever that was.'

I bring up Dad's number and dial as Harrison stands closer, leaning against the door.

'He's still touching you even though your boyfriend person is in the same building. He's a menace. You obviously weren't honest with him.' Harrison's voice is low, and the deep tone curls through my body.

I shake off the vibrations from Harrison and whisper, 'I was getting to that part.'

'Didn't seem like it when I walked up.'

'He was touching me, not the other way around,' I say with more force because the timing was bad.

'You still get to decide who touches you.'

'You touched me, and I don't remember deciding that.'

'I did warn you I was a touchy-feely boyfriend.' I glance up, and thoughts of what a touchy-feely boyfriend means to Harrison run through my head. My gaze must linger too long on Harrison's lips because his eyebrows lift in question. I shake my head, and any thoughts of Harrison's touch away.

I can hear the call connect, so I whisper, 'Stop. You're enjoying this too much.'

Harrison leans in so his lips are positioned behind my ear as he says, 'Truth is, if you were my girlfriend, I would

94

have said and done a lot more than I just did.' I feel the rumble of his voice down to my toes.

Oh my. I rub my neck where I can feel the tingles lingering from where Harrison's thumb grazed my neck back and forth. I don't have a chance to acknowledge that before Dad answers.

'Aggie? Everything all right there?'

'Hi, Dad. Are you okay?'

'Yes, I'm fine. Are you busy? I thought the weather might have kept people away?' Dad immediately talks about the restaurant and asks if the weather has affected the night. Next week, he will be in deep mourning because I don't know what will occupy his thoughts every waking moment.

'We've had some no-shows, but it's still been steady.'

I can hear Dad shuffling around in the kitchen while I imagine the phone is squeezed between his ear and shoulder. Dad never uses the speaker function, even though I've shown him countless times.

'You feeling okay, Dad?'

'No. I'm pissed those weather people finally decided to get it right on the one night when we didn't need this bloody storm.'

The noise from the rain is constant now. It's getting heavier every minute, and the wind has picked up. 'It might still blow over.'

Harrison huffs.

'Hold on a second, Dad.' I cover the phone with my hand. 'What?'

'Ernie shouldn't be driving in this, and I'm not sending Noah out. It's not safe for me to put the kid on the road in these conditions.'

'So, Dad just misses out on saying goodbye? I need to give him some hope that there's a chance he can make it.'

'That's not hope. That's a lie.'

'Stop. It's me trying not to break my dad's heart.'

Harrison shakes his head. 'He's a big boy, Agnes. He can handle it even if he misses out on the last night.' Harrison at least looks upset about the idea. 'It's not what anyone wanted, but it's not safe. Put Ernie on speaker.'

Dad will want Harrison's opinion on this decision, so I stab my phone with my finger to show Harrison how I feel about his demands.

'Dad, Harrison's here now, too.'

'You guys under control?'

'It's quiet,' Harrison answers. 'I think we should start sending people home.'

Dad sighs, and it's laced with sadness, but I think he's surrendering to the disaster that tonight has become. I submitted to that fact hours ago.

'You probably should. The Whalleys okay to get home?'

'I'll go and check on them,' I say because I'd like to chat with them again. Devin and his issues have kept me distracted.

'Thanks, sweetie. I can try and make it now before it gets worse.'

Harrison and I make eye contact as we let that idea float around the room. There's no stink-eye or evil glares for a change, only both of us weighing up the pros and cons of sending Dad out into a storm. I give a resigned nod.

'Dad,' I say at the same time as Harrison rumbles, 'Ernie.' Harrison steps back and gestures for me to speak.

'We all want you here, but it's not worth you driving in this right now. You're better off waiting, and let's hope it clears soon.' Dad can still drive, but it's getting harder for him, and I've noticed he rarely drives at night.

'We can send Noah out the second it slows and come get you, Ernie.'

There's silence at the end of the phone until more shuffling starts again.

'Okay, okay. Here's the plan: start sending the staff home if they have a safe way to get home. Otherwise, keep everyone there. Let the customers leave now if they want and cancel any other bookings for tonight.'

'Will do.' I watch Harrison as he drops his head. What a way to go out. This is one hundred times worse than I imagined, and I'm devastated for my dad.

'What a fucking shitshow, hey?' Harrison and I chuckle at Dad's assessment, and I'm glad he can still laugh about this. 'Keep me up to date with what's happening there, you two.'

'We will. Love you, Dad.' I hang up the phone, then Harrison and I linger beside each other as we ponder what tonight has turned into.

'You want to talk to the kitchen staff? I'll first talk to the Whalleys and then the wait staff.'

'Good plan.' I can tell Harrison is pissed, whereas I feel blue. This was meant to be a celebration, and now it's a 'shitshow' as Dad put it.

'We forget it's the last night and getting everyone home safely is the priority. Are you okay to stay? I can manage if you want to get home.'

Harrison's head flings back like I slapped him across the face with a wet fish. It's clear he doesn't like me asking that question, and his stare is positively pissed.

'Don't ask me stupid questions.' I put my hands up in defence because it's only polite for me to ask. 'I know it's not my name on the paperwork or my family, but this is my restaurant, too.' Harrison points in the direction of the main dining room. 'I'm not leaving until every single person is out that door.'

Harrison doesn't let me reply before he storms off. I somehow poured vinegar on a wound I didn't realise existed.

Chapter Ten

Mr and Mrs Whalley both take a sip of red wine as Mr Whalley strokes his thumb over the back of his wife's hand. They're constantly holding hands or smiling at each other. I imagine they can't always be like that, but it's how they are when they come out to dine.

'I'm sorry to interrupt.' I kneel down so they can hear me. 'The weather is getting worse, so we're going to send some of the employees home.'

'That's lovely of you.' Mrs Whalley takes her hand from Mr Whalley's and rests it on my shoulder.

'I wanted to make sure you both can get home safely. The conditions aren't great outside.'

'We were just talking about that. If it's all right with you, we'd prefer to stay. Neither of us like driving at night and especially not in this weather,' says Mrs Whalley.

'And we're enjoying our last meal here. It doesn't feel right that this place won't be open tomorrow,' adds Mr Whalley. There's something in the way he says it with such sincerity that it pushes the stress and guilt I'm feeling to the surface, and a tear breaks out before I can smother it.

'Oh, my dear. Come here.' Mrs Whalley pulls me into a side hug as I lean in. I wipe the tears before they become too many to hide. 'Such a shame it's ending this way, but there is something fitting about it.'

'There is?' I stand up because my calves are burning, and I don't want to be tempted to burrow into Mrs Whalley and sob like a baby.

'Your parents never told you that story?' I shake my head as I reach for my necklace because I sense I'm about to hear a story about my mum. While I love those stories, they're also hard to hear when I'm feeling vulnerable. I clench her locket on my chain for support. 'Opening night there was a terrible storm. Your mum was worried it was a bad omen, but it was a blessing.'

'How so?'

'It's how we all got to know each other. People talk when there's a crisis. We would have eaten and left, but we stayed and helped clean up instead. It's how I got to know your mum and dad. Something about the weather tonight feels just right. I know your mum would be laughing about how it's turned out. She had the best laugh.'

I didn't realise she knew Mum so well. I thought they were regulars, our most loyal customers, but I didn't know Mum might have called her a friend. No one talks to me about Mum. Dad rarely mentions her, and we have so little family that I rely on the tiny memories I have of her.

I bite my top lip, trying not to cry, but the tears fall down my face.

'That's nice to know; I don't remember her laugh,' I say, my voice just a little hoarse. I wish it were recorded so I could hear the sound of her laugh again. I remember her laughing but I never memorised the sound. I never thought I'd need to.

'Well, your dad has the best laugh as well.'

'That is true.' I would know that laugh anywhere and wish he were here right now to boost morale. 'I'm still hopeful Dad can make it. I hate that he's home alone.'

Mrs Whalley takes my hand again. 'He'll get here somehow. These storms normally blow over.' *That's what I've been saying!* Finally, someone agrees with me.

'Let's hope so.' I wipe my tears again and hope I'm not all blotchy. 'You can stay with us as long as you like. I'll get Harrison to bring you some dessert.'

'Thank you, that's kind of you. He's such a sweetheart.' *Is he?*

'I'll see the staff get away safely and I'll be back.'

'No rush, we're very happy here.' Mr Whalley tips his wine glass at me and I am jealous of the contentment that surrounds them both.

I wipe my face again as I push through the door into the kitchen.

'Eight-fifteen! You all saw it. Give me my money!' Scout is far too excited about seven dollars. I check my watch because I didn't realise that was the time. Noah hands Scout her winnings as she does a little dance.

Across the room, I spot Harrison talking with the kitchen hands. They hug him and then make their way to the staff lockers. His eyes find mine across the room, and he studies my face with concern. I must be red and blotchy. Damn, Mrs Whalley and her kindness. I didn't want to cry tonight.

I say goodbye to the employees leaving as Scout flicks a coin in the air. She doesn't look like she's going anywhere.

'You can go too. I'll work the bar.'

'Nah. With the drama at home I'd rather stay here.'

Harrison catches the coin Scout tosses in the air, and she smacks his arm before he hands it back.

'She actually cracks some tears. I didn't think she had it in her.' Harrison is talking about me, in front of me, but not to me and there's an odd bitterness to his tone.

'Eight-fifteen on the dot.' Scout winks at Harrison and then pushes through the doors to the restaurant, leaving Harrison glaring at me.

'Fake tears then.' How I'm feeling tonight is not his or anyone's business, so I don't correct his wrong assumption.

'Scout is staying. She's avoiding her place with Ria moving out. Mr and Mrs Whalley don't want to drive, so they're also staying.'

Harrison nods, but it's clinical. We're back to business mode, Harrison and Agnes.

'Noah's staying. The four of us can cover things.'

'Agree.' I clap my hands. I'm not sure why, but it feels like a way for me to end this conversation and leave.

'Your ex staying?'

'No.' I sigh. 'I need to go see them now.' Harrison doesn't say anything as I step away.

'I thought you were having feelings. Shame they weren't real.' Harrison's voice sounds like he's disappointed in me and it raises all my walls.

I don't turn back as I say, 'You have no idea what you're talking about, as usual.'

'Enlighten me then.'

I twist back to rake my eyes over Harrison. His expression is guarded. 'No. You never answer my questions and get to walk away when you don't feel like talking, so no.' I change my tone to professional before continuing, 'Mr and Mrs Whalley would like dessert. They'll be happy with whatever you choose for them.'

'Right on it, boss.' Harrison gives me a combination of a bow and a salute to piss me off and it works.

Devin's dad spoons the remaining gelato into his mouth in three giant scoops. He then wipes his mouth and stands. 'Let's go.'

That's all Frank says before he pushes his chair in and walks over to pay the bill. I've given Scout instructions to discount their bill, but I hope they didn't think the meal would be free. I wouldn't be surprised if they did.

Luckily, Devin had seen the warnings before I got to the table, so the Spork family were already getting ready to leave. I feel like I can breathe for the first time this evening. Maybe Mrs Whalley was right and storms can be a good thing because it's pushed Devin out the door early.

'Devin, you'll be okay getting home on your own?' He's a thirty-one-year-old man. Why is Barbara asking that question? I internalise my sneer, which gives me a burning sensation in my chest.

'I'll follow behind you and Alma so we can all get home safely.'

'My sweet boy.' Barbara comes around the table to give me a one-arm hug. 'It was lovely to see you again. We might see you next week then?'

I make a mhm sound, but it's not enough for her. I'm trying not to lie openly to her face, but it's getting hard. 'We'll see.'

'We'll see?' Barbara cocks her head to the side.

'There's still a lot to do with closing down the restaurant, so I just need to see how much help Dad needs.'

'Surely, you can't work nights?'

Leave me alone, woman! I fix the smile on my face so she can't tell how irritated I am by her whenever she opens her mouth.

'We'll just see.' I repeat myself, so hopefully she'll leave it.

Barbara leans in to speak in a soft, calming voice, but there's a fakeness to it that I feel in my bones. 'Men need attention, Agnes. Devin's patient, but best not to test it.'

Barbara and I eyeball each other for a few seconds, and I would love to tell her that her precious Devin can shove his patience. I've had more patience than a saint dealing with this woman, and I'm done.

'Thanks, Barbara. You better get on the road before the storm gets worse.'

'Yes, that is correct. Let's go, everyone.'

Barbara waves her hand to herd the family out of the restaurant. I make an effort to hug Nelly because she's the best one.

'Take care of yourself,' I whisper to her, hoping she doesn't read too much into it. Alma squeezes me before saying she'll be in touch about the hen's night. I hope that idea will disappear once she knows we've broken up.

Devin lingers by my side as his family all leave. My father's restaurant is flooding. I've got a million things I need to check on, so I hope Devin doesn't want a long-winded goodbye. 'Goodbye and get out' is almost all I can manage right now.

'I'll walk you to the front door,' I say, but it's so I can get him out the door and end this fiasco.

The rain is bucketing down, and through the front door, I watch the water pooling in the car park while I wait for Devin to put on his jacket.

Devin's shoulder brushes against mine as he joins me in inspecting the rain. He doesn't move away, but his shoulder seems to get closer. I step away, putting some distance between us. This is my moment – time for the ridiculousness of the night to end. If I want a clean break, I will need to do two things right now: be brutally honest about my feelings and be the bad guy. Both seem horrible, and I would avoid them if I possibly could, but after tonight, I do not want to partake in any more Spork family gatherings. That's a firm boundary.

'I'll call you later in the week,' Devin says casually.

I usually wouldn't reply, but here I go.

'Devin.' My face must reveal all my intentions because he cuts in before I can get more out.

'Still okay for us to be friends, right?'

I rock on my heels because I need to be honest. No softening the blow. No bending of the truth. Rip the Band-Aid off and leave a big gaping wound. Devin can see the hesitation on my face.

'Don't tell me, Harrison won't let you? That's not healthy, Aggie.' Devin's voice fills with concern like Harrison is someone I need to be wary of, which is ridiculous given the situation tonight.

'It's not Harrison,' I snap back because Harrison's the last reason.

'Okay, then I'll text you tomorrow. Maybe we can get some coffee during the week and make plans to take Nelly out.' He's a steamroller. It's only hit me now that he's exactly like his mother and steamrolls people until he gets what he wants.

I was his perfect target because I never speak up and can easily get pushed over by anyone. I'd struggle even against a forceful mouse. Everything in our failed relationship becomes clear, and it makes me mad. He's not listening, and it's up to me to finally make him hear me.

Devin cups my arm as he leans over and kisses my cheek. He lingers for a moment, inhaling deeply and making me feel many layers of uncomfortable. He's taken too many liberties tonight and my patience has run out. I place my hand on his chest and push him back.

'I don't think that's a good idea.'

'It's just a kiss on the cheek. Harrison has you on a short leash.' Ugh. I hate that saying and that he thinks I'm now controlled by a man.

'Not the kiss, the coffee. Taking Nelly out. I don't think any of it is a good idea.'

'Why?' Devin's lips pull back in a snarl and I don't appreciate the attitude in his voice.

'Because the truth is Devin—' What's the truth? Where to start? At the beginning, I suppose. 'We weren't friends before we started dating.'

'So?'

'I don't think we'll likely be friends after.' This contradicts what I told him when we first broke up, but it's been the truth the entire time.

'You don't think it's likely? Because you have a shiny new boyfriend?' Devin's face contorts when he says the word 'boyfriend'.

'Because we didn't get on that well when we dated, so why would we want to hang out now?'

'We didn't get on? What are you talking about?' Devin's voice rises, and I quickly look across the restaurant to see that no one has heard. Nearly all the customers have gone now and the Whalleys seem blissfully unaware or are politely not listening.

I lean in and lower my voice, hoping Devin will do the same. 'We fought a lot. You know that.'

'I told you, Mum said it was just an ironing out of issues. Those things go away. I told you to talk to Mum

106

'about it.' Devin does not lower his voice, and my patience is slipping.

'I didn't want to talk to your mum about our relationship,' I say through gritted teeth.

'Why?'

'Because it's weird. I wanted to talk to *you* about our relationship.'

'Mum knows these things. She could have helped.' There's that condescending tone that Harrison mentioned. It's never bothered me as much as it is at this moment.

'Helped who? Me and you or just me?'

Devin at least has the decency to look sheepish when he replies because we both know he was referring to only me needing help. 'We all have stuff we're working through. Mum explained why you're closed off. It makes sense based on the way you grew up. You're just not used to having a mum around.' Devin coats his voice in what he believes is kindness, but I could burst into tears from the red-hot anger flowing through my veins. Patronising arsehole!

There is nothing that will infuriate and hurt me more than telling me I'm deficient because my mum died. How dare he and his mum think it was something to fix in me.

My voice is firm, and I maintain direct eye contact so Devin knows I'm not messing around.

'I remember my mum. I remember what it was like to have a mum. I am not broken.' I bring my hand to rest on my chest with Mum's locket resting under my fingers. 'I prefer parents who aren't constantly interfering with their children's lives. I didn't have to run to my dad every time we disagreed for backup. How was I ever going to get through to you when it was always two against one?'

'We're back here.' He rolls his eyes and my temper ignites to volcanic levels. 'My mum is not the problem. What a load of rubbish. She was trying to help us.'

'When she's talking to me about our sex life, you're sharing too much.'

'We're a close family.'

'You can say that again!' I proclaim loudly, and it's a joy to let it out.

Devin's not at all embarrassed that he overshared with his mum. That was the last straw for me when I decided to cut and run. I wish this was how I ended things the first time because I wouldn't be in the midst of a second break-up while I'm working, but at least it's finally coming out now.

'Listen, there's no need to go over this because we broke up. You and your mum can discuss whatever you like now, but I don't want to be involved in the, to be very honest, icky closeness of your relationship. So, no, we won't be friends. We won't see each other, and I hope I never see your mother again.'

It's all out. Devin looks hurt, and I'm the bad guy, but I was honest. It's done.

I hear a gentle clearing of a throat behind me before Barbara steps alongside Devin and rubs his arm like he's fallen over and has a boo-boo. I thought she'd left already. Didn't she leave with her husband? I'm frozen as I try to process what I just said to Devin and work out what Barbara heard. From the expression on her face, she heard everything.

Shit. Shit. Shit.

Chapter Eleven

Barbara regards me with a superior air before turning to face Devin.

'I couldn't help but overhear, is it true? You've broken up?' The discomfort could swallow me whole right now, so I fold my arms for protection and wait for what I know is coming.

'I'm sorry I didn't tell you. It's new. We were working through things.' The hurt in Devin's voice when speaking to his mum makes me irrationally angry. It's a tone he only uses with his mother.

'You don't need to explain. I know it's been challenging for you.' Barbara emphasises *for you* before turning her steely gaze in my direction. 'I know our relationship is hard to understand for people who don't have a close family. I only tried to include you in that, but sometimes it's hard to accept something that feels unknown.'

Barbara has a sweetness to her voice that is so sickly that it makes my teeth ache. It's passive-aggressive but done with a level of skill that should be studied. She's backed me into a corner, and if I say anything to call her out, I'm the emotionally immature girl without a mother. Screw her one hundred times over. I cannot handle the dynamic of Barbara and Devin's relationship tonight. Or ever, which is why I broke up with him.

I'm not sure how to respond to her jab. I'd like to yell that my dad and I are close, but it seems childlike, or I could scream 'the thought of being in your family makes me feel physically ill', but nothing comes out. Barbara's about to take another shot when I feel a hand gently touch my back seconds before Harrison walks past me towards the front door.

'I just heard reports that streets are starting to flood. You better run before the storm gets worse.' Harrison holds the door open enough for rain to start coming in, but he doesn't seem to care. He's telling Barbara and Devin to get out but with a touch of Barbara's fake kindness. It fills my body with relief, which I thought would be impossible right now.

'Thank you, let's go, Devin.' Barbara pushes her handbag higher on her shoulder before giving me a once-over. No goodbye for me before she turns to Devin and places her hand on his shoulder. 'I'll make you a hot chocolate at home.'

He doesn't live with her, but he'll stop for a hot beverage with his mummy. I hope he enjoys his hot chocolate. He can have as many hot chocolates as he likes, as long as I never have to see her scoop extra marshmallows into his cup and wink at him as she does it. It's my villain origin story.

Devin nods like the good boy that he is and gestures for his mum to walk out first. He eyeballs Harrison before realising that may not be a smart idea and looks at me.

'Text me if you need anything, Aggie.' He thinks I've got myself into a bad situation, but he has no idea *he* was the bad situation. He was always clueless.

It's a sad way to end things, but at least they're over. As Harrison said, I no longer have to try to avoid him.

He'll be avoiding me now, and something about that feels surprisingly okay.

Harrison and Devin have a manly nod at each other, but Harrison is more stoic, so he wins the alpha-off. He closes the door quickly and deadbolts it shut.

'He's gone.' Harrison's voice startles me. I only notice now that he's holding the backup mop. The water in the bathroom must be coming in harder than I realised. I'm utterly drained from the second break-up, so I can't bicker with Harrison right now, but then I catch a flicker of emotion in his eyes.

'You know what I think?'

'No, but I look forward to you telling me.' My head drops so I can hide my face as I brace for Harrison's honesty, but he puts his finger under my chin and gently lifts my head.

'I think you're a fucking saint for putting up with those two.'

I laugh despite my foul mood and it makes me realise how much I needed to hear that. For months, I was made to feel like I was somehow wrong for not wanting my boyfriend to discuss *every* issue with his mum. They preyed on the fact that I desperately missed my mum, and instead of trying to fill that void, they used it as a way to score points against me. Harrison's statement makes me feel sane.

'The door is locked, and they're gone. For good. Okay?' Harrison drops his finger, but our eyes stay locked. The clear ocean blue of Harrison's eyes steadies my breathing.

'Okay.' I shake off the bad vibes from Barbara and attempt to smile. 'I'll come help you.' I gesture to his mop and am glad we can focus on minimising the damage to the restaurant now that most of the customers are gone.

Harrison takes two steps towards the kitchen, then swings back to face me. 'Does this mean we're breaking up now?'

I chuckle at his suggestion we were ever something to break up. 'Sure, why not another break-up? I'm on a roll.'

'You want to do it or give me the honour?'

'A gentleman would let me do it.'

'Fine. Let's see how you go.' Harrison rests his hands on the top of the broom handle as he waits for our fake break-up chat.

I take a small step towards Harrison and lower my voice. 'Harrison James, we need to talk.'

'Oh, shit. This doesn't sound good.' Harrison's acting is terrible as he holds one hand to his heart.

'I think we need to break up.'

'You *think*?' Harrison leans forward and whispers, 'No grey areas, Agnes.' He resumes his fake hopeful expression.

'No, not I think. We are breaking up.'

Harrison's mouth drops open, and he gasps. I laugh before resuming my solemn break-up voice.

'I'm sorry, but it's you. All you. I'm perfect, and you're an unreasonable grump.'

Harrison breaks character and arches his eyebrows. 'I've heard this break-up before. Pick something more original.'

'I don't like your cooking.'

'That's a kick to the nuts. Don't be so cruel.' He seems genuinely upset and I let my laugh out. It feels good to release some of the tension from tonight in this fake break-up. It's the most fun I've ever had breaking up with someone.

'Fine. You wore me out in the bedroom, and I need a break.'

'Seems like a valid reason.' Harrison smiles at me and in that moment, I'm grateful he was here with me tonight. I no longer feel stressed about what happened with Devin.

'Your turn to be the bad guy. Be kind.' I point my finger so he knows I'm serious.

Harrison rolls his shoulders, getting ready to fake break my heart.

His expression changes to thoughtful as his eyes roam my face and he says, 'Agnes Keegan, you deserve far more than the likes of me.'

Oof. I wasn't expecting that. I thought he'd say I was a stubborn mess and he couldn't put up with me any longer. Harrison's shoulders drop and his head tilts to the side as he watches me. I imagine him in an actual break-up, and that thought makes me want to hug him. For all his cocky confidence, there's something vulnerable about Harrison that I've never been able to understand fully. Something squishy and hidden underneath his ridiculously handsome face. He smiles softly as he continues breaking up with me. 'Also, your father would have my balls if he knew, so best to end it now.' Harrison has a tenderness in his expression before he looks away. 'And you're a terrible cook.'

His joke breaks the moment and the air feels lighter again. 'That's true. Friends then?'

Harrison abruptly swings the broom around and walks towards the kitchen. 'Argh, you and the bloody friend thing. *No.*'

'You're saying we're not friends?' I yell out.

'I'm leaving.'

'So, we're back to hating each other?'

'I never hated you, but it's good to know how you feel.' Harrison shoots over his shoulder. I'm about to reply to his infuriating comment, but pounding on the door cuts me off. I reach for the front door, but Harrison yells out.

'Wait. Let me get it.' He gestures for me to move behind him as he unlocks the door. It flies open, as does the thrashing rain. The wind has picked up and I can hardly see outside through the fierce storm. Through the torrential rain, I squint to see who's at the door. Harrison steps aside just as Devin and Barbara burst into the restaurant. Harrison quickly closes the door again before more water gets inside. My heart plummets at seeing these two again.

Devin and Barbara are breathing heavily, and their clothes are soaked through as they try to shake them out.

'Are you both okay? What happened?' I ask.

Devin's out of breath as he tries to talk. 'It's madness out there. We could hardly see in front of us. We got to Stanley Avenue, but it was too deep to drive through.'

'It's flooded already?' asks Harrison.

'All the way up to Petrie Road. Alma and Dad got through, but only just. It wasn't safe for us to try and drive through.'

'Oh my gosh, the water's come up so quickly,' I say as I help Barbara out of her wet jacket.

'Guys.' Scout comes out from the kitchen holding her phone. 'More warnings. They're calling the storm a "rain bomb". Everyone's instructed to stay put until the storm stops.'

'And when do they think that will be?' Harrison asks.

'A few hours, maybe. I don't think anyone knows yet.'

Great. I think the realisation hits everyone at the same time that we're trapped now together for the next few hours. *Shit. Shit. Shit.*

'I didn't know where to go,' Devin tells me. I appreciate him saying that, and I wouldn't want them stranded.

I wave away his concern. 'It's fine. Of course, you can stay here.'

We're being polite with each other, which removes some of the awkwardness. Some still lingers, and that's mostly coming from Barbara. She stays eerily quiet, but I can see she's freezing. Water is dripping from her as she has a full-body shiver.

'Let's try and get you guys dry. Harrison and I need to clean up the bathroom, and then we'll have a drink to calm our nerves.' I gesture for Devin and Barbara to follow Scout.

'Thank you,' says Devin as Scout leads them into the main dining area.

Seven hours is now turning into an all-nighter.

I can hear Harrison relocking the door as he mumbles, 'This fucking night.'

I feel the same way.

'You okay?' Harrison stands beside me. We watch our return guests warm themselves as Scout hands them towels.

'Just giving myself a moment to mentally prepare for whatever comes next.' I gesture to the dining room.

'What did your dad call it? A fucking shitshow.'

We both laugh before Harrison says, 'Agnes?' I look up, and he's got that twinkle back in his eye, but I'm not sure why.

'Yes?' I'm suspicious and don't hide it.

'I decided,' Harrison leans over and whispers in my ear. 'I'll give you a second chance. Breaking up was a little premature.'

'How kind of you.'

'This should be fun.' Harrison winks at me, and he knows how cheesy it was.

'You're enjoying this too much.'

'How could I not?' Harrison walks backwards and beams at me. 'I'm Agnes Keegan's boyfriend.'

'For tonight.' I hold my finger out like I'm schooling a child, but I want to be clear.

Harrison hooks his thumb over his shoulder. 'They don't know that.'

It scares me how much he's enjoying this. He swings the mop over his shoulder and makes his way to the kitchen.

Before he's out of earshot, I say, 'Harrison, I—'

He turns, and I don't know how to finish that sentence. Before tonight, I never would have asked for help, but this situation is unique, and I'm feeling deflated that I have to deal with Barbara again. I'm also worried about my dad, and I fear it might all have become too much. 'Thanks.'

'I'll take them both out if they give you any shit.' Harrison's statement shocks me, but it's exactly what I needed to hear.

'That escalated quickly,' I joke, but I appreciate that Harrison is in my corner right now.

'Perhaps, but still true. Let's go.' Harrison angles his head, and I follow him to help stop at least one of the disasters of the night.

The clock has been reset. Unknown hours to go.

Chapter Twelve

Everyone has broken off to hang out in different parts of the restaurant. Barbara and Devin are in the corner whispering. A towel is wrapped around Devin's shoulders as he sips on the drink Scout was friendly enough to take over for him. Harrison is cleaning the kitchen for no reason other than wanting to hide, and I might join him soon. We cleaned up as much water as possible leaking into the bathroom, but we can't stop it entirely until the rain goes away.

Mr and Mrs Whalley have joined Scout and Noah at the bar, while I linger at the side. Devin and Barbara sneak glances my way and then pretend not to notice I'm in the same space as them. I'll take the silent treatment from Barbara over any more conversations about my relationship with Devin. *Ex*-relationship.

My phone rings, and I know it will be Dad.

'Hey, are you okay?'

Dad's voice comes through the phone, but it's hard to hear now with the noise coming from the storm. 'Did everyone get home safely?' He yells so much that I pull the phone away from my ear.

'Yes. Well, mostly. A few are staying until the storm blows over.'

'The Whalleys?'

'Yes, they're here and safe.'

'Harrison, okay?'

'I think so. Why wouldn't he be?' Dad only answers with a dismissive sound that doesn't answer the question. 'Is your house holding up? No water coming in?'

'Aggie, I'm fine. Listen…' Dad pauses and I know it's from sadness about how things have turned out. 'Put me on speaker.'

I follow Dad's instructions and take the phone over to the bar area.

'Hello, everyone.'

'Oh, Ernie, are you okay?' Mrs Whalley asks.

'I'm all good – nothing to worry about. I'm sorry I can't be there, but it's still the last night, and I want you guys to celebrate. I want it to be the best night despite everything that's going on.'

I dart my eyes over to Devin and Barbara before turning away. Dad has no idea about the set-up and dynamics going on tonight and that his request will be challenging.

I sense something behind me and find Harrison standing in the doorway of the kitchen, listening to Ernie.

'Harrison, you there?'

Harrison joins Scout behind the bar and leans closer to the phone. 'Here, Ernie.'

'Use everything we have left. Whatever anyone wants, they can have.'

'Will do.' Harrison nods even though Dad can't see him and then retreats again to the kitchen.

'Mr Keegan, Noah here. Do I have permission to drink while on duty?'

'Write yourself off, son. You're not on duty anymore.' Noah raises his hand for a high five, but his hand is too high for anyone to reach. Scout jumps up and smacks his hand and Noah shakes it out like she hurt him.

'Dad, that's not the best idea…'

'Aggie, have some fun tonight. Stay safe and have fun. That's an order.' Dad hangs up before I can suggest that he maybe not give away all our stock and suggest the young staff get wasted.

'You all heard the man!' Scout lifts a bottle of tequila on the bar, screws off the lid and throws it across the room. Mrs Whalley giggles and helps Scout line up shot glasses on the counter.

'To rain bombs!' Scout, the Whalleys and Noah hold their glasses in the air. 'Hold up.' Scout waves to Barbara and Devin to join the group. Devin looks to his mum for direction. She turns her body away, and Devin sadly shakes his head. I bet he'd love a shot, but he can't go against Mummy.

'Harrison! Get your arse out here!' Scout yells over her shoulder.

Moments later, Harrison pushes through the doors from the kitchen, places a platter of leftover entrées on the bar counter and then takes his shot. He throws it back before cheering anyone. He slams it back down on the bar.

'Another.'

Scout watches him with amusement. 'You're meant to cheers with us first.'

Harrison looks up and notices the group eyeing him.

'The first one didn't count. Let's go.' He motions for everyone to raise their shot glasses.

I give in and join the group in clinking glasses. Harrison tips his glass to me before sculling his drink. He maintains eye contact with me as the drink flows down his throat. He then turns to Scout and demands another.

He slams that one down and then disappears into the kitchen. His moods this evening are next level. He's working through something, but I have no idea what. Who knows how Harrison James's mind works?

'Maybe we should play a game?' Noah's enthusiasm is met with silence. 'Come on. We're stuck here. Let's have some fun.'

'Noah's right, let's play a drinking game.' Scout starts arranging bottles and pouring drinks before anyone agrees to a game, let alone a drinking game.

'I didn't say drinking g—'

Scout covers Noah's lips with her finger. 'Shh. I'm making yummy things.'

Noah nods while his lips are still blocked from moving by Scout.

Boom! The front door thrashes violently on its hinges, but the lock holds it steady. I'm not sure if it's the weather or a supernatural being making the door shudder, but we all remain frozen, staring at the door. The door rattles again. I take a step towards it as Devin stands. He takes no further steps closer but waits to see if I'll move. I think he's trying to be my backup. I'd rather Scout, if I'm honest.

I walk over tentatively to the door just as Harrison exits the kitchen. Within seconds, he's next to me and twists in front of me to reach the door first.

He leans over and whispers in a teasing voice, 'Any more ex-boyfriends or mothers-in-law joining us tonight?'

When the door rattles again, Harrison pulls me behind his back and keeps a hold of my side as he peers through the glass. He nudges me further behind him as he carefully undoes the lock and steps aside.

The rain comes pouring in. Wind and leaves fly through the door as I brace myself for the impact of the cold rain. I peer through my fingers to see a man step out of the dark and into the restaurant.

Harrison pushes against the force of the rain and closes the door again.

Our new guest is wearing an oversized fireman's uniform, but the jacket is undone. The man takes the jacket off, revealing the tightest white singlet I've ever seen on a human body. It's wet and barely covers the mass of muscles protruding from his body. He's bumpy, toned and obviously doesn't enjoy cake. He shakes his shoulder-length hair and then flings it back as if he were starring in a swimsuit photoshoot.

Everyone in the restaurant is silent as we watch our newest guest.

Scout's mouth hangs open until she says, 'Can everyone see this, or am I that drunk already?'

Mrs Whalley's head bobs quickly up and down as she says, 'I see it, but let's pour another drink just to make sure it doesn't go away.'

'Good idea.' Scout and Mrs Whalley shot another drink while staring at the muscly fireman standing in our entranceway.

'Sorry, I'm late.' The man waves at the group and smiles at us with some hesitation.

I ask, 'What are you late for?' as Scout says, 'That's quite all right.'

Muscle man doesn't know who to answer first, so Harrison steps in.

'Did you have a booking tonight?'

'Yes. Linda's hen's night. I got lost in the storm, so sorry I'm late.'

I say, 'I think you're still lost, sorry,' as Scout says, 'No problem. You can start now.'

Harrison steps in to help again.

'There's no Linda here. Or a hen's night. Or anyone waiting for a stripper—'

'Speak for yourself,' Scout yells out, and Harrison ignores her drunk arse.

'We don't mean to assume, but you're a stripper?' I ask. Harrison turns and lifts his eyebrows at me. 'You don't know. Maybe he's actually a firefighter, and there's been a fire at Linda's hen's night,' I say in response to Harrison's stare.

Muscle man pops his head around Harrison and says, 'No, he's right, I'm a stripper. I prefer male dancer, but it's splitting hairs.'

I move next to Harrison and offer my hand. 'Nice to meet you, I'm Agnes, this is Harrison.'

The man extends his hand and introduces himself, 'Willy. Lovely to meet you.'

'Nope. That's not your name.' Harrison folds his arms over his chest as Scout descends into hysterics in the background. Willy looks confused at Harrison's comment.

'It's my name.'

'No. This is a prank.'

Willy looks even more dumbfounded. 'I can assure you that after the crappy night I've had I would not participate in any pranks. Is there really no Linda here?'

'No. I'm sorry, Willy,' I say and manage to keep a straight face.

'Don't call him that,' Harrison says gruffly at me, and I can't help but smile.

'It's his name. It's a great name.' I beam at Willy.

'I think it's a great name, too, if we're taking a poll,' Noah shouts from the bar.

'I get that a lot about my name, so it's not a big deal for me. My full name is William, but I go by Willy. Yes, I'm a stripper, but I'm also a gym instructor. I know Bill is more common, but I prefer Willy.'

'This fucking night,' Harrison grumbles to himself.

'Come in, Willy,' I say as I hear Scout laughing again in the background. 'We'll get you a towel and a drink. I don't think Linda is getting her show tonight.'

Willy shakes his head. 'This is bad. I promised I'd be there tonight. This damn storm is ruining everything.'

Willy takes a seat at the bar and hangs his head in his hands until Scout hands him a drink. He smiles at her kindly before asking, 'Straw?'

'Sure thing.' Scout hands him a straw, and he swirls his drink, which I think is some type of alcohol and soda, and then he takes a long sip.

'Delightful. Thank you.'

'You are so welcome.' I smack Scout on her arm discreetly because she's eyeing Willy up and down like she could take a bite of him any second. Willy introduces himself and shakes everyone's hand.

Devin finally decides to join the group, or perhaps he's thirsty. Scout pours him a drink, and he takes a seat next to Willy.

'Willy, nice to meet you.'

'Devin. Likewise.' The men shake hands as everyone breaks into conversations – Harrison with Mr Whalley, and Noah and Scout with Mrs Whalley. Barbara remains on her own in the corner. We'll see how long her stubbornness will keep her over there.

I fluff around behind the bar and can't help but overhear Devin and Willy's conversation.

'Lovely spot. I've heard the food is amazing. You come here often?' asks Willy.

'Used to.'

'That's right, it's closing, isn't it?'

'That and my girlfriend and I broke up.'

'And you can't eat seafood anymore? That's a bad break-up.'

'No, she works here.' Devin points to me, and I give Willy a shoulder shrug. 'And her new boyfriend.'

Devin points to Harrison on the other side of the bar, and of course there's a lull in conversation, so everyone catches that last part.

Scout and Noah have the same reaction. Their eyes pop open as they yell, 'What?!' Mrs Whalley taps her husband on the arm and says, 'I knew it. Didn't I?'

They both have knowing smiles, which they turn and direct at Harrison and then me. Harrison rubs his face roughly but doesn't say anything.

'I'm so happy for you guys.' Noah seems emotional before saying, 'But I thought you were dating Obi-Wan Kenobi?'

'Who?' asks Devin with confusion.

Harrison discreetly says, 'That's *Star Wars*, not *Star Trek*.'

'And what does either have to do with me?' asks Devin.

'I can't help you if you can't learn your lines,' Harrison mumbles to Noah. 'And they broke up.'

'Oh, awkward sauce,' says Noah.

'Were you giving me shit about my last name?' Devin says and Noah takes a step backwards towards the kitchen.

'Nope, just a misunderstanding. Sorry about the break-up. Aggie is awesome.'

Why did he add that last part? I think he was being kind but it's like pouring salt onto a wound. Noah continues to back away and places a hand on the kitchen door. 'I'll make some more treats. Maybe desserts. Bye.'

He darts in the kitchen and away from the awkwardness he created.

Scout's eyeballing me, and I discreetly wave her away and mouth, *Tell you later.*

'Your dad must be thrilled, Agnes,' says Mrs Whalley before realising Devin is still at the bar and can hear her.

'What does that mean?' Devin snaps.

'Devin, leave it,' I say, but I can tell he won't. Mrs Whalley mouths *Sorry* to me.

'He wasn't thrilled about Aggie dating me?' Devin's eyes dart around the group, hoping someone will answer.

'He was fine with us dating. Let's just leave Dad out of this.'

This little white lie is getting bigger, and I hope it doesn't make its way back to Dad. I don't want to try to explain it to him. Harrison remains quiet but catches my eye with a smirk on his face. He does not care that Devin is feeling annoyed right now. Harrison takes a sip of his drink and avoids Devin's glares from across the bar.

Willy turns to Devin and says, 'Probably not my place to ask, but why are you here then?' It's the question of the night.

Devin opens his mouth, but I'm not sure what explanation he's going to use.

'You know what…' Devin reaches across the bar, grabs the tequila bottle, takes a swig, slams it down and then sulks over to sit back with his mum.

Willy points to Barbara. 'Who's that?'

'His mum,' says Scout.

Willy nods. 'That makes sense.' The side of Harrison's mouth tucks up, but he tries to hide his grin.

Scout comes over and whispers in my ear, 'I knew it, you dirty dog.'

My head flings back in surprise because she can't be serious. She has to know it's all bullshit.

'It's not real,' I whisper back.

'Okay, sure it isn't.' She smiles as she rolls her eyes in disbelief. She's watched Harrison and I fight and bicker for years. This must be the alcohol talking.

'You know it's not.'

'I know that I just lost out on winning more money.'

'Scout, what's that kitty for?' I grit my teeth as I force the words out because I know what's coming.

'When you and Harrison would finally hook up. Nothing like making us all wait until the last minute.'

Chapter Thirteen

Everyone believes I'm dating Harrison. While Devin is distracted talking to his mother, I shimmy behind the bar and tug on Harrison's arm. He's politely chatting with Mr Whalley but stops, looks down at my hand on his arm and brings his gaze up to me.

'Sorry to interrupt, but can I borrow Harrison for a second?'

'Of course, my dear.' Mr Whalley smiles as I pull Harrison away from the group and over to the front counter.

'What do you need now, Agnes? No more favours, I hope.'

'Did you know that everyone had a kitty for us hooking up,' I whisper, but it's an angry one.

Harrison glances back to the bar and then to me. He takes a deep breath before saying, 'Yeah, I knew.'

'What? And you didn't tell me?'

'Why would I tell you?'

'Because it's about me. And you, I guess, but I should have known.'

'Who cares?' Harrison folds his arms over his chest. 'It doesn't matter.'

I suppose it doesn't matter, but I don't like the fact that the staff were watching Harrison and me for any signs of hooking up. They have misinterpreted arguing for chemistry.

'It's weird.'

'It's just silly gossip.' Harrison leans in closer and has delight in his eyes. 'And it wouldn't have been a problem if it wasn't for your little dilemma.'

I drop my head because it's all messed up now, then laugh at the absurdity of this evening, which catches Harrison off guard. I think he was preparing for a fight, so my reaction has surprised him.

'They thought we were flirting when we were fighting,' I say.

'Would you call it fighting?'

'Well, I wouldn't call it flirting.'

'True, you'd know if I was flirting with you.'

'Yes, I've seen your flirting first-hand, and it's nauseating.'

Harrison narrows his eyes and asks, 'When would you have seen me flirt?'

I wave my hand around the restaurant. 'The female guests who were desperate to meet the chef. *Oh, Harrison James. A man who can cook* and *is handsome.* Blah, blah.'

'And you think I was flirting back?'

I lean in closer to his face and say clearly, 'Every time.'

'No, I was being courteous.'

'You loved it. How will you handle not having women coming in to compliment your cooking now? Oh, may I please speak to the chef?' I pretend to feel faint, but Harrison takes my arm and holds me upright. 'Do I need to come over and compliment your cooking? Oh, Harrison, however do you fry this tiny animal and put it in some sauce.'

Harrison removes his hand as he shakes his head. 'It's a thankless task, but someone has to do it. Still, it doesn't mean I was flirting.'

'The flirting and swooning have been stinking up the place for six years.'

'Jealous, Agnes?' Harrison arches his eyebrows in question.

I fake vomit. 'No! I can't imagine anything worse than people fawning all over me.'

'Anything worse? Your imagination sucks.'

'It's unprofessional.'

'I'm always professional.'

'Not when you go home with one of them.' Harrison's eyes narrow, and I know I've pushed it too far. We've never discussed the sea of women that come to fawn over him, but I've heard the rumours. I've seen the look he gives the women before they're ushered out of the kitchen. Regardless, I know Harrison prides himself on being a professional, and I've stepped on a landmine. He leans in closely and I notice his eyes have darkened.

'When have I ever done that?' he says slowly.

I feel like shrinking back now, but I try to stay strong. 'I don't know, but the staff talk. There's always whispers.'

Harrison retreats an inch, but he's still pissed. 'The staff are wrong. That's never happened.'

'I don't believe you.'

'Why would I lie to you? I thought the one thing we had was we're honest with each other.'

'I—' I've lost the steam and the reason I started this conversation.

'Kiss! Kiss!' Scout chants from the bar, breaking the tension between Harrison and me. Willy joins in for some reason. Harrison is the first to give them a crabby look.

'The sexual tension is killing us, guys. Just go for it!' adds Scout.

I'm going to kill her when I get the chance. She's too intoxicated and relishing this too much.

'Stop,' I say as I try to ignore them and turn back to Harrison. He's not paying attention to them.

He watches me before saying, 'I should have told you about the kitty.' I was not expecting a submission from him, so I'm stunned into silence. 'I didn't know the details and thought it was silly, but I should have told you.'

'How much was it?'

My question surprises him.

'Why is that important?'

I can't answer that other than being intrigued about how much people thought Harrison and I had chemistry. Didn't they see us bickering all the time? Witness us arguing over every little detail? What did they see in those moments that I've missed?

'I, um...' I'm still trying to come up with a reason when the front door abruptly rattles. Everyone, including Harrison, jumps from the fright.

It bangs a second time with force as Harrison steps around me and places me behind his back once more. I see movement out of the corner of my eye and it's Scout rushing to grab the tequila bottle and then pour two shots.

'Quick, quick.' She hands one to Mrs Whalley, and they cheer, scull their drinks and face the door to wait.

The front door flies back, knocking against the wall as rain streams into the restaurant. Harrison must have forgotten to lock the door last time. Harrison's arm moves around me and tucks me firmly against his back. I'm hidden from the rain and the new intruder.

A man with a giant frame steps one foot into the restaurant and shakes out his raincoat before placing the other foot inside. Harrison nudges me further away before he drops his hand and helps the man in before shutting the door and locking it this time.

The man has his back to us as he takes off his raincoat, and the women in the room all pause to take in the image. Underneath, he's wearing a suit, and it's soaked, the material clinging to his body. The legs of his pants are drenched up to his knees. He removes his suit jacket before turning to face the group. He pushes back his short, brown, wet hair, revealing a handsome face with a strong jawline, and I hear Scout groan. She holds the tequila bottle in the air as she and Mrs Whalley cheer their empty shot glasses before Scout proclaims, 'It's magic!'

Mrs Whalley giggles, and I can safely assume they're both quite drunk.

'It's not magic,' says Harrison over his shoulder.

'Maybe it's an angel come to save us,' says Scout.

'He's very handsome,' says Mrs Whalley, and I'm not sure she meant to say it out loud. She wobbles on her feet, and Mr Whalley takes the opportunity to guide her back to their table. He hands his wife a glass of water.

Our new guest loosens the tie around his neck and undoes his top button as he takes in the group before him. Scout's mouth drops open, and she leaves it open while her tongue tries to find the straw of her freshly made cocktail. She closes her mouth over the straw and takes a loud sip while her eyes don't move off our latest guest. I think she's enjoying the view.

The man stands in the entryway, I assume, wondering why no one has said anything.

Noah pops out from the kitchen and notices our new guest. 'Are you a stripper too?'

'Excuse me?' Our new guest's voice is sharp, and it scares Noah enough to retreat into the kitchen.

His voice is deep but oddly familiar. I step closer to get a better look, and now realise how I know that voice.

'It's not magic. He's not an angel. He's not a bloody stripper. Close your mouth, Scout, it's just my brother,' says Harrison as he steps forward, grabs Thomas's wet jacket and throws it over his shoulder. 'Everyone, this is Thomas, and that's all the introductions I'm doing with your drunk arses.'

Harrison's younger brother, Thomas, lifts his hand to acknowledge the group before shaking his head like a dog, and water flies across the room.

He's not as tall as Harrison, but he's built. Built with muscles and a tight business shirt that's soaking wet and moulds to every dip. He runs his fingers through his damp hair, and it slicks back like he's just stepped out of a salon.

I knew Thomas when we were teenagers. Thomas James was the most popular boy in my grade in high school, but to me, he was only a massive flirt. That's why I find it hard to believe Harrison has never gone home with one of the many admirers who's come into the restaurant over the years. The Thomas brothers always had a reputation for being players, but maybe that comes with being strikingly handsome. Riding on the coattails and reputation of his older brother, who had graduated four years earlier, Thomas was a menace, but he wasn't this big in high school.

He was wildly popular, sporty and I steered clear of him. We shared two classes, and he always tried to borrow my pens. After the third pen he lost, he was on a permanent ban. He was mostly kind to me, but I was weary of the heartbreak he caused the female population of our school.

'How did you get here?' asks Harrison.

'I need a drink before I tell you that story,' says Thomas as he and Harrison join the group at the bar. Harrison gestures for me to follow them.

Willy has his head down, typing on his phone and ignoring the group, while Devin seems to be quietly arguing with his mother before he walks back over to the bar. Barbara sits alone, looking out at the view of the storm through the deck windows.

'I'll get you a drink.' Scout grabs a shot glass and fills it to the rim. 'Tequila?'

'Great, thanks.' Thomas is friendly with his reply but it doesn't have the flirty edge I was expecting.

Scout places the drink in front of him and says, 'I'm Scout, and I'll be at your service tonight. Drinks are free.'

'Free? Who's paying?'

'Insurance,' says Scout before I can say my dad. Thomas sculls his drink and then notices me standing next to Harrison.

'Hey, Aggie. Been a while, you're looking good.' Again, it seems friendly and genuine, catching me off guard. This is the guy who solely used the pick-up line: 'I play football, you should come watch,' and it worked on all my friends. It's not even a pick-up line; it's only stating a fact, yet they giggled every time Thomas looked their way.

'Nice to see you. You got bigger.' Bigger probably isn't the right word to use, but it makes him chuckle.

'Yeah, I suppose I did.'

'We haven't seen you around here?' Never. I've never seen Thomas at the restaurant, and after a few years, I forgot Harrison had a brother. He never talks about him.

'Moved away. I've been back for a few months now.'

'What are you doing here?' Harrison cuts off the conversation and our mini-reunion.

'Always so pleasant.' Thomas gives his brother a playful shove before saying, 'I was coming to have dinner, but then the roads flooded. I thought my car could handle it, but—'

'You got caught? Tell me you got the car out.'

Thomas shakes his head and holds up for a refill from Scout. She obliges with haste, and he slams down another shot.

'Car's gone. I'm guessing the water is up to the windows by now.'

'Fuck.' That's all Harrison can say.

'The streets are flooded that badly?' I ask because it's hard to believe the streets have gone under already. The rain has been heavy for hours now, so it is possible. I was hoping it wasn't true so I could see my dad.

'They're expecting two hundred millimetres, but it seems like it might get worse,' says Thomas.

'We're all going under if it keeps up,' adds Scout.

I hadn't thought about The Shark Biscuit completely flooding. I was concerned about getting through the night without feeling guilty about the closure every two seconds, and then Devin and his family, but I should have been worried about the restaurant going under. Literally.

'Why the hell didn't you turn around and go home when the weather was this shit.' Harrison doesn't care that Scout, Devin, Willy and I are listening to their conversation like it's a soap opera.

'I was thinking that it was more important to go and check on my brother since his restaurant is close to the water, and I knew you'd never leave it, even if it were sinking.' Some older versus younger brother dynamics are at play here, and no one can look away.

'You could have called.'

'I did. You didn't answer.' Harrison was probably out placing the sandbags or helping me with ex-boyfriends when Thomas called. Harrison's eyes flick to mine for a second. He must be thinking the same thing.

'We were out the back trying to stop the flooding for a while. That's nice of you, Thomas.' I give him a warm smile, but my motivation was to stop Harrison's parental lecture.

'Thanks, Aggie Baggie.'

'Aggie what?' ask Devin as he screws his nose up at that awful nickname.

'That nickname died in high school,' I say pointing my finger at Thomas as I try to keep my voice neutral.

'No way. It's staying forever.' Thomas winks at me, and I feel Harrison stiffen next to me.

I need more to drink. I hate that nickname, but I try to cover my annoyance with a light-hearted laugh. That nickname makes me want to burst into tears, but it's not Thomas's fault. He doesn't understand why it hurts.

Willy lifts his head and rejoins the group.

'Is there a private room I could use? Linda said we could do a Teams meeting for my performance.'

'You are not stripping in my restaurant,' Harrison says it slowly and firmly, leaving no wiggle room for negotiation. Or so I thought.

'I'm not going to be nude. Just shirtless.' Willy then mutters, 'And pantless.'

'We all heard that,' says Scout before looking at Harrison. 'Surely we have somewhere, please?' She begs with her hands tucked together under her chin.

'Ask Agnes, it's her restaurant.' That comment had a tone, and I'm not sure why. As much as I'd like to disagree with Harrison, I don't want a naked man dancing in the near vicinity.

'Sorry, Willy, probably not the best idea right now.'

Willy looks sad but takes it on the chin. 'I understand. Maybe I could just send her a photo of the goods?'

'Maybe,' I say, being supportive.

'Could I borrow your bathroom?'

'I'll show you.'

I walk around the bar as Noah emerges from the kitchen with a tray of desserts.

'That's lovely of you.' I hope there's one left when I get back.

'I got emotional that it's my last time plating up desserts here and cried all over the meringue.'

'I'm sorry, Noah.'

He cocks his head on the side and asks with genuine interest, 'What are you sorry for?'

That it's all my fault.

'I'm sorry you're sad.' That's all I can say on the spot.

I pat his arm as he walks behind the bar and gets introduced to Thomas. Willy follows me to the bathroom, which I hope isn't underwater by now, and as I walk down the corridor, I hear Noah say to Thomas, 'Great news about Agnes and Harrison dating, hey?'

'What?! Bullshit. When?' Thomas's reaction is honest, and what I'd have said if someone told me I'd be dating Harrison, fake or not.

I'm glad I'm not there to watch Harrison invent answers, but I'm surprised when I hear him reply, 'Why would it be bullshit?'

Oh, Harrison, you should know the answer to that.

Chapter Fourteen

The bathroom is a disaster.

Water flows steadily through the wall into both cubicles and the shared washroom. *Shit.*

I race to the storage room next door and grab more old towels and the mop.

'How can I help?' asks Willy. This man is growing on me every minute.

'That's kind of you, but you get your job done first. You can use this room.'

I set him up in the storage room, which doesn't have terrible lighting for what he's doing. It might even be the proper dim lighting he needs.

The towels and mop aren't making a dent in the water flowing into the bathroom. The sandbags must have moved. I run out the back door, and the force of the rain hitting my face stuns me. This is not normal rain. It's heavier than I ever remember – fat, loud, unforgiving rain. I try to huddle under the awning, but my clothes are instantly drenched.

With the pressure of the rain and the shots I drank too quickly, I can't tell if the swirls in front of my face are from the force of rain or a hallucination. Most of the sandbags are still in place where Harrison left them, but the water is coming too fast, and there is too much. A few have washed away from the building. I try to lift one, but the sandbags are extra heavy from sitting in the water. I heave one up against the pile on the side of the restaurant, but it's a fruitless exercise. Surely, it's got to stop soon? I've never seen it rain this heavily and for this long in my life. A rain bomb was not on my bingo card for another thing I had to survive tonight.

The Shark Biscuit will go completely under if the rain doesn't stop soon.

I sit with that sobering thought for a second before realising I can't do anything to help the situation out here, so I'm best off getting back inside. As I turn, the loudest clap of thunder snaps nearby, and I feel the force of it in my teeth. The sound is terrifying and I let out an involuntary scream.

In my fright, I jump and catch my foot on the corner of a sandbag, falling face-first onto the concrete. I try to stop my fall, but my hands slide off the wet, slippery concrete, and I come down hard on my shoulder.

Stunned from the fall and the weather, I lie on the ground for a moment, feeling the pulse of my erratic heartbeat. The rain pounds down as I lie in the puddles. They're more like large pools of mud, which is now all over my clothes, face and inside my mouth.

I push myself up, but my necklace gets caught on something and I hear it break and fling onto the ground. *No!*

I scramble around, looking for the pieces through the mud. The rain blocks my sight, and I wipe my eyes, trying desperately to see something sparkle in the water. I find my chain, but I can't find the locket. I sweep the water away with my fingers; however, there's nothing but dirt and sand on the concrete. I desperately need to find it before it gets swept away in the rain, but my hope is fading every second. My dad gifted Mum the locket when she couldn't wear her wedding ring any longer due to losing too much weight from her illness. It's more precious to me than her wedding ring because it makes me feel close to Mum while also reminding me how much my dad loved her. Through everything in life, he loved her.

'Agnes?' I hear Devin's voice coming from the doorway. He turns and yells, 'She's out here,' before rushing over to help me stand. 'What happened?'

'I fell,' I say, and it comes out like a sob. I know I'm okay, but I feel shaken.

Devin places his arm around my torso and pulls me to my feet.

'Are you okay?'

I'm struggling to catch my breath. The wind has been knocked out of me, either from the fall or the rain pelting down on us. I can't see, and my body is shivering. Devin wipes the hair back from my face and tips my chin up. I must have mud on the side of my face from the fall.

'I think you'll live.' He smiles warmly, but he's getting pelted with rain now, too.

'I think so, if this rain ever stops.'

'Here, I'll help you inside.'

Devin guides me towards the door, but I shiver and stumble forward. Before Devin can catch me, I feel a different set of arms grab me around my waist. I'm holstered against Harrison's chest, and he holds me tightly.

'I've got her.' I hear him tell Devin over my shoulder, and I'm too drenched to help alleviate the awkwardness between the two men. I keep my forehead pressed against Harrison's chest, and he rubs my back. Devin says something to Harrison, but I can't hear him over the rain. The shivering is getting worse, and Harrison pulls me closer to the warmth of his body.

I feel the stubble of his facial hair graze the side of my face as he leans into me.

'Are you hurt?' he whispers gently.

'No,' I say faintly because I know I'm okay but feel off-kilter from my fall.

'I'm going to pick you up carefully.' Before I can protest, Harrison runs his hand over my back a few more times in a soothing motion before he bends down and scoops me into his arms. My arm swings around his neck as his arms cradle under my legs and back.

I try to study Harrison's face. It's hard with the rain still pouring on us both, but he doesn't look annoyed at me for once. He looks concerned and that emotion coming from Harrison does something to my insides. He's inspecting my face like it's a medical report and he can read how hurt I am.

'Agnes, why were you out here alone moving sand-bags?' He doesn't sound angry, but I still shrink back into myself.

'I don't want to get in trouble right now. I lost my mum's locket.' I close my eyes because I'm about to cry. 'I can't lose it. Not tonight. Why tonight?'

Harrison hugs me tighter towards his chest as I try to calm myself, but an aching sadness overwhelms my body. It's not just because I've lost my mother's locket but also from being held in Harrison's arms like I'm precious, and I don't remember the last time someone held me like that. If ever.

Harrison carries me inside, closes the door with his hand under my legs and walks with haste through the restaurant, making a beeline towards the kitchen.

'Is she dead?' Noah's voice rises with concern. *Am I dead? Do I look that bad?*

'She's not dead. Don't ask that,' Harrison says with fury.

'Is she okay?' Mrs Whalley's voice breaks a spell, and I open my eyes. She and Mr Whalley are still at their table, and concern laces their faces, while Scout's at the bar with Noah. I'm not sure where Devin went, but Willy must still be taking photos.

I lift my head and say, 'I'm okay.'

'She fell. Scout and Noah, can you guys try to stop the flooding in the bathroom? Get Spoon Boy to help you as well when he reappears.'

Scout and Noah rush off, and Scout squeezes my hand as she brushes past me. Harrison turns his back and pushes through the kitchen door.

'What the hell happened?' Thomas stands in the kitchen with a mouthful of bread as he asks. There's a look of horror on his face.

'I fell,' I say again because I don't have the energy for more words.

'Did you fall down a drain pipe?' says Thomas, and I hope he doesn't expect a reply.

Harrison places me carefully on the counter. He leaves me as he gets a towel, wets it, brings it over and starts cleaning my face.

As I reach up and take it, I say, 'I can do it.'

'Just sit there.' Harrison pulls the towel away, annoyed. I've been waiting for the Harrison James lecture. I will cry more if he is too harsh. I don't have the strength to fight at the moment, so I hope he goes easy on me.

'What can I do?' Thomas must have finished his food and stands on the opposite side of me. He's looking at me like I'm a car that needs fixing.

'Under the sink is my bag. Grab me two fresh shirts.'

Thomas does as he's told and passes Harrison the shirts.

'Can you help the others? They're in the bathroom.'

Thomas nods, but I say, 'You don't have to do that.'

Harrison eyes me with a glare before saying, 'You want him to stay here while you change?' Harrison's voice is low, and it's this tone that frightens most people. It doesn't faze me. It usually gets my back up and readies me for a fight.

'I'm out.' Thomas puts both hands in the air and exits immediately.

I lift my chin and gape at Harrison. 'You think I'm changing in front of *you*?'

'No, but you need to get out of these clothes, and the bathroom is currently occupied.' Harrison continues to wipe the dirt from my face and arms. 'I'm going to the freezer to get you ice. Change into my shirt while I'm gone.' He walks away without waiting for a reply.

My body aches from the fall as I hop tentatively from the counter. My shirt is soiled with mud and peeling it from my body feels fantastic. I wipe my arms with the towel again before quickly throwing Harrison's shirt on. It smells like him. It's soft, too big for me, and it feels like hopping into a freshly made bed. I don't want to dirty it with the mud from my work pants, so I slide them off and dump them in the pile with my shirt. Harrison's shirt comes mid-thigh, so I'm covered.

'Get back on the counter, and I'll put this ice on—'

Harrison stops mid-sentence as I turn around. I must look ridiculous with wet hair, an oversized shirt, mud still on my arms and bare legs. A real treat for the eyes. I pull his shirt down to cover more of my legs, but that only pulls the neck over one shoulder, so I stand and pull that back, which pulls it higher on my thighs.

Harrison watches it all and seems hypnotised as his eyes track my movements. When he realises I'm aware of his staring, he snaps out of his trance and his detached demeanour is back in place.

'Hop back up on the counter.' Harrison gestures to the kitchen top, but I only make it halfway before slumping back to the ground.

Before I realise it, Harrison's hands circle my waist, lifting me with ease and he places me on the counter. His shirt has risen up and I quickly pull it down, which pulls the collar over one shoulder.

When I go to replace it, Harrison reaches out and pushes my hand away. 'What did you land on?'

I assess the aches and pains in my shoulder. It's not hurting, but I know I'll be stiff in the morning. Harrison places the icepack there, which is covered in a tea towel. He holds it steady against my shoulder as he gazes at the wall behind me. His outer thigh grazes my bare leg. I sneak a look at him while he studies the wall with intense focus. This may be the closest we've ever been and the longest we've gone without either of us picking a fight.

His eyes are shadowed – either from stress or tiredness. He's got a fresh shirt on but still some mud on the side of his face. Without thinking, I slowly wipe it away with my finger. A single stroke down his cheek, and his eyes flash to me. I hold up my finger to show the mud to explain my reason for touching him. His face is softer than I imagined. There's more mud under his ear, but I point to it instead of wiping it this time.

'You have more there too.'

He wipes it away, readjusts the ice and then resumes staring behind me. Still no words.

'They shouldn't bother with the bathroom. It doesn't matter.'

His eyes slowly rotate to examine me, and I go back over my words because I'm not sure what I said wrong, but from the fury in Harrison's eyes, I've said something wrong. *Again.*

Harrison places my hand over the ice, holding it in place. He then steps back and leans against the counter in the middle of the kitchen. He folds his arms, and I notice that he keeps his gaze firmly on my face.

'Why aren't you talking?' I whisper because it feels like I'm breaking a rule since Harrison is so uncharacteristically quiet.

'I'm trying to work out what's going on with you tonight.'

'What does that mean?'

He takes three long, deep breaths before he responds. I wonder if he's trying my breathing technique.

'I don't get you.'

'That's not new,' I say because I could have told him that.

'Yes, it is.'

Now it's my turn to scoff, but I move my shoulder too much, and I can't hide the wince. Harrison steps forward and holds the ice in place again.

'As much as I know you'll hate me saying this,' Harrison tries to avoid my eyeline, but his face is close as he holds the ice. He keeps his focus behind me, but now and then, he flicks his eyes to me. 'Normally I can predict how you'll react. How irritated you'd get, how much something would get under your skin, but tonight, I don't know how to read you.'

'It's been a pretty unusual evening.'

'I couldn't give two shits about your ex out there. I'm talking about our restaurant.'

This was the conversation I've been trying to avoid having with Harrison, and I can't move. He's cornered me and holding me down with ice. It might be for legitimate reasons, but I'd love to find a reason to squirm away.

'What about the restaurant?'

'You're acting like this is just another day. How can this not mean anything? Your parents' restaurant? *Your* restaurant? Where are your feelings?' Harrison's eyes stay connected to mine as he inches his face closer. 'One minute you're alone in the rain fixing sandbags, upset about your mum's locket, and the next you're saying it doesn't matter if the place floods.'

'I *meant* it doesn't matter if the water gets in the bathroom. It has to make its way up the steps before entering the restaurant.'

Harrison searches my face again, but I've closed it off. I'm not letting him extract more information. He places my hand over the ice again and takes two steps away. He swings back around, and I know he won't leave this alone.

'I feel like my *fucking* heart is breaking, Agnes. Do you know that? Scout's out there drowning her feelings with a bottle of tequila. Noah's crying into desserts. And you?' Harrison's arm gestures up and down before he rests his hands on his hips and drops his head.

'I'm fine. I've come to terms with it. I'm sure everyone will—'

'Stop. Just stop. Be honest!'

'I am. I'm fine.'

'No, you're not. I just saw how upset you were outside. Be real with me.'

'Why? The restaurant's closing. It's done.'

Harrison shakes his head. 'I want to know what you're feeling. Just tell me. What's the worst that can happen? The roof isn't going to fall in. Be honest with me.'

'You need to stop with that nonsense. I am honest. I happen to care about people's feelings, unlike you.'

'No. You care that people like you.'

'Everyone cares about that.'

'I only care about the people that matter to me. Everyone else can get stuffed.'

'Well, you're certainly honest with me.'

'And you're usually honest with me.' Harrison's angry and his voice rises but he still doesn't yell. His eyes flicker to his 'No Yelling' sign before he continues. He drops his voice so it's lower but still just as furious.

'This place,' Harrison gestures with his arm to the restaurant, 'is my home. All these people are my family, and much to your disappointment, that includes you.' He points at me, and I ready myself for his next words because I know he's on a roll. 'I'm fucking devastated, and you not giving a shit is breaking my heart.'

'I'm breaking your heart?' I find strength in my voice because I'm done with Harrison James telling me how I should or shouldn't react on one of the most fucked-up nights I've had.

'Daily.'

I throw the ice on the counter and hop down to step into Harrison's space. He wants to fight? I'm ready.

'Oh, cry me a river, prawn boy! You can't be sentimental for one day and rewrite our history. You hate me. We've done nothing but fight for six years.'

'I hate arsehole customers. I hate wrong deliveries and bad weather. But you, I don't hate. I never have.'

Harrison and I have a stand-off. His chest is heaving from his speech. We're inches from each other with our eyes locked.

'How could this not mean anything to you?' he whispers, and I decide to be honest. He's been on me all night to be honest, so here it is: the biggest secret I've held in all these years. It's the most truthful thing I can say to Harrison and the last thing he's going to want to hear.

'Because I *hate* this place! I'm counting down the hours until this all goes away. I've always hated it, and I'm glad it's all over.'

My arms fly up, my breath is heaving and it feels good to get it off my chest for about five seconds until the shock on Harrison's face turns to disbelief.

I take a step backwards so I can explain better, but a booming clap of thunder vibrates the restaurant. Harrison reaches out and grabs my arm as there's another loud crack, and the restaurant descends into darkness.

Chapter Fifteen

Harrison grips my hand tightly as we stand silently in the pitch-black kitchen. After a moment, the generator kicks in and throws a low light across the room.

'Of course, there's a blackout,' Harrison mutters.

'I'd be disappointed in this night if there wasn't one.'

Harrison's lips curl up on one side as he gazes down at me, our chests almost touching from our sparring match that was interrupted by the blackout and saved me from explaining my outburst.

'At least the generator should keep the refrigerator going,' says Harrison, still holding onto me.

'But the rest of the restaurant will be in the dark, right?' It's a cost-saving decision I'm regretting right now.

'Yep.'

'We should check on the others then,' I say as I step back from Harrison, and he drops his hold of me.

The restaurant is in complete darkness and eerily silent when we step out of the kitchen. The sound of the rain pounding on the roof is all I can hear.

I hover behind Harrison as he steps carefully to the front door and turns on the emergency light. Together with the exit light, it gives a soft glow but isn't strong enough to fully light even the nearby bar.

'Everyone okay?' Harrison yells out. At first, all I can see is the light coming from three mobile phones. I can't remember where I left my phone, and I'm going to struggle to find it now.

I bump into Harrison when I miss a step, and he reaches behind to take my hand. He squeezes my fingers tightly, navigating me through the dark restaurant. I clutch his shirt in my other hand as he takes another step forward.

The mobile phone lights get brighter as we stop briefly at the table with Mr and Mrs Whalley. Barbara has now joined their group. I pull the shirt I'm wearing down because I didn't get a chance to find replacement pants before the blackout.

'You're covered. Stop worrying,' says Harrison quietly in my ear.

I hover behind him, but Barbara notices immediately that he's holding my hand. I attempt to remove it, but Harrison clutches it firmly.

'Everyone okay?' Harrison asks.

'Yes, thanks, son. We're all good,' says Mr Whalley as he angles his phone so we can see each other.

'We'll check on everyone else and then bring you some water,' I say, but they might like more alcohol. I would.

'Water would be lovely,' says Mrs Whalley, but Barbara remains silent, her eyes still not leaving me.

'You need anything?' Harrison directs the question to Barbara, and it's curt.

'I'm fine.' Her eyes dart briefly to Harrison before returning to me. 'Are you okay, Agnes? Quite the fall you had if you lost your pants.'

My teeth are gritted and I squeeze Harrison's fingers as I reply, 'I'm okay, thank you.'

We engage in a dimly lit stand-off for a few seconds before Harrison steps away, pulling me with him.

'I'll be back shortly with your water,' I say over my shoulder as Harrison drags me away.

With the torch on Harrison's phone guiding us, I sneak a peek at the time. Ten-thirty. On any other night, the restaurant would be closed by now, and I'd almost be on my way home, but tonight, I'm stuck hanging out with Barbara.

We find the others coming out of the bathroom. Harrison slows his pace and bends down to whisper in my ear, 'Don't let the woman get in your head. She's not allowed there.'

He regards me in a gentle way that makes me feel exposed. He knew that I'd feel two feet tall after Barbara's comment. He maintains eye contact for a second and then leans to whisper again in my ear, 'You look beautiful, Agnes.'

He doesn't look at me again before Scout, Noah and Devin rush over. Noah reaches us first.

'Did someone die?' Noah shrieks.

'Stop leading with that question. Ask less dramatic ones first,' says Harrison, his patience with Noah's hysterics thin.

'So the answer is no?' Noah's voice is getting higher by the second. He must think we're keeping bad news from him.

'No one is dying tonight. Stop asking,' Harrison says flatly.

'You'll tell me if someone dies, though, right?'

'Sure, I'll mention it if one of the ten people here suddenly dies.'

'Promise?' Noah's voice is faint, and it reminds me that everyone is probably secretly freaking out from the stress of this evening.

'Yes, I promise.' Harrison softens his voice when he replies this time.

'Thomas has gone outside to see if the whole street is out,' says Scout as her phone light illuminates her face. I think the effects of the alcohol have worn off already.

'You okay?' asks Devin, and thankfully, he can't see what I'm wearing – or not – in this light.

'Yeah, thanks. The fall startled me, but I'll be fine.'

'The water's coming in steadily now. Not much more we can do in the bathroom. Sorry, boss,' says Noah and I don't know if he's talking to Harrison or me. Probably Harrison.

The light from someone's phone comes bopping down the hallway, and as Thomas appears, he angles the torch down. The light beams on me, revealing that I'm wearing Harrison's shirt and no pants.

'Oops.' He redirects the light. Harrison angles himself so I'm hidden behind his shoulder and continues as if everyone isn't assuming I've been half-naked in the kitchen with Harrison. I have been, but it wasn't the fun time they're all imagining.

'The street is completely out. Pitch black everywhere,' says Thomas.

'Shit. It could be out for a while.' Harrison flexes his fingers around mine but doesn't let my hand go. I'm not sure why he's still holding it, but somehow, I know he wouldn't appreciate me removing it right now.

'The sandbags are doing jack shit out there. There's so much water. I've never seen it like this.'

'Excuse me?!' We hear the voice and then a frantic knocking. 'I can't find the door. Help, please! Someone?'

We all look around to see where the voice is coming from and then realise it's Willy. He's still in the storage cupboard, but now in the dark. Noah rushes over with his phone and opens the door. He disappears for a while, so Harrison drops my hand and goes to help. First, he turns on the emergency light near the back door. We can at least find our way to the toilets and storage room with a bit of extra light.

While we're waiting, I tug on Scout's arm and whisper in her ear, 'Do you have spare clothes I can borrow?' My voice is frantic. I need dry pants. Stat.

Scout smiles as her eyes roam up and down, taking in my disgraced appearance. 'You look fine to me.'

I swat her arm as she laughs. 'Seriously, my clothes are covered in mud.'

'Harrison is inventive, I'll give him that.'

'There's nothing inventive about me falling and getting mud on my clothes.'

'M-hmm.' Scout gives me a knowing look, but there's nothing to know.

'I'll explain it all later if you give me some leggings.'

'Do you deserve them when you didn't even tell me you and Harrison were a thing? I could have won two hundred bucks.'

Two hundred dollars is the largest kitty I can remember. People thought Harrison and I were going to hook up that badly?

'*Please* give me pants.' I tug on her arm and plead with my eyes, which she probably can't see well with our limited light. I'd like to tell her the truth about Harrison and me, but I can't guarantee Devin won't hear us.

'Fine. I have some in my bag. Follow me.'

We've only taken two steps away before Harrison steps out of the storage cupboard and holds the door open.

Noah comes out next with his head down. He stands next to Harrison and waits.

Thomas scans his phone light over their faces, and Harrison doesn't seem thrilled. Thomas's light moves to the storage room doorway as Willy emerges. His bare chest is the first thing I see, followed by the red leather underwear. I assume by the high cut it's a G-string. Harrison's eyes stay on the ceiling and Noah tries to hide his laughter.

Willy holds his scrunched-up clothing to his chest as he sheepishly looks over to me.

'I understand now why you didn't want me to be naked. In the restaurant. In a storm.'

I shrug my shoulders at Willy because I can't say much since I'm also not wearing pants. 'It's okay, Willy. No worries.'

He smiles at me, and I can tell he appreciates not being scolded right now. I'm sure he's embarrassed enough already.

'You get dressed and we can all have a drink.' Everyone likes both parts of my suggestion, especially Noah, who claps excitedly.

'Did you get to at least finish your show?' Scout asks Willy.

'I was just getting started when the blackout happened, and I fell on my phone. Butt side down. I'm sure it wasn't a pretty sight.'

Scout walks over and takes his hand. 'I'm sure it was the prettiest butt crack they've ever seen. Let's drink more.'

They follow Scout's light to the bar.

'Scout. Clothes first,' Harrison yells across the group.

In the dim light, I can see Scout's wicked grin. She was hoping he'd forget – evil mastermind.

I step over and say to Scout, 'And you owe me some too?' Willy looks down and notices I'm pantless.

'Oh, what did I miss?'

I can't even imagine where to start to get my new friend up to speed.

'Let's get a drink first, Willy.'

—

Everyone gets cleaned up, some of us put pants on, and we sit at a table closest to the front door, so we have some lighting. Harrison delivered drinks and whatever food he could find to the Whalleys and Barbara so I didn't have to see her again so soon. After locating my phone, I checked in with Dad, and he has power, so that's one shining light in the stark darkness of tonight.

My hair is still wet, so I try to dry it with a tea towel from the kitchen. I give up trying to fix my hair and resign myself to the fact that tonight is a nightmare on every level, and plan to succumb to drunkenness to get through the next few hours. I tug on the black leggings Scout lent me, which are itchy but a relief at the same time.

'You sure you don't want to play, Mr & Mrs Whalley?' asks Scout.

'We're okay over here, dear. Thank you for the offer,' says Mr Whalley.

'We'll enjoy watching.' Mrs Whalley is positively excited by watching a drinking game. I wish I were watching and not being forced to join in.

Willy, Thomas and Noah sit on one side of the table, with Scout, Harrison and I on the other. Devin hovers nearby, clearly unsure if he wants to join us in drinking or go and sit by his mother.

At the last minute, he dashes over and sits at the head of the table near Scout and Willy. He hasn't looked my way since the blackout, and I'm trying to avoid the awkwardness. Harrison hasn't said anything about my reveal regarding my feelings about the restaurant, which makes me uneasy. Surely, he has questions. Thoughts. He's said nothing, but I can feel the tension in his body as his thigh rests close to mine. He's stressed but trying to remain calm for our guests. I think we all are.

'Everyone write down a game on a piece of paper, and we'll draw one out of a hat.' Noah is always fair.

'We don't have a hat. Next idea.' Harrison doesn't seem like the kind of person to play games and is trying to veto any fun.

'Let's use a bowl then.'

'Good idea, Noah,' I say as Noah's chest puffs out. It's easy to make the kid happy and Harrison unhappy simultaneously. Perfect outcome.

Scout grabs an order pad and hands out a piece of paper to everyone.

'No one write any games with the word strip in them,' I say, and Willy's head jolts up. 'Sorry, but you'd have an unfair advantage.' And I don't want to play strip anything with this group.

'That's fair,' says Willy before jotting down something on his paper.

Noah crumbles up his piece of paper and secretly tries to put it in his pocket. He raises his hand. 'I'm going to need a new piece of paper.'

Harrison scribbles something on his pad, and I lean over so I can try to read it.

'No peeking. Eyes on your own paper, Keegan.' Harrison shoos me away.

'I'm just intrigued about what horrible game you would suggest since you hate fun.'

'Out of the two of us, you are the fun police.'

'That's rude and wildly wrong, *James.*'

Thomas glances at Harrison and me with a coy smile and then looks away. Harrison will need to update his brother tomorrow on the truth of our relationship.

Everyone places their suggestions in the bowl, and Noah holds it up high as Scout draws a piece of paper. She hands it to Noah, and happiness breaks out over his face. In the light of his phone torch, it looks somewhat menacing.

'I won, guys! You're going to love this game.' Noah's grin widens, and I'm fearful.

A few minutes later, Scout shuffles the cards as Noah places a can of craft beer in the middle of the table.

'Everyone listening?' says Noah with a voice that reminds me of Harrison. It's commanding without raising his volume. He's as quiet as a mouse in the kitchen, but with drinking games, he's suddenly become an alpha.

I lean over to whisper to Harrison, 'Did you know he was so domineering?'

'Yes. I've trained him well.' Harrison gives me a wink which startles my brain for a moment. Harrison winking may be one of the sexiest things I've ever seen, and I generally hate winking. I can't do it and only look like I have something in my eye when I attempt it. It felt cheesy when Devin did it, but something about Harrison winking at me is remarkably not cheesy and sexy as hell. I'm putting this reaction down to stress. Even Scout raises her eyebrows and gives me a sneaky wide-eyed look as she lays the cards face down in a circle around the beer can.

'The game is called Kings. Sorry ladies, I didn't name it. When it's your turn, you pick a card. Each card comes with a different instruction or game. Once you've completed your task, you place the card under the tab. Eventually, with enough cards, the beer can will crack open, and if it's your card that tips it over, you must drink the entire can.'

Scout hops up and returns with a tray of pre-mixed alcoholic beverages – all with vibrant colours. Our bar is getting a pounding tonight, and we're not even open anymore. Scout places a drink in front of each of us. I get an orange spitz and I'm not upset at all.

She prances over to the other table and Barbara looks horrified by the bright blue bottle placed in front of her.

Harrison opens my drink without me asking and places it back in front of me.

'You're first, Devin,' says Noah.

'Why?'

'Just lucky.' Noah winks at Devin, but he looks confused by the gesture.

'Does your mum want to play?' Willy asks, and it's an innocent question, but it gets chuckles from the group.

'No, my mum doesn't want to play a drinking game,' Devin snaps at Willy. 'She's not feeling well,' Devin says quietly, and all the laughing stops.

'Can I get her something?' I ask, but I plan on asking someone else to deliver it.

'She's anxious and it makes her feel queasy. She doesn't do well in stressful situations.'

'No one does, that's why we're drinking. Numb the pain.' Scout salutes us and chugs her drink.

I lean over the table and say, 'Please let me know if we can help her feel more comfortable.'

Devin's eyes flash to Harrison and then he lingers on Harrison's shirt that I'm wearing. I fidget with the sleeve until Harrison places his hand on my leg. He squeezes my thigh and leaves his hand there, which is clear for Devin to see. It was also a signal for me to stop worrying about Devin and his mother, but it's hard not to feel awful about this situation.

This fake dating thing was meant to be for a few hours, but now this charade is carrying on into the middle of the night. There's far more touching from Harrison than I expected. I thought he was joking when he said he was a touchy-feely partner.

Harrison's large fingers cupping my thigh are distracting and confusing. His warm hand on my leg, just as I was getting over the sexy wink, is making me dizzy. I don't hate his hand comforting me and don't know what to do with that realisation.

Devin watches me before taking his card as if he's scanning me for intel. I feel like screaming over the table, *I haven't lost my mind.*

Sensing her stare, I can't help but look, and Barbara holds my gaze. She's watching Devin and me closely. She's also watching Harrison and I with an eagle eye, and she seems perfectly well to me. I break the eye contact and keep my attention firmly on Devin as he holds up a three of spades.

'That card means you have to consume your beverage,' says Noah, and he must play this game enough that he has the rules memorised. I'm not sure if I should be concerned about that for him.

'So, I have to drink? That's it?' asks Devin.

'Yes, but you also can't say the D-word. It's banned in the game. You get penalised if you say it, so you must also now consume an extra sip of your beverage,' says Noah.

'The D-word?' I ask.

'I can't say drink,' says Devin, falling for my trap. I laugh as he realises I stitched him up.

'Another beverage for you, Devin. That's three,' says Noah, urging Devin to pick up his craft beer and scull.

'Aggie, that wasn't very nice.' Devin pouts at me, and Harrison's hand flexes on my thigh.

'Sorry!' I'm not sorry, but at least the tension from the room eases a little. I'm still not going to look in Barbara's direction.

'My turn!' Scout takes a card from the pile and draws a five of hearts.

'All the men have to consume their beverages.' Noah tries to get the guys to clink glasses, but Devin doesn't reach forward enough before they all take a large gulp.

It's my turn and I draw a jack of diamonds.

'Never have I ever card. Everyone puts up three fingers, and Aggie asks questions. If you have, put a finger down. The first one with all fingers down loses,' says Noah.

'It should be the other way. Finger down if you haven't. You're rewarding people for not doing anything.' Scout has a good point.

'I don't make the rules,' says Noah except, technically, he does because he's dictating every rule but I can't be bothered getting involved.

'What happens to the loser?' I ask with an innocent voice.

'They have to drink, of course,' Noah says, but he doesn't realise he's fallen into my trap.

'You said the bad word,' Devin laughs at Noah's mistake.

'Ah, shit!'

'Drink up.' Devin smacks his hand to his forehead. 'Fuck.' His joy is gone instantly as he takes a sad sip of his drink. His beer is going down fast.

Thomas smirks at me as he says, 'You're evil, Aggie. I love this game.' Thomas reaches for his own drink and takes a mouthful.

Noah waggles his finger at Thomas. 'No drinking until you're instructed.'

'You said the bad word *again*.' It's the first time Harrison has joined in the game, making everyone laugh at Noah's misfortune – and constant errors.

Noah drinks his penalty as Thomas asks, 'I'm not allowed to quench my thirst unless it's part of the game?'

'For your information, I enjoyed you saying the words *quench my thirst*,' says Scout as she tips her drink in Thomas's direction.

'I think we all did,' says Willy and he and Scout nod at each other.

'All right. Fingers up. First question, Aggie,' says Noah, bringing us all to order.

I wriggle in my seat, and Harrison removes his hand from my thigh. My thigh feels oddly cold now, and I have the urge to grab his hand and place it back down. Instead, I think I'll mess with Harrison.

'Never have I ever worn a chef's uniform.' Harrison drops his chin to glare at me as he slowly puts a finger down. Noah drops a finger as well. 'So, you have worn them? I thought you'd be safe.'

I beam a sarcastic smile at Harrison, and he turns his hand, holding up his two fingers in my direction, essentially giving me the universal sign for 'screw you'. It makes me laugh.

'Next question. Never have I ever worn a Santa costume and passed out from heat stroke while handing out lollies to children.'

'Not fair, she's cheating,' Harrison barks out as he puts his second finger down.

'What happened?' Scout asks. I forgot it was before she and Noah worked here. It was the first Christmas after Harrison started working here. The first and last time he dressed up as Santa.

'Ernie was supposed to be Santa. It's his thing, but he wasn't well that day, and I was trying to make a good impression,' says Harrison with one sad finger remaining.

'He scared all the children. They ran out of the restaurant crying. One of them grabbed his candy before leaving, though,' I say as a tiny grin appears on Harrison's face. I don't think it was a terrible memory for him.

'I'm a chef. Not a whatever that job is called.'

'Dad took over the job again after that.'

'He's a stronger man than I am.' Harrison mumbles the comment, and it makes me look over at him. He keeps his head down as he taps his single last finger.

'Last question,' I say. I know it's the last question because Harrison is about to lose.

'Never have I ever had sex in the storage cupboard in the restaurant.'

Harrison's head flashes to mine, his eyebrows raised, but he doesn't drop his finger. He mouths, *What?* to me just as I notice Noah and Scout both slowly drop a finger each. Harrison and I continue to look back and forth at both of them as our mouths drop open.

'I'll come back to you two,' I say, pointing to Noah and Scout before facing Harrison because he's not being honest. 'Drop a finger.'

'No.'

'You absolutely had sex in that cupboard!'

'With who?' Harrison looks completely puzzled.

'I don't know her name. The one with the brown hair. Used to come in here all the time and carry on.'

'Oh, Carry On Carla? I remember her. She loved a chat,' Scout tells the others. 'Harrison didn't have to say a word in that relationship.'

'Lucky man,' adds Thomas.

'Gross,' Scout, Willy and I say in unison to Thomas. He holds his hands up, but he's still smiling.

'Just joking, guys.'

I turn back to Harrison because he's being untruthful. 'Yes, her. Everyone knew you two, in the storage room… *you know.*'

Harrison leans in closely, his arm rests on the back of my chair. I know we have an audience, but I'm not backing down from this fight.

'Yes, there was a Carla. I didn't have sex with her or anyone in any part of this restaurant. Maybe you're thinking of another chef?'

'The only other chef who's worked here is my dad, and he hasn't.' Harrison raises an eyebrow to question my statement. 'Stop it. I can't think about that.'

'Maybe your mum enjoyed a cupboard quickie.'

I place my hand over Harrison's mouth. 'Stop saying things.'

Harrison's amused, and when I drop my hand, I can tell he's still pleased with himself. It fades quickly as he waggles his finger between Scout and Noah.

'I hope you're both joking. In my restaurant?' Harrison's voice is firm.

Noah lifts his finger. 'I'd like a take back. I misunderstood the question. I thought you meant any cupboard. Not that particular one with the excellent shelf heights.'

Scout laughs but tries to hide it. 'Me too. Misunderstood. Not the one with condoms stashed in the back corner. I'm thinking of a different cupboard.' She's a phenomenal liar, but no one here believes her bullshit. 'I say this not from experience, but I feel like you both missed out at least not making out in that room. It has the perfect ambience. So, I've been told.' Noah nods and then stops when Harrison notices.

'That is true,' says Willy with confidence. Everyone starts chatting about the ambience of the storage cupboard as Harrison and I sit in silence. I can sense Harrison's mind ticking over. I'm waiting for him to say something because I know him well enough to know when he's mulling over something.

Harrison leans over, pushing his shoulder into mine and puts his lips against my ear.

'You have the wrong idea about me, Agnes. You always have.'

He straightens up without looking my way, drops his final finger and takes a drink, so my turn is over. I keep my eyes on the table as the tingles flowing from my ear down my neck slowly subside. I know Harrison James. I *know* him. Don't I?

Chapter Sixteen

Scout brings a second tray of beverages to the table and distributes them to the group. Her phone buzzes, loud enough for us all to hear.

'What's Ria saying now?' Harrison asks while sneaking a sip of his drink. I bat his hand away because he can't drink until told to in the game. He playfully bats my hand away and then waits for Scout to answer.

'I knew you were just pretending not to like gossip,' I say as Scout backs me up by saying, 'Oh, Harrison loves the gossip.'

Harrison gives Scout a flat look that conveys his lack of enthusiasm for her comment.

'It's all I've got going on tonight, except a monster storm, the end of a loved job, playing a drinking game with the weirdest bunch of people and trying to maintain my sanity. Other than that, I'm totally free. What did she say?'

Harrison would be invested in this regardless of the events of tonight. He always knows the gossip around here, even though he pretends not to care. It might be why he was surprised he didn't know about Devin and me breaking up.

'She can't move tonight. Obviously.' Scout gestures to the storm outside. 'She's packed up and going to sleep on the couch.'

'That's good then?' I ask.

'I suppose. I'd prefer if she were gone when I got home.'

'Bad break-up?' Willy asks.

'I guess. Not really. I don't remember asking her to move in, but I came home one day and most of her stuff was there. I brought it up and she flipped out.'

'How?' Harrison asks.

'Said I was emotionally cut off. Wasn't emotionally ready for a relationship.'

Devin's eyes ping to me and there's an aspect in his expression that I hate. It makes my blood boil because after everything he's done tonight, he still believes I'm the one who needs to grow and change. He can bugger off. I try to project my thoughts into my facial expressions and Devin stands abruptly.

'I'm going to check on Mum.' He slinks away and joins the others.

'*I* thought it would be mature to have a conversation before you move your fish tank into my lounge room and discuss chipping in for rent, but apparently, that makes me high maintenance.'

We all jump in with versions of *You're not* or *Of course, you aren't.*

'I know that!' Scout says it with such conviction I wish I had her confidence, some of her self-assured attitude. 'I said she and her school of fish need to move out.' Scout throws a thumb over her shoulder, and I do not doubt she made the same gesture when she told Ria to get out.

'You never know, we might be stuck here for days. She'll be gone by then,' says Thomas, like it's a possibility, and the alcohol in my stomach starts trying to make a reappearance.

'Please don't say that. My fiancé will be beside himself with worry,' says Willy.

We're taking turns now to use the torches from our phones because everyone's batteries are draining quickly.

Harrison flicks his torch on before asking, 'What's his name?'

'Yael.' Willy beams when the name flows from his mouth.

'Do you like being a male dancer?' Noah asks like he's been waiting for a chance to ask that all night.

'It's not unpleasant. Meet some nice people.' He throws a warm expression across the table to our group.

'What if the ladies get too grabby?' Scout asks. It seems everyone had their questions ready for Willy.

'It happens, not often, though. I know how to handle it. I'm only doing it until September when we get married.'

'Your partner doesn't approve?' I ask.

'He does, but I won't need to save money anymore. We've got a big wedding planned in Maleny and woo wee, weddings are expensive. Yael is doing private catering on the weekend while I'm stripping, so we can have the wedding of our dreams with no debt.'

You can tell Willy is so proud of them as a couple, and I am, too. I kind of wish Yael was here right now. 'I won't get any more work if Linda gives me a one-star review, though. She's not happy with my performance tonight.'

'We'll all jump on and give you five stars, Willy,' says Scout, and we all agree.

Willy puts his hand on his heart. 'Thank you, guys. That's so kind of you. I can give you an actual show if you morally don't feel comfortable doing it without seeing my work.'

Thomas and Harrison both put their hands up, as Harrison says, 'No need. We're all good.'

Scout pouts at Harrison, but he ignores her pleas.

'Okay, less chat, more play.' Noah claps his hands together. 'My turn to draw a card.'

We've been around a few times and through enough alcohol for us all to be on the path to drunkenness. There are enough cards under the beer tab now that I'm worried on my next go, I'll be forced to skull that beer.

Noah drags it out for dramatic effect and then holds up a king of clubs.

'Big card, guys!' Noah is excited, but no one knows why. 'With this card, you get to make a rule. You can change one of the card rules or make up something brand new.'

Again, no one reacts, and the fact that Noah is excited worries me.

'Guys, I can create a new game within a game. This is big.'

'You've mentioned that. What's the new game?' asks Harrison.

Noah jumps up and whispers in Scout's ear. She laughs while nodding her head. He bends down, and they have a whispered conversation while the rest of us wait. Noah walks around the group, slowly eyeing each of us and then sits down with confident posture.

'New rule. If you draw a king card, we play a game.' Noah picks up his empty bottle like it's a trophy. 'We play Spin the Bottle.'

'No.' It's a collective 'No' from the rest of the group except Scout, who yells, 'Yeah!'

'No. I'm not playing a game of Spin the Bottle with employees and my brother. Willy's my only option, and no offence, Willy, but we just met,' says Harrison. 'Oh, and I'm not twelve.'

They are all great reasons. I am not playing Spin the Bottle because I'm in my thirties, my ex-boyfriend will be playing, as well as my current fake boyfriend, two employees and possibly a married couple in their seventies. My options for a non-awkward kiss are non-existent. Willy is my only option as well. Or Thomas, but no.

'We thought you might say that, so I have an idea.' Scout pauses for effect, and it works. She leans in a little closer. I imagine everyone is hoping she comes up with a better idea than Spin the Bottle.

'Spin the Cupboard.' Scout doesn't offer any further explanation, and she needs to.

'Explain,' says Harrison.

'Please?' I add.

'Maybe, if it's a good idea,' Harrison counters.

'We each take turns to spin the bottle. If it lands on you, you can nominate two people for seven minutes in the storage cupboard.' Scout finishes and beams at all of us. I know she thinks her idea is brilliant.

'So, instead of Spin the Bottle, we're now playing Seven Minutes in Heaven?' asks Thomas. 'I'm not saying it's a bad idea; I'm just checking.'

'Essentially, yes. You can do nothing in the cupboard. You can talk. You can rearrange the stock, or you can use your imagination. Whatever you like.' Scout winks to no one or all of us sitting at the table. 'And let's call the cupboard by its proper name: The Shag Room.'

'What!?' Harrison and I say in unison. Scout winks in our direction.

'What do the rest of us do for the seven minutes?' Willy asks, and it's a great question.

'Drink and eat,' says Noah. 'I'm getting hungry.'

'Me too. Not hating this idea,' says Thomas.

Devin rejoins the group and doesn't look my way. Harrison puts his territorial hand back on my leg, and I almost reach out to cover his hand with mine but stop the impulse. 'What did I miss?'

Noah brings Devin up to speed, and his face contorts with every word.

'And you are all in?' Devin asks, and his face lingers on mine for a second. Harrison's hand moves up and down my thigh while he looks across the table to Thomas. His face is unreadable, but I don't need to read his face because I can feel the tension in his fingers.

'But if we do this, everyone has to agree to play along. No opting out. Ruins the fun,' adds Scout.

Everyone takes a moment to eye each other and see who will be the first to opt in or opt out.

'I'm in.' Thomas pulls his chair closer to the table, signally he's ready to play. Everyone else mumbles *okay*. All it took was Thomas's firm interest and everyone fell like a poorly formed salmon stack.

'Who wants to go first?' Noah asks as Barbara walks over to the table. She places her hand on Devin's shoulder and says, 'What are you playing? I'm feeling a little better. Mind if I join in?'

Everyone hides their sniggers except for Scout, who laughs loudly before saying, 'Of course you can. Devin, get your mum a seat.'

'Mum, it's probably not—'

'Shh, Devin. Let the woman play,' says Scout as she retrieves Barbara a chair herself.

Barbara sets up next to Devin as Mr and Mrs Whalley also come over to join. We have a full house. Noah blushes as he explains the game to the Whalleys, and he deserves to feel embarrassed. I wondered if he would abandon the game when they came over.

'So, it's Seven Minutes in Heaven?' Mr Whalley asks directly, and Noah nods. 'We haven't played that in years.' He nudges Mrs Whalley's shoulder, and they both chuckle together. It's so sweet. I hope they get picked, and then I can eat and drink within the rules of the game.

'Everyone ready?' Noah takes the bottle and spins it too fast. It wobbles out of the middle of the circle. Thomas has to catch it.

'Try again. Gently this time.'

'Yes, sir,' says Noah.

'Don't call me "sir".'

'You can call me sir,' says Scout to Noah, who laughs off her joke.

Noah gently spins the bottle, and it comes to land on Scout. Everyone whoops as Scout throws a fist into the air. I don't know what prize she thinks she just won.

'I nominate.' Scout pauses as she looks around the room. 'Devin and his mum.' She can't get the words out before she doubles over in laughter.

'Fuck you,' Devin says, but it's in a friendly, affectionate way. He knew it would be the first couple anyone would pick. We all join in, except for Barbara. Of course, she doesn't want to have any fun.

'I don't think I've heard you swear like that, Devin,' says Barbara.

'Go into the storage cupboard and you'll hear even more,' says Thomas, and even Harrison can't resist laughing. Barbara is again not impressed. She takes a sip of her drink and faces away from the group.

Scout signals for everyone to listen to her again. 'All right, that wasn't serious.' She nudges Devin, and he smiles at her. I'm glad he's finally loosened up, but that could be the result of playing a drinking game for too long.

'My real choice is Harrison and Agnes! Off you go, you two.' I knew it was coming, but it's still awkward as hell.

'A lady would never—' But Barbara cuts off her words mid-flow and gapes at me as I slowly stand. 'Well, never mind.'

I duck my head from the glares from Barbara and Devin as Harrison takes my hand and we walk to the storage cupboard.

'I want my drink refilled when I get back. And food, Noah,' Harrison yells over his shoulder.

It's only seven minutes. In the dark. With Harrison James.

Chapter Seventeen

Harrison softly closes the door while still holding my hand. The light from my phone gives us minimal vision in the storage cupboard. It's enough not to trip on one of the boxes. Harrison and I walk over to lean against the shelves, and he drops my hand as he slides down to sit on the floor. His knees are bent, and he dangles his arms over them.

He looks back up at me. 'Sit. We have six and a half minutes to go.'

I sit beside him and place my phone face down so the torch can shed a glow over the room and our faces.

'How are you feeling from your fall?' asks Harrison.

I haven't thought of it since we started drinking, but I'll probably wake up tomorrow with a killer bruise somewhere on my body.

'I feel fine now or the alcohol numbed me enough not to feel anything.'

We sit in silence for only a few seconds before I can't wait any longer.

'Do you want to talk about it?' I lean against the shelves and face forward. Not that he can see my face well, but I'd prefer that it was entirely hidden.

'What? You pretending you hate this place? No, because I know that's garbage.'

It's not. I stay silent because I'm happy not to talk about it. Harrison crosses his arms and leans further back against the shelves.

'Fine, I'll bite. You hate the restaurant. Why?'

That's a tricky question to answer without a lengthy explanation, so I simply say, 'I'm not built to smile and talk to people every day. Not the way my dad is – he loves it. Or my mum. Somehow, I skipped that gene, it just exhausts me.' While that's true, it's not the only reason I hate this place.

'Tell me then, do you *hate* this place or hate it the same way you hate me?'

'There's a difference?'

Harrison scoffs before saying, 'You know there is, Agnes.' I don't know what to say to that. Harrison swivels his body in my direction and watches me with a thoughtful gaze, and I can't look away.

'You can hate this place, which I don't believe for a second, or maybe you really do hate me, but what I realised out there is that we may have the completely wrong idea about each other.'

Now it's my turn to scoff. 'You really think that?'

'If you think I'd have sex in here while I was working, then yes, we don't know each other.'

'I heard whispers from the staff back when you were dating her—'

'We only dated a few months. There couldn't have been many whispers.'

'She visited a lot, and people were talking one night.'

'They were wrong.'

Harrison's not backing down about that, so I may have to admit I was wrong. Painful as that is to do.

We've worked together for six years, so we know each other. You get to know a person in that time.

'If we don't know each other like you think we don't, we can use these seven minutes to rectify that. Anything you're dying to know?'

'You first.' Of course, I have to show my cards before Harrison is willing to play.

I blurt out the first question that comes to mind, 'Do you cook for your girlfriends?'

'Yes. Of course I do.' Harrison sounds like it's a preposterous idea that he wouldn't.

'I just wondered if it was a case of hating cooking at home since you do it every day.'

'I do it every day because I enjoy it.'

'Do you like people cooking for you?'

'Yes.' Harrison drags out the word, and it sounds like he's unsure about the answer.

'No, you don't. You're a control freak. You would be monitoring every ingredient they use.'

'As long as it's edible, I think I'd like it.'

I twist my legs, so I'm facing Harrison. 'What do you mean by that?'

'No one's ever cooked for me before.'

'What? How is that possible?'

Harrison shrugs his shoulders, but there's some vulnerability in his posture.

'I've been in the wrong type of relationships.'

'Yeah, but surely you shared a meal. They didn't make you cook every time, did they?' Harrison averts his gaze. 'Oh, right.' I think I'm finally catching up. 'You didn't have the kind of relationships where you shared meals together, just a bed.'

Harrison darts his head back to mine, and I can see his eyebrows drawn together in irritation.

'That's not it. Some were like that, but I think I always offered to cook. Most weren't long enough to get into stuff like that. I would have loved for someone to cook for me. I think it's how you show people you care.' Harrison looks away again.

My mind drifts to all the meals Harrison has made me over the years. We'd bicker and debate, but he always ensured I was well fed. He'd plop a plate down in front of me regardless of whether we were on speaking terms or short one-word answers. Even today, he's fed me multiple times. I could dismiss it as being leftovers and he hates waste, but it was always the food I love. He knew that about me. It seems I've jumped to conclusions about Harrison *again*.

'I'll cook you my famous two-minute noodles, egg and mayo meal. It's mouth-watering.'

Harrison glances at me again and the stress in his brow has disappeared.

'Your family runs a restaurant. You should hang your head in shame. But I'll try it.'

I nudge his leg with mine. 'Your turn to ask those questions about me festering in your brain.'

I'm mocking him, but he shuts me up by saying immediately, 'Did you and my brother ever hook up in high school?'

My head flies back because I was not expecting that question. 'No. One hundred per cent no.'

'He was pretty popular,' says Harrison like that's enough reason to assume Thomas and I made out in high school.

'I am well aware of his popularity. I never saw the appeal of knowing he'd never be interested for more than a second. I had too many friends cry on my shoulder over your brother.'

'But never you?' He gazes out into the dark storage cupboard as he asks.

'Never. I don't think I would have caught his eye anyway. He had a type.'

Harrison's silent for a moment but then says, 'I imagine you were the girl in high school that had no idea boys were interested in her.'

It feels like a compliment, but I can't be sure. Perhaps he's calling me aloof. Harrison was four years above me in high school, so we never crossed paths. I realise now that I may have assumed Harrison was like Thomas when it comes to dating. Perhaps that assumption was unfair. 'So, no interactions with Thomas?'

'You want me to repeat it? If you don't believe me, ask him yourself.'

'I believe you. Just checking. I've always wondered. I thought maybe Thomas broke your heart in high school, and that's why you instantly disliked me.'

'You disliked me first. Not the other way around. And you've had six years to ask, why didn't you?'

'That's not true. It was you first, and I didn't think it was my place to ask. I knew you guys knew each other in high school. He loves calling you that ridiculous nickname.'

'That nickname haunts my dreams. Aggie Baggie.'

'Does it even mean anything?'

'I'm sure he doesn't remember, but I do.' Harrison circles his hand to signal that I need to share. I'm not sure it's the best idea to tell him. It's handing more ammunition directly into my enemy's hands. 'It's one of those silly things that somehow stuck.' I brush a piece of non-existent fluff from my sleeve, hoping Harrison will move on.

'We have another –' Harrison checks his phone for the time – 'four minutes, so you might as well tell me.'

'This is not just a burning question. This is *sharing*, so you need to share something with me.' Harrison opens his mouth to reply, but I jump in first. 'Straight afterwards. You're not getting out of this on a technicality or some clever loophole. I share, and then you share. Something.'

'Just share *something*?'

'A secret.'

'Now we share secrets? Next, you'll be texting me all the time.'

'If you're lucky. You want my secret or not?'

Harrison nods. 'You have a deal.' Something about the look on his face makes me believe him. There's no smug expression on his face. It's neutral, like I can see past the puffed-up version of Harrison and perhaps, just maybe, have a normal conversation.

'Okay. Get your secret ready.'

'Done.'

'That was quick.'

'I don't have many secrets. Just a few very juicy ones.'

'Now I'm intrigued.'

'You should be.' I roll my eyes at his confidence, which is stifling. Harrison laughs, which seems genuine. His laugh is hearty and real. 'Come on. Time's ticking.'

'Fine. I was always called Aggie at school. That's a normal nickname.'

'You know Aggie means aggravating, right?'

178

'It does not!'

'You didn't know that? I thought that's why everyone called you Aggie.'

'Very funny, *anyway*.' Somehow, Harrison and I always get way off track, and I lose sight of why I started the conversation with him in the first place. 'Everyone knew me as Aggie, but Aggie Baggie started the first year of high school after Mum died.'

Harrison's eyebrows furrow when I mention my mum. I assume he thought it was a silly nickname, and it probably was to Thomas and the other kids. To me, it hurt.

'My dad tried but never knew what clothes to get me. He always bought the wrong size. We had a free dress day, and I had to wear these huge shorts and a T-shirt. I'd grown out of my other clothes, and Dad didn't have time to change the new ones. They were swimming on me. I tried to tuck the T-shirt in, but it was enormous.'

Harrison shifts in his seat, but his attention stays laser-focused on me. I check to see if he's about to jump in and say something, but he's silent. No silly remarks or comments. He's listening.

'Your brother and a few of his loser friends came up with Aggie Baggie, and it stuck. All through high school.'

Harrison still doesn't say anything. He blinks, so I know he hasn't fallen asleep, but he usually would have a smart reply by now. 'I'm done. That's the end of my story.' I think that's what he's waiting for.

He folds his arms over his chest and leans backwards. 'I'll make sure he never calls you that again.' Harrison's voice is low and earnest.

'It doesn't matter now. I'm used to it.' My hand waves around, flicking Harrison's concern away. I don't know how to handle Harrison looking out for me *again*. The feeling swirls in my belly and makes everything feel warm. I can imagine Harrison protecting his loved ones fiercely. No one messes with Harrison James except me.

'It does, and I don't think you ever get used to a nickname you hate.'

'Don't tell him why.'

'Because you don't want him to feel bad?'

'Because he didn't know.'

'It's okay if he feels bad. People are allowed to feel bad if they do shitty things. The nickname has probably made you feel shitty for years.'

'It's just high school crap. I've moved on.'

'Okay, I won't give him details. He still won't call you that again.'

'Harrison, you being nice is making me feel nauseous.'

'I'm always nice.' The scoff comes out of my mouth so quickly that I cough afterwards. 'That idea makes you almost vomit?'

'Almost.'

Harrison shakes his head but smiles in my direction. 'You'd be surprised how nice I really am, Agnes.'

'It's not something people normally keep hidden, *Harrison*. Anyway, it's time for your secret. I want the juiciest one.'

Harrison stands, wipes his hands and then reaches out to help me. Our time in The Shag Room must be up.

Harrison holds my hand for a second before he lets it drop to my side. Harrison's gaze studies my face. If I had to guess, Harrison looks nervous. I'm unsure because I don't think I can remember a time when he was ever nervous. Or that I could tell. He grounds me in place with the way he's surveying my face. He licks his full bottom lip, and my eyes drop involuntarily. I watch his tongue before it disappears again. I meet his eyes again.

'You ready? The juiciest secret I have.'

'Bring it on.'

Harrison leans in closer. Our faces are only inches from each other. He might be drawing this out for effect, but it's working on me. I've never been this intrigued. Harrison could be an actor in a soap opera. He'd have me hanging out for whatever his next big reveal would be. I hope Harrison's secret isn't that he's a long-lost relative that's been presumed dead.

'I tried to buy The Shark Biscuit from your dad.' *What?* My mouth drops open, and Harrison seems pleased with my reaction. I'm not sure why. None of this makes sense. 'And he turned me down.'

Chapter Eighteen

Harrison bolts from The Shag Room before I can get a single sound out of my mouth. Let alone one of the many questions flooding my brain.

I race out to the dining area and am met with cheers and woof whistles from the group. Clearly, no one needs any more alcohol tonight. Devin and his mum have disappeared somewhere, so at least I'm spared from the awkwardness of facing them after everyone assumes Harrison and I made out for the last seven minutes. Harrison sits at the drinking table and sculls the entire beer in front of him. The bottle bangs down on the table, catching everyone's attention.

'Wowsers.' That's all Noah can say. Harrison doesn't lift his head to acknowledge any of them.

'The power of The Shag Room,' says Scout as she waves her hand towards Harrison and me. If only she knew how wrong she is. No shagging. No touching. But sharing of secrets, which might be more of a surprise than if we made out.

Thomas sizes up his brother, I assume, trying to guess his mood. Good luck with that.

'Okay, since you are not giving us any details, let's move on. Willy's turn.' Thomas drags his gaze off Harrison as Willy retrieves a card. He holds up a queen to the group before putting it in the discard pile.

'Queen card means you have to ask a person a random question. When they answer, they have to ask a different person another random question quickly. We keep going around until someone doesn't answer or can't think of a question.'

I spy Devin, Barbara and the Whalleys talking at a nearby table, and then Devin rejoins the group.

'Mum's going to sit out for a while. She's feeling the effects of that cocktail.' Scout looks away from Devin sheepishly, but she shouldn't feel bad. I warned everyone she knows how to make a mean cocktail. At the same time, Noah explains the rules of the queen card to Devin, and I jump on the opportunity to whisper at least some of my questions that flowed from Harrison's Shag Room revelation. I tug on his shirt. His eyes skirt over to me, but he barely moves his head. I lean in and talk directly to the underside of his ear.

'You can't tell me something like that and just run off.' I keep my voice low so no one else hears. To them, I could be whispering sweet nothings in his ear. 'When? How? Did Dad say why?'

Harrison angles his head close. Our eyes examine each other for a second before Harrison looks away. 'I shouldn't have told you. I just needed to know whether you knew or not. I figured you did, and that's why you've been weird lately. With me. Like you felt guilty.'

I've felt guilty for months, but not because I didn't want Harrison to buy The Shark Biscuit. I felt guilty because I thought I was the reason it was closing. Now, I find out that's not the case. I need to talk to Dad to find out what the hell is going on.

Harrison leans away from me and settles back in his chair like our conversation has concluded. We're only getting started. He should know I don't let him get away with the final word. Ever.

'I'll call Dad and find out.' I go to stand, but Harrison places his hand on my thigh and gently pushes me back down.

'Don't.' He leans forward and is now the one leaning in to whisper into my ear. Except now, the gravelly vibration of his voice sends a shiver shooting up the back of my neck. I hope he didn't notice the tiny shiver my body involuntarily did when his breath hit my skin. 'He must have had his reasons. If he wanted you to know, he would have told you.'

'Harrison—'

'*Please*, Agnes. Just once, I need you to leave it.' Harrison moves his head back, and his eyes bore into mine. He's pleading with me to leave it. I don't want to leave this, but I give him a slight nod.

'Ahem,' Thomas clears his throat from across the table as Harrison and I jump away from each other. Every person at the table is staring at us. Thomas's eyebrows are as high on his forehead as humanly possible as his eyes dart between Harrison and me.

'Seven minutes wasn't enough for you two, hey?' Scout winks in my direction as she places a new drink before Harrison. I shake my head to clarify, but Harrison rests his hand on my thigh and squeezes it. He rubs my thigh up and down, and I know he's telling me to just play along. It's distracting as hell, though.

'Can we play now, or do you two need a minute?' I didn't realise Thomas was so into the game that he'd be impatient.

'Let's go.' It's all Harrison says for the group to finally look away. Devin's gaze lingers for a second before he reaches for his drink. It seems like I'm telling secrets in front of him with my new boyfriend but I can't explain that I'm not that cruel – another thing to swirl around in my head. I'm going to max out soon and need a lie-down.

'First question is for Aggie Bagg—' Thomas doesn't get a chance to finish that sentence before Harrison interrupts.

'That nickname is done. For good.' Thomas laughs, but Harrison lasers him with an expression that means he's serious. Thomas's laugh dies suddenly.

'Are you serious?' Thomas isn't sure what's happening, and I don't blame him.

'We'll talk later, but find a new nickname. Or use her real name. Okay?'

'Ok-ay.' Thomas says it slowly to convey the weirdness of this conversation.

I wish I could hide under the table but take a sizeable drink from my cocktail instead. Harrison stops rubbing my thigh, but his hand stays in place.

'Agnes,' Thomas nods in my direction as some sort of formality as he uses my correct name. 'What's your favourite body part of my brother's?'

I choke on my drink and cough into my hand. I wipe the water from my eyes and I don't think I can be strategic or clever right now. My brain is completely maxed out.

My mind is swirling from Harrison's revelation, alcohol, stress and the heat coming from Harrison's hand on my thigh. I gaze at his large, calloused fingers spread against my thigh, and I blurt out the truth before I can stop myself.

'Forearms.' I take another sip of my drink to help clear my throat. I'm not sure alcohol is designed for that, but it will have to do. I can sense Harrison watching me, but

I avoid looking his way. I hang off until the last second, catching the hint of a cheeky grin as he turns back to the group. I could have lied, but it's our last night together, so I'll gift him with the truth about his glorious forearms.

'That's weird.' Willy holds up his toned, bronzed forearms and inspects them. 'No one has ever complimented my forearms.' He leans over to compare his next to Harrison's, but Harrison gives him a look that makes him retreat to his side of the table.

'I get it. Not about Harrison, but the forearm thing.' Scout salutes me with her drink before taking a sip. 'Your turn, Agnes.'

'Umm,' I don't want to ask Harrison or Devin a question, so I ask Scout, 'Are you upset about your break-up?'

'It's meant to be random, not personal, Agnes.' Scout says it in a friendly tone. 'But the answer is no. Glad. Relieved. I want my side of the bed back. Want her shit out that was cluttering the apartment.'

'That's pretty clear.' Noah laughs at Scout's pragmatic view of the ending of her relationship. 'Your question. They have to be much faster, or this game will never end.'

'Okay. Harrison, what's your favourite body part of Agnes?'

'Scout!' I cry out across the table.

'Sorry, but it was the next obvious question.'

'Smile,' says Harrison quickly, with conviction.

'That's not a body part,' says Scout.

'Fine. Lips. Next question: Thomas, would you rather have sex with a mermaid or a centauride?'

Thomas's eyes bug out of his head as he struggles for an answer. It looks like he's running both scenarios through his head. 'Fuck. That question broke my brain.' He shakes his head like that will somehow help organise his thoughts. 'In a good way.'

'No answer. Next card.' Harrison points to Scout whose turn it is to take a card. I feel like he knew Thomas couldn't answer that question, which ended the *fun* question card.

Scout debates over which card to take and then reveals another king. She cackles loudly as Noah places the bottle in the centre of the table. Scout spins the bottle, and it lands on herself. I feel like she planned that somehow. Her grin is wide and smug.

'You want to go into the cupboard?' Scout cocks her chin in Thomas's direction.

Thomas does a double-take to check she's talking to him. He was not expecting that proposal. 'Didn't you just break up with your girlfriend?'

'Yes, which would mean I'm single,' says Scout with no shame, and I love her for that.

'You like guys too?' asks Thomas.

'You'd hope so. I'm not going in there to crochet together.'

Noah laughs and Thomas looks unsure how to proceed. This is a complete role reversal from the Thomas I knew in high school. He would be the one nudging people towards a cupboard to make out without a second thought, but tonight, he looks hesitant.

'Don't worry, sailor, I'm just messing with you. The big ones normally can't handle the bi thing.' Scout winks at Thomas, and he stiffens at her comment. 'I was always going to pick Agnes and Harrison.'

I'm not sure I can handle any more time in The Shag Room tonight.

Chapter Nineteen

Harrison closes the door to the storage room and we take our seats again. I turn off my torch because I only have 10 per cent of my battery left. Harrison leaves his torch on and places it beside him so I can see his face in the soft light.

'I don't understand why you won't let me call my dad. There's been a mistake. He told me he couldn't find a buyer.'

'It's pretty clear what happened.' Harrison shuffles beside me. 'He doesn't want to sell it to me.'

'Did he give you a reason?'

'He said he had a better offer.'

'So, you think there's another buyer?'

Harrison moves a little closer and his shoulder brushes up against mine.

'I have no idea. I was hoping you knew something, but I wasn't sure how to ask.' I can hear the sadness and exhaustion in Harrison's voice.

'I didn't think you'd ever be shy asking me anything.'

'There's a lot we never talked about,' says Harrison as he rubs the back of his neck.

'Ask away. This is what the room is for: spilling secrets.'

'I thought this room was for shagging.'

'Not shagging.' I point my finger at Harrison, and he must be able to see it in the dim light because he chuckles quietly.

We sit in silence for a few minutes before I say softly, 'I'm sorry my dad did that. I have no idea why. I know he loves you.'

Harrison seems to appreciate my words, and I now realise why he's been upset all night. He thought I didn't want him to have the restaurant when the opposite is true.

'I hope you don't hate Dad,' I whisper.

Harrison shakes his head firmly. 'I could never. I would have killed to have grown up with a dad like your old man.'

'That's because you would have loved cooking with him.'

'No, because he loves you.' There's a sadness in Harrison's tone that catches me off guard. I thought it was a given that all parents love their children, but he makes it sound like Dad is a rarity.

'You don't think your parents love you?' I ask delicately because I'm not sure I can jump straight into this territory with Harrison. We did say it's the sharing room, but this would be asking Harrison to share at a level of vulnerability we've never ventured into.

'Um.' Harrison somehow looks smaller. He's managed to shrink himself in size without even moving. I've touched a deep wound without realising it. Perhaps it's more like an infected boil that needs lancing.

'Harrison?'

'I'm sure they love me.'

'That was carefully phrased.'

'It's not something my family talk about.' Harrison breathes out the words slowly.

'Feelings?'

'Yep. Feelings, love. Any of that stuff.' He waves his hand around.

'But your parents told you they love you, right?'

'No. It's not said in our family.'

'Never?' Harrison shakes his head. 'You and Thomas?'

'You can keep asking in different ways, but it won't change the answer.'

'Sorry, just trying to work out the—'

'Level of messed up in my family?' Harrison doesn't snap or say it with tone but more with a melancholy edge.

'Not at all. Some people prefer to show love than say it.'

'My parents aren't like that either.' Harrison shifts his body again. He's uncomfortable but I'd like to find a way to make him feel comfortable so he'll keep talking. This is the most he's disclosed with me in years. He might need a break from the sharing, so I take my turn, hoping it will keep him chatting.

'My dad says it all the time.'

'Thanks for rubbing it in.' He's got a smirk on his face, so I know he's joking.

'I mean, he says it all the time and he did growing up. He wasn't around much, though.' I feel awful admitting this out loud because my dad is the best. But I missed him when he was constantly working.

'And that was hard?'

'Hard after Mum died. One parent down, and nothing about our lives changed. Dad didn't change his work schedule. Didn't cut his long hours. I know he may not have had a choice, but I was alone a lot. I was loved and alone.'

'We could have hung out. I wanted to be anywhere but at home. Alone would have been a dream.'

I get the feeling Harrison is only sharing a small window into what his home life was like growing up, and it doesn't sound ideal.

'You see your parents much?' I ask.

'No.'

'Thomas?'

'We're back here again. You'll get the same answer no matter how you swing it.'

'Neither of you see them?'

'I take their calls. Thomas talks to them occasionally, but otherwise, we don't see them.'

'You miss them?' It's a stupid question, and I realise it the second it leaves my mouth. You don't cut off your parents lightly. I'm about to tell him to ignore my question, but he tilts his head in my direction. The light only kisses the side of his face, but I can see the vulnerability in his expression.

'Yes. I miss them.' Harrison takes a moment to think before he says, 'I don't think you stop missing someone even when you realise they're not good to have in your life.'

'Do they call at Christmas? Birthdays?'

'Sometimes. Sometimes not. It's not something I expect, so it's not a big deal.'

I place my hand on Harrison's arm and say, 'That's a lot to handle. You seem so well-adjust—'

'Stop. Don't be nice.'

'It's true. It takes a lot of—'

'Enough, Agnes.' I lift my hand back off his arm.

'I'm giving you a compliment, so be quiet and take it,' I snap at him.

Harrison chuckles at my outburst. 'It's too easy to rile you up.'

We sit in silence, and I can't help the little smile that forms because he did know exactly how to rile me up instantly. It was too easy for him.

'I've shared far too much, so it's your turn,' says Harrison.

'I don't think I've got much left in the tank you don't know.'

'What the hell did you see in that guy?' The question comes out of nowhere, but it must be what Harrison has burning on his mind.

'We've been over this. When I met him, I thought he was nice.'

'No. He's not.'

'I suppose he was pleasant.'

'What a fucking awful reason to date someone.'

'You can't comment if you don't even date,' I say, throwing a scalding look at Harrison.

'I didn't say that.'

'Yes, you did. You said, "I don't date". I love how guys can say that, and it's all cool. I'd be judged if I said I don't date.'

'Have you finished your rant?'

'I'm not sure. Let me think about it.' I tap my finger on my chin while I make Harrison wait. I can't see his annoyance, but it's still fun making him wait. I drop my finger. 'Yes, I'm done.'

'You misunderstood what I meant when I said I don't date.'

'How could I have misinterpreted that?'

'I don't date as in I took a self-imposed…' Harrison pauses again and something about his voice makes me want to see his face. I turn on my torch, and it puts a brighter glow over our faces.

Harrison runs his fingers through his hair and casts his eyes downwards. I think Harrison James is feeling self-conscious, and I never thought that was something I'd see. I study him for a moment while I wait for him to continue. He's not looking at me, so I get full access to admire his face. It's a face worth admiring – he's always clean-shaven, being a chef, but I can see his five o'clock stubble coming through already.

'Take a photo, Agnes.' I jolt back at his words. He's still not looking at me, so I'm not sure how he knew I was staring.

'I was concerned as you finished mid-sentence, and while I know communication isn't your strong suit, that's bad even for you.'

Harrison scoffs at my remark and it has a different tone than usual. Something about the sound he made makes me want to apologise, but I'm not sure he'd like that either.

'Are you going to explain why "not dating" means something else in Harrison language?'

He runs his hand over his face and tips his head back.

'Fine. Here it is. More *fucking* sharing. I put myself on a self-imposed sabbatical. My therapist suggested some changes. I haven't been on a date, a dating app or had any contact with a woman for a while now.'

'What's a while?'

'That's your first question?' Harrison cocks his eyebrow at my question.

'I think it would be everyone's first question, but you don't have to tell me.'

'I haven't kept count. I know it will be coming up to a year soon, but it's not about the time.'

'What's it about then?'

'Making better choices. Not repeating old patterns. A whole heap of shit I've been working through.'

Harrison folds his arms and then uncrosses them. He's trusting me with this information, and it feels monumental. He's handed me a huge secret I don't believe anyone else would know. The weight of that gesture makes me feel nervous but warm all over.

'I had no idea,' I whisper.

'Just like I had no idea you'd broken up with cutlery king.' I ignore the jab at Devin because I want to stay on topic.

'And you see a therapist?' Harrison nods. 'And it helps?' Harrison nods again. 'Now the cat has got your tongue. Normally, you never shut up.'

'You would be the only person to say that to me.' There's a hint of sadness when Harrison says that, and I sense it wasn't a joke.

'I doubt that.'

'It's true. The feedback –' Harrison does air quotes when he says the word feedback – 'I've received is that I don't know how to talk. I don't know how to communicate. I'm a closed book. Locked up.'

I angle my body towards Harrison and tuck my knees against my chest. 'This feedback is from who?'

Harrison turns and looks me straight in the eye when he says, 'Every girlfriend I've ever had.' His eyes dart away quickly.

That doesn't feel like the Harrison I've known, but everyone is different in relationships. It's not the same as our relationship, however one would describe our relationship.

'And the therapist suggested you stop dating?'

'No. I did that.'

'More words Harrison.'

'The last break-up was brutal.'

'When are they not?'

'True, but the whole relationship wasn't right. Reminded me of my parents.'

'Your parents? Why?'

'Yelling. Lots of yelling. Toxic shit. Not fun.'

'It's good you got out.'

'The thing is that I wasn't good in that relationship either. It wasn't one-sided. We were both toxic.' Harrison clears his throat before he says quietly. 'I don't want that. Never again.'

'And so you started a sabbatical.' Harrison nods slowly. 'No wonder you've been so moody lately.' Harrison laughs, and I feel it all the way down to my toes. 'It's admirable. Knowing what you don't want and drawing a line in the sand.'

We sit silently for a moment, my mind ticking over and putting the timeline together. Harrison turned up with the 'No Yelling' sign last year and made a hard rule that there was no yelling in the kitchen. *Ever.*

'I can hear you thinking in the dark. Just think out loud. You can't say the wrong thing to me.'

'The sign? No yelling...'

Harrison ducks his chin as he says, 'Yes. I saw the sign at a charity shop one day and got it.' Harrison scuffles again, and our legs stay brushed up against each other. 'I want you to know I was never verbally abusive, but I kept picking people who liked to yell, and I'd shut down.'

'Emotionally?'

'And physically. They would say I was emotionally unavailable, but it felt physical.'

Harrison takes a deep breath, and I know it's taking a lot of trust to tell me this, so I place my hand on his leg, and he immediately holds my hand tightly. I thought maybe he would flinch, or I'd have to drag it away awkwardly, but he holds it like he was waiting for me to comfort him.

'I worked out I can't handle being yelled at. It feels fucking pathetic to say, and I know it's from my childhood, but yelling puts my body under stress and I normally tap out. I shut down. My body can't handle yelling, but I kept choosing people who didn't know how to fight any other way. And I can't anymore. It's a physical thing for me. I'm six foot three and can't handle yelling. What do you think about that?'

I turn my hand so I can link our fingers together. I want him to feel that I'm holding onto him and not him only grasping me. His eyes stay on our hands, so I lift his chin to look at me with my other hand.

'I think it makes perfect sense. I hate being yelled at, too.' I lean closer and whisper, 'I secretly love the "No Yelling" sign.'

'I knew it!' Harrison throws his head back and cackles.

'You did not,' I playfully laugh and it feels lovely to feel relaxed together. Harrison holds onto my hand tightly as silence takes over the conversation. Now, I'm the one who can hear Harrison overthinking in the darkness.

'It dawned on me a little while ago that *you* are the person I communicate with the best. Funny, I know.' Harrison moves his other hand and places it under mine. My hand is engulfed in Harrison's strong fingers. 'But I trust you'll tell me exactly how you feel. We can fight without my body ever feeling threatened. I never have to walk on eggshells with you because you tell me. You don't yell or storm away. You stay and tell me. I can't tell you how much comfort I find in the way you fight with me.'

I can't speak. It's possibly the nicest thing anyone has ever said to me, and it's a compliment about my fighting style. The way Harrison explains it makes so much sense and makes me realise something.

'I can fight for what I want with you,' I whisper into the still air. Harrison's face slowly turns, and I catch his eyes in the soft light. This man isn't emotionally unavailable or closed off. He's private. He's intense, but he knows how to communicate and listen. 'I don't know when that happened, but I feel safe saying no to you. I don't have to put my feelings aside to make you happy. I can't tell you how amazing that feels.'

Harrison's eyes roam over my face, and there's a fondness in this expression. His fingers move to caress my arm up and down.

There's nothing more to say. It feels like our first official truce. A laying down of our weapons and finally revealing ourselves to one another. I don't feel exposed or vulnerable; I feel safe. All the things Harrison has revealed tonight feel like the missing parts of a puzzle I've been trying to figure out. I never felt like I had the whole picture of him, and now that out of focus image is in clear view.

Harrison continues to stroke my arm, and I do the thing that feels natural. I lean down and rest my head on his shoulder. He lifts his hand, and his fingers curl into my hair. He clutches me against him with more affection than I've ever experienced.

'We waited until the last night to really know each other,' I say quietly, a deep sadness welling at the time wasted not knowing Harrison James and all his hidden pieces.

'It's not—'

Harrison is cut off by a pounding on the door that startles us both.

'Ding ding. Time's up, lovers.' Thomas's voice crashes into our moment.

Harrison and I slowly unfold our bodies and he helps me to my feet. He reaches for the door handle but hesitates. The next moment he spins around, cups the back of my head and leans in slowly to place a kiss on my temple. He retreats quickly, and he's out the door. I place my fingers over the spot where his lips were moments ago.

Maybe it was a thank-you kiss or perhaps a goodbye kiss. All I know is that something about it makes me want to stay in here and cry.

Chapter Twenty

When I return to the group, Harrison is nowhere to be found. The tables have been pushed back, and the torches set up to make a small dance floor.

Scout and Noah dance in a way that only severely drunk people know how to, with chaotic arm and leg movements. Willy rolls his hips with skill, and Scout laughs so hard that she has to bend over to catch her breath. Thomas sits in a chair, and I notice he's watching her intently. Maybe he regrets not accepting her offer for crocheting in the cupboard.

Mr and Mrs Whalley dance slowly together off on the side. Barbara and Devin are in the corner, and Barbara rests her head on Devin's shoulder. She looks half asleep, and Devin looks like the most bored and trapped man in history. Somehow, the image feels fitting.

I tiptoe over to Devin, trying not to disrupt Barbara mainly because I'd rather not talk to her and whisper, 'Do you want to try and find a spot for her to lie down?'

Devin gives me the coldest side-eye and mumbles, 'We don't need anything from you.'

He turns his head away, dismissing me. I stand in shock for a moment, feeling my cheeks heat from various levels of humiliation. No matter what he thinks I've done wrong by him, I don't deserve that level of rudeness since I was offering to help his mother.

Once again, I've let Devin make me feel small. I don't know how he does it, but I'm annoyed at myself for letting it happen so easily. I shake off his horribleness and walk over to stand next to Thomas. He's sipping another drink and offers me his chair. I wave him away and wrap my arms around myself because there's a chill in the air, but also for self-protection.

Scout, Willy and Noah start a dance-off and it lightens my mood. Mr Whalley joins in but quickly regrets it when he holds his back and rejoins Mrs Whalley in slow dancing.

From behind, I hear the kitchen door push open and Harrison comes out with two large platters of bread rolls, cold seafood and chocolate cake. He places the platters on the bar and Thomas hops up and grabs two bread rolls before anyone notices they're there.

Noah and Willy stumble over to the bar and devour the food. One look at Noah and I can tell he's hammered. I don't know how much drinking went on while Harrison and I were in the cupboard, but Noah is feeling the full effects. Scout continues to dance on her own and looks like she's having a wonderful time. Thomas's eyes can't stop bouncing back to her, and they eventually linger.

I join the group and position myself next to Harrison. He takes a napkin, places a bread roll in it, and holds it out for me before I reach his side. He's constantly feeding me.

'Thank you,' I say softly because the gesture feels loving, and it thaws some of the coldness from my inter-action with Devin.

Noah holds his head back and throws an oyster down his throat. He wipes his mouth and says to Willy, 'All I'm saying is you must have picked up some moves from your work.'

I hope they're in the middle of a conversation that got interrupted, or Noah is even drunker than I thought.

'Dance moves, yes, but not what you're asking,' Willy says as he inspects the platter and points at the assortment. 'Thank you for this, what a delightful treat.'

'You're welcome, Willy,' says Harrison before opening a can of beer.

Willy cocks his head to the side and beams at Harrison. 'You called me Willy.'

'It hurt.' Harrison smiles back at Willy before Noah clicks his fingers in Willy's face.

'Excuse me. We're focusing on my problem.'

'Ask him. He might know.' Willy points to Thomas, and I catch the cheeky grin he is trying to hide. Noah steps over and drops his forehead onto Thomas's chest. Thomas stumbles back, but Noah keeps his face snuggled into Thomas's torso.

He then lifts his face and places his chin on Thomas's chest as he looks up at him with appreciation.

'Can you show me how to use my penis?'

'Absolutely not.' Thomas lifts both his hands. One is holding a prawn, and the other cake. Noah still looks at him with childlike wonder.

'That's what everyone says. I know how to cook, but I don't know how to pleasure a woman.' Noah sulks away and slides down the wall. He places his head in his hands. I quickly pour a glass of water, and we pass it down the line until Harrison leaves it on the ground beside Noah.

'I don't think they require the same skills.' Thomas says it like a question and that he's not 100 per cent sure pleasuring women and cooking don't require the same proficiencies.

Willy slides down next to Noah and taps his knee.

'One day, you'll be just as good with your penis as you are a cook. It just takes practice.'

Willy's advice seems to give Noah some comfort. Mr and Mrs Whalley join Thomas, Harrison and me to enjoy the late-night snacks.

'You think the rain is slowing?' I ask with equal amounts of hope and stress in my voice. It's almost one o'clock, and I don't think I'm any closer to leaving this place than I was hours ago.

'I do. I just said that to Dot,' says Mr Whalley. 'I think we'll be right in a few more hours.'

A few more hours?

'Your mum would have loved tonight,' says Mrs Whalley, surprising me, because people rarely talk about my mum.

'She would have loved the chaos?' I ask because I'm unsure what part of tonight would have appealed to Mum, and that thought sobers me.

Mrs Whalley has a small chuckle, and I think she still might be tipsy, but then she says with a straight face, 'She would have loved chatting with everyone tonight.' She takes my hand. 'She loved talking and hearing people's stories. You're just like her in so many ways. Taking care of everyone tonight.' I reach for my locket and the heaviness of realising it's gone sweeps over my body again. Harrison must notice because he watches me with a melancholic expression.

'Do you mind if we get a coffee one day and you tell me more stories about her? I don't know that many.'

'I would love that.' Mrs Whalley tenderly smiles at me, and I fall in love with the creases that form around the sweetness of her eyes. She keeps my attention for another second before her eyes swing over to Harrison. 'You know what else her mum loved?'

Harrison has his mouth open and a piece of cake halfway to its death when she asks. It might be the first time I remember seeing Harrison wholly caught off guard. He drops the cake and says, 'I don't. Sorry.'

'She loved to dance.' Mrs Whalley dips her chin, giving Harrison a signal before she looks back at me. 'Your dad and her used to dance all the time in here.'

'No. My dad would never.' I shake my head because I would remember that, except she may have already been sick by the time my memories kicked in. Or at least started her treatment. She fought the cancer for years before it finally overcame her body.

'Oh, yes, he did. You ask him. They danced all the time.' Mrs Whalley repeatedly taps Mr Whalley's forearm, 'Play that song, Scott.' It dawns on me that their names are Dot and Scott, and my parents were Ernie and Birdie – no wonder they all became friends.

'What song?' Mr Whalley asks, and I agree that he will probably need more hints to narrow it down.

'The Sam Cooke one.' That's enough for Mr Whalley. He pushes a few buttons on his phone and a song plays softly through the speaker. I lean over to read 'You're Always on My Mind' on the screen.

'Come on, dear. For old times' sake.' Mrs Whalley pulls Mr Whalley onto the dancefloor, holding each other tight as they sway to the music.

'Harrison, that was your cue,' Mrs Whalley bellows with a wink at Harrison.

'Right.' Harrison brushes his hands on his pant leg, as I've seen him do one hundred times, and he holds out his hand, 'I've been given instructions.'

He pulls me towards the dancefloor before I can refuse the offer. I wouldn't have anyway because, for every hour the night goes on, I'm becoming more drawn to Harrison. My reflex is to lean in when he's close, and it's frightening to admit that to myself.

Harrison spins me into his arms and pulls me against his body in a swift motion. My hand rests on his shoulder as he slides his arm around my back and inches me closer. Harrison holds my hand and brings our joined fingers to rest on his chest.

We sway together without any words until Mr and Mrs Whalley dance to our side, and Dot leans over. 'You remind me so much of your parents.' She winks at us, and they dance away.

She's making me an emotional wreck, and to hide the impending breakdown, I rest my forehead against Harrison's chest. I'll bury myself here until the sadness disappears. Harrison cups my head and holds me tightly while swaying us to the music.

'Sorry. Dad never talks about her, so I'm not used to someone speaking so openly about her,' I whisper into Harrison's chest. 'I love it, though.'

I lift my head and give Harrison a watery smile. He strokes my hair and places it behind my ear.

'You should make your dad talk about her more.'

'Make him?' Harrison and I have been over this already tonight.

'Yes, Agnes.' Harrison leans forward and stares at me intently. 'You can be very forceful when you want to be.' He raises his eyebrows while I let that sink in.

'You're the only person who would think that,' I mumble as I duck my chin again and rest my head against Harrison's shoulder.

'Then they don't know you,' Harrison says quietly, ending our conversation. Another Sam Cooke song plays as Harrison and I and the Whalleys continue to slow dance.

As Harrison twirls us slowly around, I see Scout, Willy and Noah on the ground playing cards again. Perhaps they're trying to help Noah feel better or less drunk. I'm out, though. I'm done with any further drinking games.

Scout picks up a card and laughs so hard that she falls backwards. Thomas puts his hand on her thigh and pulls her back to a sitting position. She shows the boys the card and Noah also falls back with laughter. Thomas pulls him back to a sitting position and keeps a hand on each of their thighs for stability.

Scout cups her hands over her mouth and shouts to the group, 'I got another king card.'

Harrison and I shake our heads as Scout yells, 'Mr and Mrs Whalley, it's your turn. The Shag Room awaits your arrival.'

Noah covers his mouth like it's the most scandalous thing he's ever heard.

'I don't think we're playing anymore, sweetie,' says Mrs Whalley, as Scott walks his wife towards the storage cupboard.

'Rules are rules, dear.' I see him wink at Thomas on his way past and Thomas gives him an understanding nod.

I drop my shoulders, which were holding the tension from the possibility of another cupboard walk of shame.

'I think I'm offended by that exhale. Was it that bad?'

I know Harrison's not upset, and he's only teasing.

'I'll look at that room in a new light after tonight. And take to it with disinfection.'

Harrison chuckles as the next song comes on, and I realise we're still dancing. The Whalleys have gone to the cupboard doing things I don't want to think about so Harrison and I can stop at any time, but I like it. I've never slow danced with a partner. Harrison takes the lead with our rhythm, and it's comforting. Scout, Willy and Noah have stopped playing their drinking game, thank goodness, and are happily chatting while sprawled out on the floor. Devin and Barbara are still off to the side. I sneak a peek and regret it instantly. Devin's death stare has more venom than I expected. If I'm not mistaken, I think Barbara did the tiniest disapproving head shake at me.

My body tenses, and Harrison must sense it because he swings us around, so my back is to them.

'Ignore them,' Harrison mumbles under his breath.

'Easier said than done.'

'I was talking to myself.' Harrison's lips snarl on one side.

'You needed to give yourself a pep talk?' I say jokingly, but Harrison responds immediately with a 'Yes.' He then looks over my shoulder, and the warmth leaves his face, 'Because if he keeps looking at you like he's a wounded puppy, I'm going to lose my shit.'

Harrison's eyes continue to glare behind me, and I assume it's at Devin. Or maybe Barbara. I place my hands on Harrison's face and angle it back towards me. Nothing good can come from Harrison eyeballing The Sporks.

'Remember your pep talk?' I say, teasing, but Harrison's dark mood hasn't left him yet.

'Yes, but now I'm thinking that I'll have a word with Devin about how sulking is unbecoming of a man. Have some fucking pride.' Harrison's disposition lightens, and I know if I can keep him looking at me, his mood will improve.

'I didn't think we'd be in his face for this long. It's not ideal.' I duck my chin because I didn't mean to be so openly visible with Harrison in front of Devin. It was an extremely short-term arrangement that involved no touching, but now we're slow dancing in front of him.

Harrison lifts my chin and keeps his thumb on my jawline as he says, 'You don't owe him anything. Stop feeling bad.'

There's a faint sound of a tsk behind us, and Harrison's eyes snap over my shoulder.

'You trust me?' Harrison slowly brings his eyes down to me as he asks.

'Why would you ask—'

Harrison drags his fingers down my spine to rest on my lower back. I don't have a chance to mutter a word before he thrusts me forward into his body. My hands fly out and land on his chest to steady myself. His black shirt is soft under my fingers, but I can feel the firmness of his chest. I'd never let myself think of the firmness of his chest. My mind normally fixated on his forearms but never travelled further. I gave myself the forearm and no more. Harrison nudges me closer. There was a little gap before, but now we're fully pressed against one another.

Harrison leans in to whisper, 'Heads up, I'm going to kiss you.'

'What?' My brain doesn't have time to compute before Harrison says, 'Say no now, Agnes, or I'm kissing you.'

Harrison leans in slowly, his eyes dipping to meet mine to gauge my thoughts. The first thought that hits my brain is *I like being this close to Harrison*. It startles me, but something about the way he's looking at me makes my stomach drop at the same time I lean in closer. The sensation of his arms surrounding me is delicious. I feel surrounded, safe and electric. I shut my brain off and let the words slip out of my mouth.

'Oka—'

I don't have time to get the rest of my answer before Harrison's lips envelop mine. My mouth was already open, and Harrison used that to his advantage to deepen the kiss as the hand on my back moves higher and spreads between my shoulder blades. He angles his head to kiss my top lip, kiss the side of my mouth and then pulls back slightly.

'Kiss me back, Agnes.' Harrison's whisper is almost silent. 'Or are you just a terrible kisser?' He says over my lips as he lightly pecks the corner of my lips.

I was too stunned by the force and the captivating nature of Harrison's kiss to react. His comment snaps me from my stupor.

Challenge accepted.

I give him one steely gaze before I lift my hands from his chest and cup his face, pulling his mouth down to mine. My tongue thrusts into his mouth as we both angle to deepen the kiss. At first, there was a need to prove Harrison wrong, that I am indeed an excellent kisser, which I've somehow forgotten as the kiss lingers. Harrison's hands cup my back, and my hands move higher into his hair. I continue pulling him down so I'm in control of our kiss. Maybe sensing that I'm winning whatever game of cat and mouse this is, Harrison reaches down and lifts my legs. I wrap them around his waist, and his hands settle on my backside, cupping it firmly. He's moving us somewhere, but I have no idea where. I'm still exploring his mouth and tongue when I faintly hear some cheering coming from the dining room.

I thought the drunk idiots were cheering us, but Scout yells out, 'You dirty dog, Mr Whalley!'

As Harrison sweeps us into the kitchen, I hear Mr Whalley say, 'Best night of my life, kids.' The drunken trio laugh as Harrison flings open the kitchen door, and we disappear inside.

Chapter Twenty-One

Harrison walks backwards into the kitchen while still kissing me. He takes three giant steps back before he bumps into something, and the sound of pots crashing to the ground is startling enough to break us apart. Harrison's hands still cup my backside, my legs are firmly wrapped around him and my hands are locked behind his neck.

His breath glides over my cheek, and the soft sigh makes me angle my body closer to him, my eyes stay fluttered shut. This was a prank to alleviate Harrison's frustration at Devin or to finally get him and Barbara off my back, but neither Harrison nor I have loosened our hold of each other. There's no one else here, so there's no need to pretend we're together, yet neither of us moves away.

We could sit in here and twiddle our thumbs, and everyone would still believe we're making out. I pull back a fraction, and Harrison gently lowers me. I sway when my feet touch the ground, but Harrison clutches my arm to hold me steady.

No words are said between us. That was hands-down the best kiss I've ever had in my life. Harrison James kisses better than he makes bug rolls. The thought is equally unsettling and a turn-on.

We haven't stepped away from each other. Harrison's hand still holds onto my elbow. His grip tightens, and I slowly open my eyes so I can read his face.

The soft, dim light from the generator makes the room feel inviting and not as cold and sterile as the kitchen usually feels. Harrison peers down at me, and his expression makes my breath hitch. It's the strong, handsome version of Harrison I've always known but now I can see the swishy, vulnerable parts. The parts I never understood. It makes him irresistible because now I see the whole picture. I've always been drawn to Harrison, to bicker, to get his attention, but I'm drawn to him in an entirely new way right now. His eyes are heartbreakingly beautiful as they roam my face.

Another round of the bull and mule, and I still have no idea which one I am, nor do I care. All I know is that kissing him was a fucking dream, and I want to do it again. Tonight will be my last chance. This moment right now could be my last chance. He could reject me. He could laugh in my face since we're alone in here, and there's no need to pretend.

I want to gauge his thoughts, so I run a finger across his jaw to see how he'll react. His hand flexes again on my elbow. He drops his chin and angles it closer to my finger, and that slight movement is all I need to know Harrison won't laugh at me. I think, for once, we might be thinking the same thing. It's pretty amazing that it's come to this to find something we agree on. I could ask him or find a reason why we need to kiss again, but I don't want to wait another second.

'Screw it.' I launch myself at Harrison, climb back up his body and loop my legs around his waist. Luckily, he catches on quickly and holsters me up by holding under my thighs. Harrison spins us, and my backside hits the counter as he brings one of his hands to cradle my neck. I guide his mouth to mine, but we find each other effortlessly. His lips open, and his tongue plays with mine with give and take, which we both don't usually allow. He angles my head to the side to deepen the kiss as I place my hand on the counter for stability. There's another sound of utensils dropping to the floor as I tighten my legs and pull Harrison closer. My hand on the counter slips, and a container flies to the floor.

Harrison pulls back and kisses down my throat. 'You're not looking for my knife, are you?'

I chuckle at the thought. 'Not right now, no.'

'Good to know.' Harrison puts his hands on the top of my thighs and thrusts me forward so there's no gap between our bodies. His hands move to hold my waist, and he returns his lips to mine, and we forget all about knives, storms, ex-boyfriends and hating each other.

We move together back and forth as Harrison continues to kiss me with a passion I've never experienced. He pulls down the left side of my collar and kisses down my neck and across my collarbone. As I wait for his lips to return, I slip my hand into his pants, dipping my fingers just past the waistband. It's enough for Harrison to lift his head. He hovers an inch from my face. His fingers graze my forehead as he pushes the hair off my face. My hand still lingers under the waistband, and I'm unsure whether to move.

'Your hand is in my pants, Agnes,' he whispers.

'I know.' I try to say it confidently, but it doesn't sound as strong as I'd hoped.

'Just checking you knew.'

'Your hand has been on my arse, so it only seemed fair.' That logic holds up.

'So, this is about making sure we're even?' I have no idea what this is about, so I remain silent. 'If that's the case.'

Harrison slowly untangles my legs and lowers them to the ground. My body slides down his, and he doesn't allow us to break contact the entire time. I feel every part of his body. My hand slips out of his pants and hangs by my side.

Harrison moves slowly and dips his hand into the front of my newly acquired leggings.

'What are you doing?' I ask with mischief in my voice.

'Evening things up.'

'Is that right?' I say as Harrison kisses the side of my mouth.

'Yes, you know I'm always right.'

'I do no—' Harrison covers my words with a kiss. Between the kissing and his fingers edging closer to the side of my underwear, my brain doesn't know what to concentrate on. I realise my hands only hang loosely between us while Harrison takes the lead. Screw that. I grip his shirt in two full fists and pull him down further. One of his hands reaches behind the counter for support as the other glides up and down my inner thigh. He's teasing me, and we both know it. Bastard. I break our kiss and whisper, 'Are you finding your way down there, or does Harrison James need help?'

His lips linger over my mouth, and I feel his mouth curve into a smile.

'Oh, Agnes. You have no idea—'

A knock on the kitchen door interrupts Harrison, and then, after a few seconds, the door slowly opens. I push

Harrison away as he turns his body to stand in front of me.

Noah enters the kitchen with a hand covering his eyes. He's holding the empty platter from our late-night snacks.

'Drunk people were asking if there was any more food?' He peeks through his fingers as I try to stay hidden behind Harrison. Noah spots me and covers his eyes again. 'Also, the water from the bathroom is coming in pretty hard now. Can't be stopped.'

Noah drops his hand but keeps his eyes closed. 'And the roof has started leaking. We need buckets. We're going down, Captain. Just keep swimming. Just keep swimming.' I think he's saying it to himself.

'Are you quoting Dory?' I ask from behind Harrison's shoulder.

'Who's Dory? It's from my favourite movie, *The Meg*.' He salutes us, feels around for the counter, places the platter and leaves the kitchen again, all without opening his eyes. 'Sorry to interrupt, boss.' He throws over his shoulder before leaving, and again, I'm not sure who he's referring to, but he's gone before I can clarify.

I'm mortified. My cheeks heat at the thought of being nearly caught by a staff member. Or ex-staff member. My head is muddled, but getting caught by anyone is enough to let some logic enter my brain.

I straighten out my clothes as Harrison turns slowly and waits for me to finish putting myself back together. Neither of us says anything. The spell has been broken, and we're back to being normal Agnes and Harrison.

We watch each other. Is he thinking the same thing that I am? We made out. We made out in the kitchen which is unsanitary. Did he like kissing me? Would he want to do it again? I bite my lower lip, and Harrison's eyes dart to my mouth. I know that instinct took over, and kissing him felt right. It felt amazing, but was it simply the vibe of the night? The pretending? The sadness of never being in the restaurant again?

I feel like we're both teetering on the edge of leaning in and kissing all over again or pulling back and never mentioning the kiss ever again.

I'm about to nudge closer or make a joke to see Harrison's reaction, just as his phone beeps with a message.

He takes his phone from his pocket and says, 'Ernie, just checking in.'

'My phone is on the bar.' Dad has probably texted me, and when I didn't reply, decided to message Harrison. 'I better check it.'

'Okay.' Harrison doesn't lift his head when he replies as his fingers tap out a message on his phone. I wonder what update he's sending.

Dad interrupting us has changed the energy between us, and I need a timeout. A thinking timeout from Harrison because although I enjoyed it, it's the last thing I expected to happen tonight. Harrison and I have chemistry. It seems the staff knew it, but I didn't. Did Harrison? My brain is tying itself up in knots, and I know I need some fresh air.

'I'll text Dad and check the bathroom,' I say softly to try and hide the panic in my voice.

'Yeah, okay.' He steps back, and my heart drops at the sound. I'm not sure why, but it did. 'I'll find more food and then join you.'

'Deal.' I nod. Harrison eyes me for a moment before he turns, yanks open the refrigerator door and disappears inside. I realise now I would have preferred if he leant in to kiss me again.

It's just after two o'clock in the morning – I'm exhausted, tipsy, wearing clothes that don't belong to me and it hits me that kissing Harrison has been the best part of my day. Kissing Harrison James might be one of the best things I've ever done. That thought is enough to make me run from the kitchen and hide in the flooding toilets.

Chapter Twenty-Two

When I stumble out of the kitchen, I find Thomas and Willy sitting against the wall, asleep on each other. Willy's head is on Thomas's shoulder, and Thomas's is resting on Willy's head. Scout and Noah sit cross-legged in front of them, rolling up napkins and throwing them at the sleeping boys. Noah hits Willy directly on the forehead and throws his arms up while doing a silent celebration.

Mr and Mrs Whalley are back at their table, but Dot rests on Scott's shoulder with her eyes closed.

I quietly walk over and ask if they need anything, but he shoos me away with a genuine smile. Devin and Barbara are in the opposite corner, but I'm not asking if they need anything. I've asked enough.

I place two buckets under the drips falling from the ceiling in the back corner of the restaurant near the deck. The leaks are minor, so the buckets should be sufficient for a few hours.

The bathroom is worse than I imagined. I carefully walk down the few steps into the hand-washing area, but my shoes touch water by the second step. The whole area is under and won't be long until it starts flowing out to the rest of the restaurant. I can't do anything but put my hands on my hips and watch a soggy toilet roll float across the room. *Fuck.* I need the rain to ease up so we can try to minimise the damage.

'Are we totally screwed?' Scout looks at the disaster area over my shoulder, and I nod to respond.

'Any ideas?' I hope Scout has some miraculous idea that no one has thought of, but that might be wishful thinking.

'I say we just close the door, block it with sandbags, and never go in here again.' It's not the worst idea because I don't know what else to do. It's probably better to destroy one area than to flood the whole restaurant.

'Let's do that.'

'I was joking, but okay.' Scout and I rearrange the sandbags before closing the door to the restrooms and then barricading it shut. We wipe our hands as we step back to look at our handiwork.

Scout raises a finger to signal she's had a thought. 'Small problem. We can't use the toilets now.'

'Shit.' I rub my forehead because I didn't think about that either.

'Boys can go outside, but you and me and the other ladies, well, we're holding it until we're free.'

'Do you need to go?'

'I didn't until we started talking about it.'

'Me either. Never mention it again.' Scout and I eye each other for a moment before she starts bouncing on the balls of her feet. 'You really need to go now?'

'So badly.' Scout's bounces are now more rapid, and I suppose her bladder can only hold so much alcohol.

'Shit.' That's all I can seem to say at the moment. 'New plan. We move the sandbags. Go to the bathroom. Bag it up again.'

'Terrible plan, but let's do it.'

We both roll our pants up, slip our shoes off and walk through the floodwater to use the toilets. The water is well past my ankles, which means the walls will need replacing because they'll swell from being exposed to moisture for this long.

If it wouldn't upset Harrison, I'd call Dad and find out the truth about his plans. I assume he has another buyer, but didn't want to mention it before our last night. The damage from the storm could be a major problem for the sale. Who wants to buy a damaged, aging restaurant? He must have got an offer he couldn't refuse if he turned down Harrison's. I wonder if the new owner is hoping to keep Harrison on – Harrison, who I made out with and whose pants I just had my hand in.

A knock on the toilet door stops my brain from going around in circles and achieving nothing.

'You okay in there?' asks Scout. 'No judgement, but it's cold, and my feet are wet, but I don't want to leave you.'

I push open the door because I had finished a long time ago.

'Sorry, I...' I don't know what to say because I have too many thoughts jumbled in my head. I walk to the basin and wash my hands.

'Tonight has been a lot, hasn't it?' asks Scout.

I lean on the wall and let my shoulders drop because they were inching closer to my ears. She has no idea how accurate her statement is.

'It's been a lot for everyone tonight.'

'Stop with that crap,' says Scout, but it's in her direct but kind way. She stands next to me, leaning the back of her head against the wall.

'What crap?'

'It's been a lot for everyone crap.'

'But it has.'

Scout puts her hand on her chest. 'It's not *my* family's restaurant that's flooding and closing forever. *I* don't have an annoying ex-boyfriend giving me the guilts all night and the awkwardness of my new boyfriend being a jealous green monster whenever my ex slightly looks in my direction.' I laugh at her assessment because there are a few inaccuracies. 'My night has been pretty fun in comparison. Free drinks and fun with some cool people.'

I wish I had Scout's attitude to life. Only she could think a night where we're trapped in a restaurant is 'pretty fun'.

'It's not what you think, Scout.' I rest the back of my head against the wall too and get ready to admit the truth out loud. It's embarrassing, but I know Scout would never judge me. 'Harrison and I aren't together. That was just to get Devin off my back.'

Scout drops her chin and gives me a look that screams *Yeah, right.* 'Not believing that for a second.'

'It's true. Didn't you think it was weird I didn't mention it until tonight?'

Scout shrugs her shoulders. 'Not really. You're pretty private, and you and Harrison hooking up is A-grade gossip. And fucking exciting.'

'Exciting?'

'Oh yeah, you two together is hot. And not that surprising.' People really did see something amongst our bickering that I didn't see.

'Again, it's not true. It's all fake.'

'Hmm, was it fake when you started mauling each other on my dancefloor?' I love that she called it *her* dancefloor, and I focus on that and not her question. 'And I assume you two were cleaning up in the kitchen, and not going at it so hard that pots were getting knocked all over the floor?'

I avoid her eyeballing me and feel heat flush my face at the memory of kissing Harrison. That part wasn't fake for me, but I don't know what it was for Harrison. That kiss will haunt my dreams because it was so good, but I don't know how to interact with Harrison now and considering we're still trapped, it will be hard to avoid him.

'Well?' Scout pushes because I haven't answered and don't know how to.

I push the words out my mouth, but they're only a whisper, 'I don't know.' I cover my face with my hands and repeat, 'I don't know what that was.'

Scout steps forward and gently pulls my hands away from my face. She holds them as she says, 'I think that was you and Harrison finally giving in to the thing everyone else has always seen.'

'What? Hostility and sarcastic banter?'

'Intense zing.' She moves her face closer and waggles her eyebrows to bring home her odd comment. Her facial contortions make me laugh as I push her away.

'I don't even know what that means, but you're wrong.'

'Am I?' She moves her eyebrows again but has a more serious tone this time. I take a moment to think, and perhaps she could be a tiny bit right. Harrison has been a comfort to me tonight in a way I never would have expected. The way he kissed me was also unexpected, but it felt like we clicked in a way I never have with anyone else.

'I honestly don't know.' I slump back further down the wall. 'I also can't feel my feet now, so I can't think straight.'

'Yes, standing in floodwater is gross.' Scout grabs my hand and pulls me out of the flooded bathroom. We wipe our feet carefully, put on our shoes, and then barricade the room again. Noah appears behind us, bouncing on the balls of his feet.

'Toilets are closed,' Scout says, guessing what he was about to ask.

'I'm busting!'

'Out you go.' She points to the back, but as she does, I notice the water coming in under the back door.

'Shit,' all three of us say at once. There's no stopping it. We're going under. I don't think I can *just keep swimming* any longer.

Chapter Twenty-Three

After realising that The Shark Biscuit will flood, I also realise that I am no longer drunk. I can only fix one of those problems.

Scout pours another drink, but it seems like she's pouring from random bottles before passing the glass to me. I take a large gulp and then cough because it burns my throat and does not taste like something that a living creature should consume. I wave her away when she tries to give me another. She's evil. She shrugs and drinks it herself with no reaction. Her stomach is much stronger than any part of my body.

'I don't know what to do.' I hang my head in my hands. 'Where's Harrison gone?' Perhaps he'll have a plan to stop the damage, but I haven't seen him since he put his fingers down my pants.

'He's outside with Noah,' says Scout, shaking something liquidy. 'Inspecting the damage.'

'I need to get out of here.'

'You will soon.' Scout pats my shoulder, but I can feel my heart beating through my chest. It doesn't feel normal. I try to calm it down by tapping it, but I don't know where my heart is exactly, so I just tap around my chest, hoping to get it eventually. My breath hitches, and now I can feel a pulse in my throat, trying to compete with my heart.

'I think I'm having a reaction to, umm, something you gave me. Scout, I can't—'

'Breathe, Agnes. You're just drunk.' Scout cups my head in her hands, but it doesn't help.

'I can't be drunk. I'm not. I'm having a reaction. I must be allergic.' I push away from the bar to get some fresh air. I'm not sure where I'll get fresh air because we're trapped – trapped in a restaurant that's about to flood. Where will we all go? Should we go sit on the roof? In the rain? Could Mr and Mrs Whalley get up there? Who am I kidding – *I* can't get up there. Do we sit on the tables and wait for the rain to stop?

'Agnes, breathe.' I can hear Scout's voice, but she seems further away and faint over the sound of my heartbeat. I rub my eyes, trying to catch my breath.

'What's wrong?' Harrison's sharp voice breaks the throbbing for a second, but I can't see his face. I can only see black dots.

'I'm having an allergic reaction to the thing, umm… drink.' I stumble over the words, but I think he gets the gist.

'She's drunk,' says Scout, but I don't think that's it. 'And she's freaking out.' I close my eyes because the spots are distracting my thoughts.

'Why are you freaking out?' Harrison holds my face, and I sense he's close, but I keep my eyes closed. 'Agnes, look at me.'

I shake my head because things feel better with my eyes closed. With them closed, my father's restaurant isn't about to be destroyed, and I don't have to deal with Harrison James touching me and my feelings about that.

'Open your eyes. *Please.*'

When I slowly peel my eyes open, Harrison's concerned face is directly in line with mine. Something about the tenderness that covers his face slows the pace of my breathing. He pushes back my hair and leaves his hand on the side of my face.

'It all became too much?' he whispers, and I give him a watery nod. I'm stronger than this. I don't break, but my thoughts ran ahead of me, and I couldn't stop them. I close my eyes again and lean in to rest my head on Harrison's shoulder. I don't want to break. Not now and not in front of other people. Somehow, Harrison understands that, places his arm around my shoulders, and guides me away from the bar.

'I'll get her some food. Be back in ten,' Harrison says over his shoulder as he walks us into the kitchen.

As soon as he opens the door to the kitchen, he scoops me up by the waist and deposits me on the counter. I run my hands over the clean, shiny steel and take some calming breaths. Usually, Harrison is the reason I need the slow breathing but tonight he's the one helping me.

'This is against the rules.' It's unsanitary for me to sit on the counter, but it's not the first time tonight and I am trying to stop my mind from thinking about our last visit to the kitchen.

Harrison takes out a brioche roll and cuts it in half. I hope it's for me. He cleans his knife before he puts his head down and chops an heirloom tomato at an unnatural speed like it's the easiest thing in the world. I can't watch too closely. I had a deep fear when I was young that my dad would cut off his finger. He cut his fingers multiple times. Lots of blood. But never entirely off. Even though I know Harrison is more skilled than my dad in the kitchen, I am still wary of knives.

'Everything about tonight is against the rules.'

'That is true. We made out.' I waggle my finger back and forth between us. 'Against the rules.' I may concede that I may have fallen victim to one of Scout's very potent alcohol concoctions. I don't think I would have said that otherwise.

'Not in my rule book.'

'You have a rule book? Of course, you do. Let me guess what's in it.' I pretend to pick up a book and run my finger over the imaginary words. 'Number one: must disagree with every suggestion Agnes makes. Number two: must pick on Agnes's purchase orders every second Thursday. Number three: must not cover my forearms as requested by Agnes.'

I peek at Harrison, who's trying to hide the small smile turning the left side of his face upwards.

'My forearms? That's interesting. They're mentioned again. I thought it was for professional reasons.'

'It was!'

Harrison slides the diced tomato onto a dish and starts working on a purple onion. 'Why did you want me to hide my forearms, Agnes?'

'I didn't.' I can't admit out loud how much I've thought of his forearms over the years.

'I call bullshit.'

'Of course, you do. Back to your rules. Must seem grumpy on Monday, so I get out of dealing with the delivery guy who talks too much.'

'Now that one is true. Him I won't miss.' Harrison dices basil into a gazillion pieces with extra force.

'He was friendly.'

'To you, yes. I wonder why.' Harrison finally looks at me to give me a pointed stare.

'Because I'm nice.' I smile with extra teeth.

'Looking. He asked me three times if you were still seeing someone.'

'He did not!'

'He did.' Harrison nods, confirming information I never knew.

'You should have taken the deliveries then.'

'Nah, more fun watching you be completely oblivious that he was flirting with you. You have no radar.'

'Well, you just assume everyone is flirting with you.'

'Not all. Some. Maybe most, but not all.' Harrison has a coy smirk, and it makes me laugh. I know he's joking, and it feels nice to not feel awkward with each other. Harrison does some other fancy chef stuff before loading the tomato salsa onto a slice of the bread roll and placing it on a plate for me.

'It's not ideal or how I'd normally serve it, but eat. Soak up whatever Scout gave you.'

I take a bite without any arguments because it looks divine and let Harrison enjoy the quiet groan of appreciation I let out.

'Thank you.' I say once my mouth isn't full. 'You've fed me a lot today.' I wipe the side of my mouth and then sneak a look at Harrison. His eyes were already waiting for me to look up. We let our eyes linger on each other in a way I never usually allow myself.

Harrison stuffs his hands in his pockets before he says, 'Are you freaking out because I kissed you?' His stare is unwavering. 'Honest answer, Agnes.'

I put the plate down beside me and slide off the counter. I walk to the other side of the kitchen because I need some distance from Harrison while I process my thoughts.

'That bad, hey?' Harrison says without looking at me.

'Harrison, I—' I cover my face with my hands and say, 'Maybe, but honestly, not really.' I know it sounds muffled, but it's the truth. 'The kiss didn't freak me out.'

'Good to know. Not the general reaction you want after kissing someone.'

His attempt at humour gives me the confidence to drop my hands and turn to look at him for this conversation.

'The kiss was—'

'If you use any word less than phenomenal, know I'll be offended.'

'Of course, I would expect Harrison James doesn't get bad feedback.'

Harrison crosses the kitchen in a second and seems unsure where he can touch me, so his hand hovers near my face and then down my arm. I reach out and take it so he knows it's welcome and lace our fingers together.

'I wasn't referring to me, but *our* kiss as phenomenal, and I fucking hope that feeling wasn't one-sided.'

I shake my head as I say, 'Not one-sided.' Just the memory of that kiss makes me blush.

I glance up at him, and a softness in his face catches me off balance. Did he think I was about to make fun of him after everything that's happened tonight?

'And?' Harrison says as a smile forms on one side of his mouth. I reach up and place my fingers on his chest because I think it will be allowed.

'I've never been kissed like that,' I whisper as I close my eyes.

'Not the kiss then, which we can discuss in length shortly, so what is freaking you out?'

I know I won't be able to keep the tears back when I try to explain this to Harrison. I hope he understands.

'I saw the water come under the doorway, and it will all be ruined. Dad's going to come back, and it'll all be gone.' Harrison wipes the tears from my cheek with his fingers.

'It's all over after tonight anyway. We'll all be fine. We just have to wait it out.'

I shake my head and extract myself from Harrison's intoxicating embrace.

'You don't understand.'

'Then help me understand.'

'I hate it! Okay?' I throw my arms out and gesture to the kitchen. 'I hate this stupid restaurant. I hate everything about it.' My tears don't help bring home my point because Harrison shakes his head.

'You already said that.'

'I know you don't want to believe it, but it's true. I'm sorry, but I hate it.' I look at Harrison through my watery eyes, and my whole body feels instantly lighter. 'I've never told anyone that. No one knows. Except you.'

'So, you can't stand this place? A job you stayed back for and did more overtime than anyone?'

'Yep.'

Harrison takes a step closer and asks, 'And you hate the place that you made sure was clean and served the best produce every single day?'

'Yep.'

He steps closer again, but his voice becomes gentle. 'And you hate it so much that you bought personalised goodbye gifts for all the employees?'

I can't speak through the tears as Harrison stands in front of me, covers my arms with his strong hands, and strokes them up and down.

'And are now crying because it's going to have some water damage. You hate it right now?'

'Harrison, stop. You don't understand.'

'Tell me. I'm listening.'

The way Harrison says that makes me stop. His entire focus is on me, and he's waiting, and I know he'll listen. He won't twist whatever I'm about to say into something else or make me feel inferior for my feelings. Harrison has never done that. He's honest, but in a way I love. I glance away as I explain my feelings in the only way that makes sense in my brain. I've been sitting on these thoughts and overwhelmed with guilt for so long that saying them out loud is terrifying, but it's a huge relief to finally talk about this with someone.

'This place stole my dad from me,' I whisper and then wait for Harrison to say something. When he says nothing, I glance back and see he's waiting for me to keep going. 'I know I'm an adult, but you have to understand this place – it's like a member of our family. He was always here, never at home. I'd come straight here after school. I don't remember eating dinner at home after Mum died. We ate dinner here, or I ate alone. This stupid restaurant stole my dad. It stole my mum, too. She was working a double when she collapsed.'

'This place has taken a lot away from you. More than I or anyone could realise.' I'm relieved it doesn't sound like he's judging me for my feelings. 'Maybe you don't hate it though. Maybe you resent it. Resent the absolute crap out of it.'

I've never thought of it like that. I always thought the feeling I had was complete dislike, utter loathing, but it's anger. Anger that could have twisted into resentment.

Harrison closes the distance between us again. 'The same way I don't hate my parents, but I sure as hell have resented them. Trying not to anymore, but some days I still do.'

'That's your parents, Harrison, and it sounds like you have every right to resent them. I can't resent a building. A business.'

'Of course you can. It stole so much from you. Your time. Your parents.'

I nod my head emphatically, and thankfully, Harrison understands this. 'And I couldn't let it steal anything more from me. I had to get out.'

'What do you mean?'

'Dad offered me the business. Handed me the keys and said things could continue as normal.' I wipe my eyes and take a leap of faith when I say, 'And I turned him down.' Harrison cups my face when my breathing ramps up again. He bends down so our faces are aligned. 'I saw that water coming through the door and thought, I'm the worst daughter. I can't do this for him. I couldn't do it for my mum either – keep her memory alive with this place. I've changed my mind a hundred times, but I can't. I just can't. I'm so sorry, Harrison. I couldn't tell you because I know what this place means to you.'

Harrison pulls me against his chest and holds me tightly as I cry on his shoulder.

'This isn't all on you, Agnes. Ernie had other options. He could have made another choice. This isn't your fault.'

'You don't understand. He wanted me to have it. He wanted it to stay in the family.'

Harrison kisses the side of my face, and I stay burrowed into his shoulder. Harrison's scent calms me, and I let my eyes close for a moment to relish snuggling in to him.

'I'm assuming Ernie is blissfully unaware of how you feel?' I nod quickly. 'Knowing how unhappy you are here – have been for years – would break his heart more. I would have made you a bloody bug roll every damn day if I'd known. You should have said something.'

'I couldn't.' I pull back but stay in Harrison's arms. 'I thought I was free six years ago. We were almost going to close then, but—'

'Ernie hired me.' We share a soft smile as Harrison understands the implications of him joining the business.

'I could have said something. I almost did, but Dad was so happy when he found you. I thought maybe I could duck away after you got set up, but Dad's health got worse, and you know the rest.'

'That's why you hated me? I always wondered.'

I place my arm on Harrison's shoulder and let my head rest against his chest. 'I never hated you.' Annoyed on the daily, but I know deep down that I never hated Harrison.

'The day I started, your dad told me you didn't want to hire me. I think his exact words were, "I don't think she's keen on you working here, but let's see how this goes."'

I stumble back from the shock of Harrison's admission, but Harrison pulls me close. 'What?! I didn't know Dad told you that. Why would he tell you that?'

Harrison cups my face, and I can see that any lingering resentment is long gone.

'Ernie's not known for his tact.' I can't believe Dad would tell Harrison that. No wonder he was snippy with me from the get-go.

'It wasn't about you. I didn't want to hire *anyone*. It was never personal.' I slap Harrison gently on his chest. 'That's why you had a chip on your shoulder about me the second you started here.'

'I thought, who is this beautiful woman, and why does she hate me so much? I'll charm her with my bug rolls and make her realise the error of her ways.'

I drop my forehead onto Harrison's chest and laugh.

Harrison moves his hand to hold my neck under my hair. 'You're not going to like this part, Agnes, but it's time to be honest with your dad. Fuck everyone else's feelings and tell him. Just imagine he's me, and you'll be fine.'

I lift my head, and Harrison gives me a cheeky grin so I know he's joking. He's right, though. I feel sick to my stomach, but he's right.

I let out a giant breath because the prospect of telling Dad is scary. And heartbreaking. Harrison continues to hold my neck tenderly.

'There's one last matter to discuss before we go and deal with the mess outside.' Harrison's thumb runs back and forth over my cheek.

'Kissing?'

'Kissing. And if I remember correctly, you said "screw it" before kissing me. That was a first.'

A laugh bursts out because I can't remember whether I said that. Harrison continues to stroke my cheek while his other hand settles on my hip and slowly pulls me against his body.

He leans forward and whispers against my lips, 'I want to be clear if you ever want to say "screw it" again, I'll be there.'

'Do I have to say "screw it" every time?'

Harrison cocks his head like he's thinking about the question. 'While I did enjoy it, it's not required *every* time.' Harrison's got a wicked grin, and I feel like wiping it off – another challenge. I trace my finger up his neck and up to his lip. I let his bottom lip hang open with my finger resting on it lightly. Harrison's playful nature disappears, and his eyes darken as he stares at my lips. I lean in even closer, our lips a whisper away from each other as I say, 'Harrison?'

'Hmm?'

'Screw it.' The hand that rests on my neck pulls me close as Harrison's lips close over mine. I throw my arms around Harrison's hips and pull him closer. Our bodies glide against each other in delicious motion as Harrison angles his head and our tongues explore each other. Harrison drags the back of my shirt up and runs his hands up my spine.

He kisses up the side of my face and whispers in my ear, 'You have the softest skin. I always knew you'd feel amazing.' Harrison kisses and bites my earlobe, and I let out a sigh that I normally wouldn't, but it snuck out.

'At some point, we need to let them know we're here, or it's just us being pervy.' Harrison and I hear Scout's voice at the same time, and we both freeze. Harrison turns around slowly and leaves a hand on my side. I can't see his face, but I know what signature Harrison glare Scout's getting. I peek over his shoulder to find Scout, Noah, Willy, Devin and Barbara all standing in the doorway watching us. It seems Thomas and the Whalleys are the only ones who didn't come in for the show.

'What are you all doing?' Harrison's voice is low, and Noah flinches at the tone. He sheepishly looks away, as does Scout. Willy smiles at me, and his face is filled with kindness. He has no idea that any of this is awkward. Devin and Barbara are at the back of the group, but I can still see the disgust on their faces.

No one speaks for several moments until Barbara straightens her spine and says, 'If you haven't noticed, the restaurant is flooding.'

'We came to see what you want us to do,' adds Scout.

'But you were too busy doing that.' Barbara flicks her wrist in our direction like we're irresponsible teen-agers. Devin slightly shakes his head in my direction, and Barbara notices. 'Come on, Devin. You've been subjected to enough tonight.'

Barbara pulls Devin's arm, and he follows her back out to the restaurant.

'Sorry guys, we're coming to help.' I push Harrison's back, and he relaxes enough to grab my hand and link our fingers together.

Scout catches my eyes, and I see her mouth the word, *Zing*. I can't deny there's something between Harrison and me, but I have no idea what that is.

Chapter Twenty-Four

Thomas and Harrison work together to drag all the tables to the front of the restaurant near the bar. Everyone else piles them on top of each other, and then we stack the chairs against the far wall near the kitchen. We moved the sandbags against the back door so, hopefully, we can stop the restaurant from flooding. Scout pulls the pictures off the walls, and I'm not sure it's necessary, but I let her do it anyway. She carefully takes the photo of Mum and Dad off the hook and hands it to me. I wipe off the dust before laying it on top of the tables.

There's nowhere for any of us to sit now, so we awkwardly stand in a huddle near the tables. Scott and Dot look exhausted, the evening must be taking a toll on them.

The rain still hasn't stopped, and just when I thought it couldn't get any harder, a large gust of wind rattles the windows, the rain appearing to double in strength. It's hard to hear now over it pounding on the roof.

I shout to Scott and Dot, 'Why don't you find a spot in the kitchen and try to get some rest?' The kitchen should stay safe for now. Scott nods as he takes Dot's hand and guides her towards the kitchen.

Scout and Noah are loading alcohol into a crate, but Harrison tells them to leave it. He talks to them quietly, and they grab one bottle each before taking Willy's hand

and disappearing into the kitchen. I think Harrison just put the kids to bed.

Thomas climbs onto a table, his back against the wall, long legs dangling over the edge.

'You want to try and get some sleep in there too?' I gesture behind me.

'Nah, I'm all good here.' Thomas rests his head against the wall and closes his eyes. Leaving the hardest to last, I step closer to Devin, who's on the other side of Thomas. As I get closer, I see Barbara's crying. Devin's rubbing her arm and consoling her.

'Would you like to try to sleep in the kitchen?' I say softly with kindness because as much as I dislike Barbara, I don't want to see her upset. I understand she must be stressed by everything tonight, too.

'Mum's not doing too well,' says Devin, and there's a whole lot of spite in his delivery.

'It's been a tough night. I'm hoping it's only a few more hours.'

'I'm sad because I didn't think someone could be so hurtful to my son.' Barbara lifts her watery eyes and I realise she's not crying about the storm. She's crying about me. 'After everything our family did for you. You throw it back in our faces tonight. Carry on with...' Barbara glances in Harrison's direction. He's cleaning up the bar area and doesn't lift his head. I'm sure he's listening, though. I notice Thomas lift an eyelid before closing his eyes again. 'It's all very disappointing.'

She means *I'm* disappointing, but instead of feeling shame, I feel anger. After everything that's happened tonight, she is the last person whose opinion matters to me. I glance over to Harrison, and he's finished packing the crate and watching us. He raises an eyebrow at me, and

I think he's asking: *Are you going to say something, or am I?* I think this time, I should be the one to say something.

'Barbara, I'm sorry you're disappointed, but the truth is that your son and I aren't together anymore, so it's none of your business.'

I notice Thomas's mouth curve upwards, but his eyes remain shut. Barbara doesn't enjoy my direct response and straightens her spine.

'And I, for one, am delighted about that.' She turns and speaks into Devin's ear, 'This is all for the best. You'll see in the long run.'

'Why don't I find you a spot in the kitchen where you'll be comfortable?' Harrison holds open the kitchen door and gestures for Barbara to follow him.

'I'm fine just here.'

'But it's not safe, so I must insist.' Harrison and Barbara have a stand-off, and Harrison doesn't waver in his eye contact.

'Fine. Let's go, Devin.' Barbara takes a step and motions for Devin to follow. He looks at me for a second before addressing his mum.

'I'll be there in a second.' Barbara looks me up and down with evident disgust, and I focus on Harrison. The muscles in his jaw are ticking as Barbara walks by. He keeps his eyes on me as he mouths, *I'll be right back.*

He eliminated one problem for me, but I still have Devin here, and I can tell he wants to hash things out. To me, there's nothing left to hash. I figure it's best to get on the front foot.

'Devin, I know tonight has been awkward, but—'

'Awkward? I would have enjoyed awkwardness. Tonight has been brutal. I come here to support you, and then you treat me like this all night.' Devin gestures towards the kitchen, and I assume he's talking about Harrison.

'I never asked you to come. I didn't know you were coming. We had broken up.'

'Yeah, broken up because we were born in different months of the year or under different moons or whatever bullshit you told me. Was it because you were already with *him*?' says Devin, with hostility.

'No. Harrison has nothing to do with this. We broke up – nearly four months ago – because we weren't compatible. We fought all the time.'

'Everyone fights.'

'But fighting with someone isn't meant to make you feel worse about yourself after every fight.'

I think about the way Devin fights and how he'd try to knock me down, or worse, dob on me to his mother. In all the fights with Harrison, I've never felt small. I never came out feeling like something was wrong with me. Devin made me feel like that. Barbara made me feel like that *constantly*.

'That's something you need to work out. That's got nothing to do with me,' says Devin like, once again, I need coaching in relationships.

'You better stop talking, mate, before Harrison gets back.' Thomas opens one eye and stares down at Devin before closing it again, but Devin keeps going.

'It's bullshit that I have to watch you fucking around with that dickhead. I didn't think you were cruel, Aggie.'

I am done with this and with Devin. I've done nothing but tie myself in knots all night, trying to be kind to him and his family. Devin doesn't get that courtesy from me any longer. I hear Harrison's voice in my head saying, *Be honest, Agnes. What's the worst that can happen?*

'Cruel? I am not cruel.' I lower my voice, but it's forceful, and I don't waver as I square my shoulders. 'Cruel is turning up tonight without telling me, not caring about what tonight meant for *me*.' I poke my finger to my chest because Devin hasn't once asked about my feelings tonight. 'Cruel is putting me in a position where I have to lie to your family. Cruel is once again making *me* the bad guy. Cruel is making me feel like I'm doing something wrong with moving on and finding a new partner.'

Devin throws back his head and laughs, but it's an empty, unkind laugh. 'Come on, Aggie, you've hated that guy for years. It's got rebound material 101 all over it. It's embarrassing. I'm embarrassed for you.'

'You got this, Aggie, or am I stepping in?' Thomas says quietly, but I nod because, for once, I have got this.

'I'm not embarrassed at all. For once, I'm with someone who doesn't make me feel inferior. Who makes me realise my feelings are just as important as everyone else's.' I point to the kitchen before saying, 'That man has taken care of me tonight and has been in my corner more than you have *ever* been. As soon as this fucking storm is over, I want you and your mother to leave, and I'm never going to see either of you ever again. And it can't come quick enough.'

'I think you've said enough, young lady.' I spin around and find Barbara standing at the kitchen door. Her arms are crossed, and she's giving me one of her disapproving looks, but it does nothing. *Finally*, I don't care. Harrison's beside her, beaming at me like he's never been prouder. Scout pokes out the other side of Barbara, and I can tell she's enjoying the show.

Barbara opens her mouth to speak again. 'After everything my family has done for you and how Devin has taken care—' I put my hand up to stop her talking because I'm not hearing any more bullshit tonight.

'I'm going to stop you there, Barbara, because that's not true. Devin didn't take care of me; your family did nothing. You've been rude to me all night when, even with the chaos, *I've* tried to help you.'

'You expected a thank-you?' Barbara says with disbelief in her tone.

'Yes, it's awkward, but I've been trying. You, on the other hand, have been nothing but ill-mannered and a crabby mean so-and-so.' It's not eloquent, but I'm new to giving people a dressing-down. She gets the gist.

'Hear hear!' Scout yells out and then hides behind Harrison's back.

'I agree, too!' Noah shouts from the kitchen as Willy says, 'We just met, but me three.'

Barbara stares in the direction of the kitchen as she takes in the feedback from everyone. Harrison remains quiet, but his facial expression tells Barbara exactly how he feels about her. He'd never cook another meal for this woman in his life.

Barbara must regain some confidence because she squares her shoulders and returns to face me.

'The thing you don't understand—'

I raise my hand to cut off Barbara's fake cream puff voice because I am never going to listen to a lecture from her again.

'It doesn't matter what I do or don't understand because I don't care what you think.' I step in front of Devin and Barbara to address them both one final time. 'If you both can't understand how wrong you were tonight, I can't help you. But I beg you, no more opinions. We're done.'

Barbara starts again and I thought she would finally shut up, but no. 'You little ungrateful—'

I look to the ceiling and break one of Harrison's rules. I'm going to yell because I need to get it out. 'Oh, just fuck off, Barbara!'

The words leave my mouth, and they feel fantastic, but then three things happen all at once. Scout gives me a little clap as Harrison rushes forward and pulls me behind him just as the ceiling over the back end of the deck crashes to the floor and smashes a window. Everyone rushes towards the kitchen as Noah calls out, 'Did anyone die?'

Chapter Twenty-Five

Harrison, Thomas and I stand together, looking through the doors to survey the damage on the deck. A piece of the skillion roof dangles in the corner of the deck. Glass covers the floor at the back of the restaurant. The rain is starting to slow, but we still have a few hours until sunrise.

I can't recognise the deck and back of the restaurant with this much damage. I never really believed it was over. I thought someone would buy it, but looking at it now, I see it's done.

Harrison turns in my direction, and his face tells me he feels the same way. Devastated. He extends his arms, as I walk into him, and he holds me.

'I'm sorry, Agnes,' he whispers into my hair.

'I need to tell Dad before he sees it,' I say, and I can feel Harrison nod in agreement.

'Sure, it will be a shock, but it might save him money in the long run. Storm did him a favour,' says Thomas.

'What do you mean?' asks Harrison.

'You know he's knocking this place down, right?' says Thomas like it's common knowledge. Harrison and I both tense and then slowly turn to face Thomas together.

'Guessing not, by your faces. *Shit.*'

'First of all, Dad wouldn't, and second, how would you know that?'

Thomas looks at Harrison first and then says, 'When he turned our offer down—'

'Our offer?' I look back at Harrison.

'Thomas and I put an offer in together. Partnership.'

'It's why I'm back here. I thought I'd be running a restaurant, but Ernie called me tonight to say sorry he was rejecting the offer.'

'He only told you tonight?' I ask.

'Officially told us tonight, but we figured it wasn't good news since he hadn't given us a straight answer for a few weeks.'

'He told me officially as he was leaving tonight,' says Harrison, and that must have been the conversation they had at the doorway before Dad left. It wasn't very professional of Dad to do it then, but what does Dad know about selling a business?

'And he said he's knocking it down? He wouldn't,' I say because I can't believe he wouldn't tell me that either.

'This is an amazing piece of land. I imagine he got an offer he couldn't refuse,' says Thomas.

'No.' I shake my head sternly. 'Dad doesn't care about money. He would never knock this place down.' He built this with Mum. This place has too many memories for it to be knocked down.

Harrison takes my hand and gently pulls me closer. 'He didn't want to sell it to us. You might have to be open to the idea that he's knocking it down.'

I shake my head again because he's wrong.

'I'll give you guys a moment. Might try and get some sleep,' says Thomas before I hear him disappear into the kitchen.

I step away from Harrison and rub my temples, trying to make sense of this. Dad's asleep now, so I can't call and clear everything up.

'It's okay, Agnes.' Harrison's voice is soft, and I don't want him to be soft right now. He should be mad.

'Don't you get it?'

'Obviously not.'

'He's knocking it down because I told him I don't want it.'

'That's a long bow to draw. He's knocking it down because you don't want to work here anymore? It's about money.'

I take a breath before I explain this to Harrison because he won't like it.

'I didn't exactly say I didn't want it.'

Harrison cocks his head to the side, and the glare I'm getting makes me feel even more uncomfortable. 'What half-version of the truth did you tell him then?'

I fight the urge to look away as I say, 'I told him I'd be too sad to come here every day knowing he wasn't a part of this and that The Shark Biscuit without him would break my heart. That's why he must be knocking it down.' *And why he didn't sell the restaurant to you*, but I can't say that bit out loud even though we're both thinking it.

Harrison crosses his arms and takes a moment before he replies. I know I'm not going to enjoy the reply.

'And somehow we're back to you not telling the truth again.'

'I was trying to save his feelings. Let him down gently.'

'I know. *I know*, Agnes. So, you weren't the bad guy, but you were manipulating your dad. Is that better?'

'I was not!'

'You were telling him what he wanted to hear. Not giving him the whole truth. Is that not manipulating his feelings?'

'I was being kind. I was taking care of my dad as I've always done.'

'Without giving him all the information. Without telling him you couldn't care less if Bob from down the street ran the restaurant, and now he will have it knocked down to keep you happy.'

'I'll fix it. He wouldn't do it. I know it.'

Harrison steps closer and gestures with both hands. 'News flash, Ernie loves you.'

'Yes, but he also loves The Shark Biscuit.'

Harrison shakes his head. 'Not even in the same realm as you. Do you seriously believe that? What's the worst thing that could happen if you're honest with him?'

How can I say it out loud? All the thoughts running through my head. I know immediately the worst that could happen.

'Say it.'

I suck in a juddering breath. 'I'd see my father's heart break for a second time. I remember his face after Mum died. This is his special place. The place he and Mum built, and it would break his heart that I don't want to be a part of that. I should be keeping this place open so Mum's memory lives on.' I whisper the last part. 'I'd disappoint him.'

'And you losing six years isn't a disappointment to you?'

'It's not the same.'

Harrison steps forward and clutches my face in his hands with a softness that makes my stomach jump.

'You're allowed to be honest, and people will still like you. You're brutally honest with me every day, and I still *really* like you.'

'You didn't up until tonight.'

Harrison lowers his head so our eyes are aligned. 'You know I never, ever hated you. Working with you, debating with you, losing to you—'

'So, you admit I did win sometimes?'

'Rarely, but it did happen – all of it was the best part of this job.' Harrison bends down and kisses me. It's sweet, tender, and he pulls back before I can kiss him again. 'And I'm fucking annoyed it's all over.'

I can't say 'Me too' because it wouldn't be true, but there will be parts that I will miss.

'In our own way, we were a good team.' I lean up and kiss Harrison softly on the lips.

The rain slowly stops, and there's an eerie stillness in the air. Harrison links our fingers and pulls me towards the kitchen.

'This will all be over soon. Let's try and get some sleep.'

Everyone has retreated to different spots in the kitchen. Now that the rain has stopped, we just need to wait for the streets to clear so we can leave.

Harrison and I find a spare spot on the floor near Scout, Noah, Thomas and Willy. Noah and Thomas are passed out and snoring loudly while Scout and Willy chat quietly.

The Whalleys are asleep on each other in a corner, and Devin and Barbara are up the other end. It's a reasonable distance away from everyone else, and it's a smart move.

Harrison pulls me close and wraps his arm around me, and I rest my head on his chest. His head is tilted back, and I think he's trying to sleep. I'm exhausted – to the bone exhausted – but I doubt I'll be able to sleep.

The restaurant is destroyed. Harrison strokes my shoulder while I revisit the shock of watching the roof of the deck collapse before my very eyes – the water pouring in and the window smashing – and the shock of finally telling Devin and Barbara my true feelings.

Harrison reaches up and runs his fingers through my hair as he whispers, 'Relax. Try and get some sleep. We'll deal with everything once the sun is up.'

I snuggle into Harrison, and I can't believe the comfort I feel throughout my body. I feel safe and warm, wrapped in Harrison's strong arms. My head feels heavy and, as Harrison continues to stroke my hair, my body starts to unwind.

As I drift off, I hear Scout and Willy's conversation.

'I decided to take my fiancé's because I like it better and want the same last name as my kids. When we eventually have them,' says Willy.

'That's lovely,' replies Scout in a sleepy voice. 'What's his last name?'

'Fitzgibbon.'

'Strong name.'

'I think so, too.'

'Willy, you better not let anyone shorten your last name, though. No nicknames.'

'Why not?'

'Because your name will be Willy Fitz.'

'Oh, shit.'

Harrison tries to hide his laughter and I chuckle into his chest.

'Stop listening to our conversation, you creeps,' Scout whispers to Harrison and me.

'I hope it fits,' says Harrison as he cuddles me closer.

'Trust me—'

'Nope. No details. Good night.' Harrison relaxes further back against the wall and holds me tight as I finally succumb to the exhaustion of the stressful, confusing night that is ending with Harrison James holding me like I'm treasured.

–

I wake with a fright, and Harrison holds me tighter to his chest. Various snores come from the kitchen, so I think everyone is asleep. I don't know how long I was out of it.

My eyes roam around the kitchen, the place I've spent more time in than the kitchen in my apartment. Harrison's sign hangs in its usual spot, but it doesn't have the same effect on me now. I'm going to miss that sign. I'm never going to stand and debate with Harrison while he taps it with his coy smile, teasing me with his antics. It's a sobering thought, and it makes me instantly miserable. I angle my neck and kiss Harrison because it's all over. We're no longer Agnes and Harrison – the dynamic team that run The Shark Biscuit and bicker until we've worn everyone else down. I kiss him again, and it must wake Harrison up because his eyes open as he leans forward to kiss me with sleepy, open-mouth kisses.

We could be strangers this time next year, and it makes me want to savour every moment I have before we're free to leave. I deepen the kiss as Harrison's fingers cup the back of my head, and he bends down to explore my mouth.

An idea hits me; I'm putting it all out there for Harrison to reject me, but I think he'll like my idea.

'You know, there's one thing left that we never did,' I whisper closely so I don't wake anyone.

Harrison's eyebrow lifts in contemplation.

'You want to yell at each other in front of my sign?'

'No. There's a few people sleeping that I don't want to disturb, and I'm not a yeller.'

Harrison sneaks a kiss before asking, 'What could you and I possibly not have done in the six years we worked here together?'

I kiss him slowly before lacing our fingers together and pull him up as we tiptoe out of the kitchen.

Harrison follows me silently until I stop outside the storage cupboard. The sun is finally starting to peek over the horizon, which means this awful night is nearly over. The blue in Harrison's eyes shimmers with desire and affection. We changed tonight. We're not the same Agnes and Harrison we were before the rain started. I feel closer to Harrison in a way I have never felt with anyone, and the thought that this is the last time we'll be together at The Shark Biscuit makes me feel panicky.

'We can't be the only ones who haven't experienced The Shag Room. That wouldn't be right.' Harrison's eyes widen as he realises what I'm thinking. 'It would be fitting if we were the last ones to christen that room. Don't you agree?'

A grin breaks over Harrison's face as he bends down and throws me over his shoulder. His large hand on my backside holds me there securely.

'I've always secretly loved your ideas, Agnes.'

Chapter Twenty-Six

Harrison closes the door, and I hear the click of the lock. He slides my body down and places me on the edge of one of the shelves. Some light filters under the door, but from the night's events, we now know how to navigate our way in this cupboard. I loop my arms around Harrison's neck and keep us close.

His hands run up my thighs as he pushes them apart, and he steps closer. I wrap my legs around his waist as he cups my neck.

'Did you really not know this was The Shag Room?' I whisper against his lips. He tries to kiss me, but I pull back slightly. Teasing him.

'You should know by now that I don't lie to you. *Ever.* I'm the honest-to-a-fault type.' Harrison moves his fingers up into my hair as he gives me a cheeky grin. 'And I'm a gentleman. I wouldn't come in here with just anyone.'

'I feel so special,' I say with a nip at Harrison's lower lip.

He lets out a gruff sigh as he says, 'I know how to treat a lady. I thought it was more romantic to wait until the place was about to fall down and your ex-boyfriend's mother was next door.'

I drop my head and laugh into Harrison's shoulder. It's the worst timing for us to be in here, but in another way, it feels completely perfect. Lifting my head, I can only see the outline of his face and the sharp cut of his jawline from the sunlight coming under the door. I know the expression he's giving me, intense but laced with affection.

'Agnes.' He brushes my hair away from my face before running his thumb over my cheek. 'We've never been in a position to say kind things to each other, so before it's all over and the chaos of cleaning up starts, I want to say a few things.'

'The Shag Room isn't for talking,' I tease because Harrison saying nice things might be too much for my heart to handle.

'Depends on what you're into, doesn't it?' I laugh again as Harrison continues to stroke my cheek with his thumb back and forth. The length of each stroke is getting longer and longer each time. His calloused thumb makes its way down the side of my neck, and I feel it in my core.

'What nice things have you been holding back from me, Harrison James?' I try to make my voice sound light, but there's a heightened intensity in the air now. A sense of anticipation and even the simple caress of his thumb feels significant. The area around us has shrunk and I can only feel the palpable energy between us. Harrison continues to stroke down further, now reaching my collarbone, and I place my hands on his chest. I move them down to the top of his pants and then back up again. We can both distract each other.

'Of all the people I've worked with, known and spent time with, no matter how much we argued, I want you to know,' he leans in closer to say, 'I admire you the most. The way you treat others, and your kindness. I learnt so much from you, and you have no idea how much I'm going to miss battling with you every day.' Harrison's full lips brush mine softly before he continues. 'I'm going to miss you pretending not to watch me work.' He then kisses under my ear and whispers, 'Pretending you weren't admiring my forearms in all their glory.' He pulls back and I know he's joking, but it's not funny now because he's right. I could never deny my attraction to those forearms.

I run my fingers down his shirt and slowly lift it as I trace my fingers over his taut stomach.

'I'm going to miss your bug rolls,' I say, and Harrison laughs into my neck.

'That's all I get? A bug roll?'

'They're so good,' I say as I continue to pull Harrison's shirt until it's clear I want it off. He steps back, and the shirt is gone in seconds before he returns to kiss me. My legs automatically wrap around him again.

'Fine, I can think of something nice.' I lightly run my fingers over Harrison's chest and his collarbone. There's enough light for me to see the cluster of freckles on his tanned shoulders and as my fingers swirl over them, I feel goosebumps breaking out over his skin. I lean forward, kiss him, and then hover over his lips, 'I'm going to miss you pretending not to see when Dad was having a bad day and I was stressed. You always seemed to have my favourite dinner ready for me on those days.'

'That never happened.' Harrison darts forward to kiss me, and it's deeper this time.

I pull back, kiss down his jaw and whisper into his ear, 'You take care of people, Harrison. I never realised it, but you've taken care of me. You do it quietly, in the background, making it even more special. You don't need an audience for it.'

Harrison pulls my mouth up to his, angles his head and kisses me with a fierceness that wasn't here a moment ago.

My hands skate over his chest, over the erratic beating of his heart. His skin is warm and I want him closer.

'As much as I love that you've been wearing my shirt all night, it's time it comes off.'

I put my hands in the air and Harrison pulls it off in one swift motion. It's discarded somewhere behind him in the cupboard.

He widens my legs and tugs me to the edge of the shelf so our bodies are aligned. 'These ugly leggings need to go as well.'

Harrison glides the leggings down my legs, and I'm not sure where they end up because Harrison immediately skims his hands up my bare legs as he kisses me again.

In between kisses, I mumble, 'Your pants are pretty ugly, too.'

'Is that a fashion statement, or you'd like them off?' Harrison kisses down my chest, and I run my fingers through his hair.

'Off, Harrison.'

'Yes, Agnes.' Harrison's pants disappear, and his palm rakes down my back while I angle my body closer. Only thin material separates us, and I regret never knowing about The Shag Room until this moment. What a waste of time.

'Wait, protection?' I say when Harrison starts to play with the edge of my underwear. He instantly withdraws and starts scrummaging through a crate in the back corner. Miraculously, this room isn't damaged. The kitchen and this room are the only parts of The Shark Biscuit that were not destroyed tonight.

Harrison returns, a condom in his hand. 'I don't know whether to be grateful to Noah and Scout or furious that they weren't joking.'

'Grateful now, furious later.'

'Good plan.'

Harrison forgets all about Noah and Scout as he deepens our kiss, but I match him with every angle. His tongue tangles with mine and I let out a sound that's not too different from when I'm enjoying one of Harrison's bug rolls.

'Do I need to get the "No Yelling" sign?' He's teasing me, but I'm making sounds I'd never usually make.

'You rate yourself that much?' My voice hitches as Harrison's hands move to my legs, his fingers tracing the inside of my upper thigh.

Harrison whispers with a nervousness that I never hear from him, 'Agnes, what do I have permission to do here?'

'Anything,' I answer immediately because I don't want him to stop.

'Where can I touch you?' His nose nuzzles behind my ear and his breath glides across my cheek.

'Anywhere.'

Harrison's body tenses before he pulls back and holds my face in his hands. His eyes find mine, looking for further clarification. I jerk his body closer with my legs in response.

I can feel the roughness on his fingers, and there's something alluring about Harrison's hands. His movements are confident but tender as they lower to undo my bra, and his thumbs caress my breasts.

In the dim light, Harrison explores my body with devotion, his skilled hands knowing how to move over my body in a way that makes me feel like I'm on fire.

It's my turn to explore Harrison, and I dip my hand into the waistband of his underwear. His breath hitches as I grip his hardness.

'Your hands have found themselves in my underwear again,' says Harrison between open mouth kisses.

'You going to even it up then?'

'I'm going to do one better.' Harrison lifts me with one hand around my waist and swiftly pulls my underwear off before placing me on the edge of the shelf again.

'You always have to win,' I say because Harrison envelops my mouth again, and his fingers roam my body, knowing exactly where to touch and circle as he kisses down my throat.

I pull his underwear down because I was never going to let him win for long, and it's really a win for us both.

When our bodies finally connect, a rush of pleasure creeps up my spine. Our naked bodies are completely in synch, and there's no more need for talking. Harrison understands what I need and how I need it.

I imagine Harrison making love slowly in the mornings, taking his time while covering my body with his while we're tangled in the sheets. Or him using his strong hands to strip my clothes off after we've arrived home from a long night at the restaurant and how he'd bury himself in me to wash away our stress.

Now that I let myself indulge in these thoughts, they overwhelm me. Harrison's signature scent on my pillows. His distinct cupid's bow as he leans in to kiss me before leaving for work. Harrison standing in my kitchen shirtless while he happily cooks us something to eat. All the moments that could have been.

Harrison pulls me back from my thoughts with a short gasp. His hypnotic blue eyes disappear under his eyelids as he tilts his head back.

'Agnes, yes,' Harrison breathes out. Seeing him come undone is all I need to let go and let the intense pleasure wash over me. He holds me fiercely, our ragged breaths all that can be heard in the silence of the storage cupboard, the storm outside long since died down. His hand spreads out between my shoulder blades and his lips return to my throat – nibbling, sucking, sometimes just resting to breathe against my skin – as our bodies come back down from the pleasure and intensity.

Harrison holds onto me, his kisses never stopping, and I feel raw, seen and adored. It's never felt like this. I've never felt connected to someone like this. It's not meant to be this good the first time with someone and in a cupboard.

I don't want to separate from Harrison or this moment. We've created a bubble where it's just us, and too much will change the second we step out of this room.

I think Harrison feels that, too, because he hasn't let go yet, almost as if he's afraid to. He rests his forehead on mine. I place my hand over his heart, which is still beating erratically.

'Harrison—'

'Not yet, Agnes. Not yet.'

I grip his face and get him to look at me. Only now do I realise there's more sunlight in the room, which means people could be waking up. Harrison's eyes hold mine, and I close the distance between us and kiss him to show him what this moment meant to me. I pepper more kisses over his cheek and whisper in his ear, 'It was perfect, Harrison.' His hand flexes over my back to pull me closer. 'It was the perfect way for this all to end.'

Harrison rears back and says, 'What?' as the door to the cupboard flies open. The light is blinding, and I cover my eyes as Harrison darts to the side to hide me behind him.

'Oh, oh, oh my!' Unless I'm too sleep-deprived to think clearly, that voice sounds like my dad.

'Ernie, do you mind closing the door?' Harrison has the clarity of mind to say, but I blurt out, 'We locked it.' As if that point matters at all now that Dad has found Harrison and I tangled together naked.

'Right, yes.' Dad is completely frazzled as he tries to close the door. Before it's fully closed, Dad adds, 'That lock hasn't worked since the Eighties, Darl.'

Thanks for clarifying that point, Dad.

Chapter Twenty-Seven

It's a beautiful sunny morning. The Shark Biscuit is a disaster, but at least the sun is shining again.

Harrison and I sneak from the cupboard, but Harrison takes off in the opposite direction to me. Dad talks with Scott and Dot near the front of the restaurant, which is still intact. My face is blushing – my whole body is blushing – from the embarrassment of what just happened. There's not much I can do except to straighten Harrison's shirt, square my shoulders and do the most horrific walk of shame over to my dad.

I try to avoid looking at the disaster of the restaurant and the deck where the roof has collapsed. My heart can't take looking at the damage, so I avert my eyes.

'The roads are cleared, Aggie,' Scott shouts across the restaurant with a thumbs-up. I'm not sure anything about this moment requires a thumbs-up, but I return the gesture anyway.

'A few cleared an hour ago. I was waiting for the green light to get down here,' says Dad as I join their group.

'We didn't think they would clear that quickly,' says Dot.

She looks exhausted and we need to get her home and in bed quickly. She's been such a trooper, but the night must have taken a toll on them both.

'I tried to call, but I figured you all must have been sleeping when I couldn't get through to anyone.' Dad reaches his hand out and pulls me into a hug. I curl my head onto his shoulder.

'I'm so sorry it's all ruined, Dad,' I whisper.

'Nothing's ruined, sweetie.' Dad rubs my back and asks, 'Are you okay?' I nod into his shoulder while I wipe a tear that snuck out before turning back to the Whalleys.

Dot steps forward, her eyes shining with love, and reaches out her hands. I lean in for my hug, and she still smells like lavender perfume. I have no idea how that's possible, but it's comforting, and I want to cry again. I think the exhaustion has taken over my body.

Dot pulls back and links her arm through mine as she tells Dad, 'This girl took care of us all night, Ernie. You should be so proud.'

'We all got drunk, and the roof collapsed,' I say flatly, but it sums up the night's key moments.

'We had a wonderful night. Everyone made the most of a hard situation,' adds Scott.

'It's a disaster outside. Roads are still backed up. Lots are destroyed,' Dad says, shuffling on his feet. 'I'm relieved you're all okay. The reports say we had a year's worth of rainfall in one night. I'm surprised as much of this place made it.'

Dad's relieved? This place is ruined, and lucky it was our last night because we'd be closed for business today either way.

'Have you seen the others?' I ask Dad, hoping to avoid us ever talking about what he walked into moments ago.

'Everyone was sleeping like babies when I walked in. Scout's waking everyone now and organising how to get everyone home.'

'We couldn't find you, dear. We told your dad you and Harrison have been busy the entire night,' says Dot before making an awkward situation even worse. 'Those two just never stop, Ernie.'

Dad coughs and I study the ceiling because I have nowhere to run and hide. I smother the wince that wants to escape because neither Dad nor I know how to reply to that comment.

There's a knock on the front door and Devin's sister, Alma, pops her head through the entrance. She sees me and bursts into tears, rushing over to squeeze the air out of me.

'Aggie, we've all been so worried.' She pulls back and then notices the damage to the back area of the restaurant. Her mouth drops open as she says, 'No! That's terrible. Is everyone okay?'

'Everyone's fine. Barbara and Devin are in the kitchen. I can get them.' I'm sure they're ready to run out of here and never see me or this restaurant again.

The kitchen door swings open, and Devin only gets a hand out before Alma crushes him with her arms around his neck.

'How did you get here?' Devin asks. He looks worn out, and I can only imagine how I look. He must have got a little sleep on the floor because it seems he's only now coming out of a sleep coma.

'They opened Luna Avenue, but not all the way. I only just made it through.'

'Thanks for coming. Mum's inside.' Devin and Alma disappear into the kitchen, and I can breathe again.

'Is that your ex?' Dad asks slowly. I nod without saying anything else. 'And he was here all night?' I drop my chin again as Dad glances down the hallway to the storage cupboard.

'And his mother too,' adds Dot.

Dad chuckles. He must have thought it was a joke but realises quickly that it's not when Dot lowers her voice and says, 'I said to Scott earlier in the night that I had a bad feeling about that woman, and I was right. She's got a stick well and truly up her arse.'

A laugh flies out of my mouth at the same time Dad has a loud belly chuckle. I love my dad's laugh. He uses his whole body.

Dot adds, 'You were so nice to her all night, dear.' She then turns to Dad and says, 'She was awful to our Aggie.'

'Is that right?' Dad says it under his breath, but when Devin, Barbara and Alma exit the kitchen, Dad excuses himself from our group and then guides The Sporks to the front door.

Dad and his amazing conversation skills thwart any attempts to look my way. He politely and graciously pushes them out the front door. Devin catches my eye over his shoulder, and I give him a sad wave. He tucks his mouth up in the corner and gestures in return. We're done. We're not friends and no more texting.

Barbara is gone without me having to speak to her again. My last ever words to her will always be *Fuck off*, and I feel content with that closure.

Dad rejoins our group, puts his arm over my shoulder and pulls me close.

'What kind of last name is Spork anyway?' He kisses the top of my head and I smile into his shoulder.

The Whalleys leave shortly after when their daughter comes to pick them up. Before they go, I arrange to see Dot next week for coffee and I can't wait.

My brain is running on nothing but fading alcohol fumes, but I need to have a conversation with Dad. It can't wait any longer.

'Dad, we need to talk. I heard about your plans for The Shark Biscuit.'

'Right, I suppose we do then.' Dad places my hand in the crook of his arm, guiding me out the front door and around the side so we can view the ocean. The car park is backlogged with water, and at least six cars are destroyed with water damage, including Noah's. I know Dad and Harrison will help him with the repairs. Dirt, leaves and broken tree branches cover the paths. We ignore it all and focus on the beautiful, calm ocean water.

'What a night, hey?' Dad chuckles, and I'm glad he can always see the lighter side of life. I'm the one who was worried about his heart breaking, but he seems to be handling this okay.

'Please don't knock this place down,' I blurt out because I don't know where to start with this conversation, but that seems like the most urgent point.

'I figured Thomas wouldn't wait long to tell everyone.'

'Why, Dad?'

'Money.' He says it plainly, and I can't believe it's a priority for him. 'For you.'

'For me?'

'Of course, you. Everything will be yours one day. Selling the land gives you the most.'

'I don't need the money.'

'One day you will.'

I shake my head because it's not right.

'I won't let you destroy it for me. I don't want that.'

'Storm already started the job for me. Anyway, it's better that way. The Shark Biscuit is gone, and we can both move on. It won't be as sad if it's a block of apartments.'

I help Dad sit on a bench seat, but remain standing. I can't stay still for this conversation.

'I honestly thought you'd sell it and someone else would make it their own, but when I heard you turned Harrison down—'

'I couldn't exactly say yes to him, could I?'

'Why not?'

'You clashed with the guy since day one, so I thought he'd be the last person you'd want to run the family business.'

'You turned him down for *me*?' This is not good. I've been feeling guilty about the wrong thing this entire evening. The restaurant could have been Harrison's if Dad and I had talked openly in the first place.

'I did, but I see that may not have been necessary since what I witnessed back there. Not that we need to talk about that.'

'That's good with me.'

There's a moment of silence before Dad can't help himself and adds, 'That is the last thing I thought I'd find—'

'Not talking about that, Dad.'

'Right. Sorry. Harrison has been suspiciously absent since I got here. Do you think he's hiding from me?'

'Probably. I'd hide from you too if I could.'

Dad has a small chuckle as he says, 'That cupboard.'

'That cupboard what?'

A wistful expression waves over Dad's face. 'Nothing, sweetie. Nothing at all.'

'Dad...' I turn and look out at the ocean as I say, 'I wasn't honest with you when we discussed the business.'

'Huh? You want it now?' There's hope in Dad's voice, and it's painful to hear. I turn to face him as I shake my head.

'No, I don't. And I should have been honest with you. I'm ready to move on. Try new things. I didn't want to be tied to the restaurant any longer.' I sit beside him and lay it all out. 'I was only here to help you. I don't like working in a restaurant.'

'You don't like it?'

I nod sadly and go to cover it up with a pleasing half-truth, but I hear Harrison's voice in my head. *Your dad loves you. Be honest.*

'I'm not like you and Mum. I'm sorry.'

'What does that mean?'

'I want to stare at spreadsheets all day. If I can manage it, I don't want to talk to more than four people in eight hours. I don't want to get breadsticks, take bookings and deal with inventory anymore.'

'Okay. Okay.' Dad's eyes are wide and the playfulness of before is gone. 'I don't know what to say.'

'I should have told you earlier. I didn't want to let you down.'

'You would never—'

'I didn't want to let Mum down, either. This is part of her legacy as well.'

'That will never change.'

'But it will because you never talk about her. She died and we worked here. That's been our life and I feel horrible that it's ending because of me.'

Dad shakes his head as he folds his arms over his chest. 'It's ending because of *me*. My bloody body is the reason. Not you.'

'I could have kept it going. I should have—'

265

'How did we get here, Aggie?' Dad asks the question softly, but his voice is laced with concern.

'Where, Dad?'

'That you think you need to take care of me.'

'I like—'

'That keeping me happy is more important than keeping you happy. Did I do that? Did I screw up somewhere?' Dad tucks his folded arms closer to his chest. 'I'm sorry if I've stuffed up. I tried. I really tried my best.'

I launch myself towards Dad and he throws his arms around me. I hold him tightly with my face pressed into his chest.

'I miss her,' I mumble through my tears and hear the quiver in Dad's voice as he says, 'Every day, love.'

'Every time something happens in my life, I miss her. In a new way, I miss her.' I pull back and lean my head on Dad's shoulder. 'I wanted to do the right thing by her. By you.'

Dad takes a moment, and I feel his deep inhales as he gets his words ready. 'You had to grow up too quickly. I'm sorry, Aggie.'

'You don't need to say that.'

'But it's the truth. I let you grow up too quickly. I never checked that this is what you wanted because maybe I didn't want the answer. I thought you were happy and didn't press any further.'

'I could have told you.'

'I could have paid more attention to my daughter. Now it's my turn to do the right thing by *you*. I'll sell the land and you can do whatever you like. I want you to be happy.'

Twenty-four hours ago, I might have said yes, but Harrison's comments have whittled their way into my brain and made me realise that I perhaps don't hate The

266

Shark Biscuit. I'm angry and resentful because I stayed in the business too long. I should have made the decision to leave years ago. I'm the one who allowed my resentment to fester.

'The honest truth is that I would be sad if it got knocked down. I'm happy for you to decide what's best for *you*, not me, but the decision is yours. I'm ready for something new. I want you to be happy too, Dad. I know this place was your pride and joy, and I want you to be happy after this is gone.'

Dad's eyes turn to gaze at me, and they look watery, though the tears don't drop.

'You are my pride, Aggie, and seeing you happy is my joy.' Dad looks out over the ocean as he says, 'I loved this place because your mum and you were here. All my fond memories of the restaurant include the people. Not this place. Not the building. It's the people who filled it, especially you and your mum. I kept it going all these years because it helped me feel connected to her. And to you. Not many dads get to see their daughters every day. I'm sorry you sacrificed so much for my happiness.'

'You'd be okay with knocking this place down, though?'

'It's up to you. We can sell the land or sell the restaurant. Although it's worth less now it's got a bloody hole in the roof.'

'That is true. Harrison would take care of it.'

Dad nods in agreement. 'I felt like a royal shit turning him down. He's got puppy dog eyes, that one. He can sulk like the best of them.' I smile because I know Harrison would hate Dad's assessment of him, but it's true.

'I think it makes sense for Harrison to take over. He'll do right by your legacy.'

'My legacy is you, not prawns.'

I drop my head back on Dad's shoulder.

'You and I need to be better at talking with each other,' Dad says as he places his chin on top of my head.

'We do.'

Dad kisses the side of my head and I curl my head onto his shoulder. He pulls me against his chest, and I hear him sigh as he rubs a reassuring hand over my back.

'I'd like it if we could talk about Mum more. Together.'

Dad's body tenses for a moment before he says, 'We can talk about her any time you like. I'm always thinking about her, so any time you want to talk about her, I'm probably already there. Living in a memory.'

'Say them out loud then. I want to hear them all.'

'I'd love that.'

Dad tells me a story about the day he and Mum found this block of land and how they had to beg, borrow and sell everything they owned to afford it. He tells me details I've never heard as we watch the sun continue to rise on a new day, a new beginning and chapter for both of us. No more guilt. No more secrets. All that's left is for Dad to talk to Harrison about his offer. I have no idea what to say to Harrison, but I know we have things to discuss. For once, I might let him speak first.

Chapter Twenty-Eight

There's noise coming from the side of the restaurant, and it's the only place Harrison could be. We've searched everywhere else so unless he took off, he must be making the racket. Dad and I come around the side and find Harrison and Thomas moving the sandbags away from the side and piling them near the car park. There are large muddy pools of water everywhere. The last thing they need to be worrying about is moving sandbags.

'What are you boys doing?' Dad echoes my thoughts out loud and waves his hands around to signal them to stop. 'Leave them all there. No use moving them.'

'That's what I said, but—' Thomas is cut off when Harrison dumps a sandbag aggressively and scowls at Thomas. 'And that's exactly why I go back to hurling heavy, muddy shit bags.'

Thomas turns away to toss another bag as Harrison dusts his hands off and looks at Dad and me. His eyes track me first and then, with some hesitation move to Dad.

'Ernie, I um…' Harrison's stumbling over his words, which never happens. He opens his mouth, and words look like they're trying to come out but are locked between his teeth. 'I wanted to, um, what happened…'

My face is burning up from the embarrassment of Harrison trying to clear the air with Dad. There's no need to be the good guy right now.

Thankfully, Dad puts his hand up to stop Harrison's word salad and my need to hide somewhere that isn't the storage cupboard.

'It's all good, son. Nothing to say. *Please.*' Thomas sniggers behind Dad, so Harrison must have told him what happened. Great, more people are involved in this now. 'I need to chat with you though. Can we take a walk?'

Dad steps forward slowly and Harrison's eyes follow him as he walks past him towards the water. Harrison looks back at me, and I know he's asking for some intel about Dad's need to chat. I could tell him it's good news, and he's not in trouble about being caught having sex at his place of employment with the boss's daughter, but that wouldn't be fun.

I mouth *Go*, and that spurs Harrison into action. He and Thomas have a few muttered words when Harrison walks towards Dad. I come closer to Thomas, and together we watch Harrison and Ernie stand near the jetty, the sun streaming between their silhouettes.

'Are Harrison's balls about to be blown off?' Thomas asks with genuine worry in his voice.

'Why would you say that?'

'It's what I'd do if I found my daughter…' Thomas's eyes shift to mine and away just as quickly. 'Well, you know.'

'We're adults. Dad doesn't care.' It doesn't stop it from humiliating me, but Dad will have already washed it from his mind. I hope so, at least. I haven't, and I'm sure my mind will be replaying our morning together for years.

Dad seems to be doing all the talking as Harrison hangs his head. His arms are folded, but as Dad finishes talking, Harrison's hands drop like anchors to his side. He turns abruptly to me, and I can't stop the bright smile that stretches across my face. I'll always remember the image of the sun-tipped ocean behind Dad and Harrison, whose beaming face is laced with surprise and awe.

I tap Thomas on the shoulder, 'I think you better join them.'

'Why? I didn't, you know, with you.'

I whack him on the shoulder for that comment. 'Just get over there.'

Within moments of Thomas joining them, the James brothers shake Dad's hand. Harrison catches my eye and we exchange goofy grins.

Harrison shakes Dad's hand again, and Dad pulls him in for a manly hug. Thomas doesn't want to be left out and throws himself into the huddle. Watching the boys have their bonding moment, I hear footsteps approaching from behind.

Scout, Willy and Noah come to stand next to me, and the four of us watch Harrison, Thomas and Dad hug past an acceptable timeframe for any hug.

'What are we watching here?' Willy asks, and it's a fair question.

'My dad handing over The Shark Biscuit to its new owners.'

'Harrison and Thomas?' Noah asks with the excitement of a two-year-old who's been given ice cream.

'It's all theirs now.'

'They do remember it's got a bloody big hole in the roof, right?' Scout asks, and I think it would be hard to forget.

'Who cares? We can fix that.' Noah's not letting anything bring down this moment. 'You know what this means, right?'

'We have to repay all the alcohol we drank last night?' There's fear in Scout's voice.

'Oh, shit. Hope not. We get to keep our jobs.'

Scout and Noah hug, so now it's only Willy and I who aren't hugging someone. He looks at me, opens his arms, and I think *Why not?* as I give Willy a squeeze.

'Shall we take a walk?' Willy suggests, but I'm confused by the idea.

'Where do you want to go?'

'The public bathrooms up there because I've been busting to go to the loo for hours.'

'Me too!' Scout shouts as she pulls back from Noah's hug.

The four of us trek down the road, past all the destruction from the storm, including abandoned cars, to find a toilet. Scout and Willy link arms and Noah hums next to me like he hasn't got a care in the world. The boys will be cleaning up from the chaos of the storm for weeks, but I think they'll have lots of friends helping them.

I look back and spot Harrison watching us. He lifts his chin to acknowledge me, and I smile back. It only hits me then that Harrison and I no longer work together; we have no reason to cross paths now. That time in my life is over. I've been counting down the months, days and hours until it's all over and now that it's here and I can put my hand out to grasp it, I'm not sure how I feel about it.

As we continue up the path, Noah turns to me with the biggest grin. 'I'm so glad no one died, Aggie.'

'Me too, Noah.'

–

When I return to the restaurant, I find Harrison standing with Thomas at the front entrance. Harrison and I haven't had a moment to ourselves yet, and the tension between us is getting thicker the longer we put off the conversation we need to have. I have no idea about how he's feeling. I can't get my own feelings straight, let alone try to gauge Harrison's thoughts.

'We'll deal with your car tomorrow,' I hear Harrison say to Thomas, who claps his brother on the back and then leans in to whisper. Harrison keeps his head down as he nods before returning the back slap. The James brothers communicate their affection for each other with back slaps.

'Yael will be here in five minutes,' Willy yells from the front door. His fiancé was able to get through the streets to the restaurant and is giving Thomas and Noah a lift home. I'm ready to collapse onto my bed but can't leave yet. Dad went to get food and supplies to tape up the window. I can't make my brain think about where to start with the damage. I need to put my head on a pillow for ten hours before I can help with that.

Willy's head disappears as Noah's pops into the doorway. He looks around the restaurant until his eyes stop on Scout. She's sweeping the dirt on a floor that will never be clean with a broken window allowing all kinds of mess inside. She could go home, but she's lingering for some reason.

'You sure you don't want a lift?' Noah asks Scout.

'I'm good. I've got my second wind now. I'll stay and help, you guys go!' Maybe she still doesn't want to be at home.

Willy pops his head back in and blows us all a kiss.

'He's here. I'll be in touch! Let's have brunch soon so you can meet Yael before the wedding!' His head disappears before we can react to the news that we're all now invited to his wedding.

Thomas gives Harrison another slap before ducking down to give me a friendly hug.

'He's a lucky man. Make sure he knows it,' Thomas whispers in my ear.

'I heard that, dipshit,' says Harrison paired with a scowl directed at his brother. Thomas only laughs it away and claps me on the shoulder. I'm part of the clapping crew now.

Scout lingers behind us with her broom doing not much sweeping. She pauses and rests her cheek on the top of the handle. Thomas's eyes roam over her as he says, 'Thanks for the drinks.'

'Anytime, sailor.' She gives him a salute and a carefree smile before returning to push dirt back and forth for no good reason.

Thomas clears his throat before he says, 'Before I go, I want you to know that I'll follow you to a storage cupboard any time you ask.'

Scout lifts her head and looks genuinely caught off guard by Thomas's comment.

'You messing with me?'

'Absolutely not. My brain didn't act fast enough the first time, but I'll never make that mistake again.' Thomas and Scout stare at each other until a sly grin breaks over Thomas's face.

He flicks his chin towards the door and says, 'You coming?'

Scout's eyes widen, and she hesitates for only a second before saying, 'Hell yeah.'

The broom drops to the floor, and she scurries past us. She blows us two kisses each as she passes by.

Thomas holds the door open for her and she ducks under his arm and disappears. Thomas looks back at Harrison and I and winks as he closes the door.

I point at the doorway. 'That's the Thomas from high school I remember.'

'He only brings it out on special occasions,' says Harrison with humour in his voice.

'Scout will decimate him.'

'I couldn't agree more.'

I pick up the broom Scout dropped like it was a sizzling seafood platter and place it against the wall. When I finally peek up at Harrison, he's staring. Watching me. He leans back on the heels of his feet and then forward. He's waiting for me to talk, but I have already decided he's going first. The silence continues for so long that he must have worked that out because a sly smile forms on the corner of his mouth.

'You want to avoid talking a little longer?'

'Is that what we're doing?'

'It's what *you're* doing.'

'I am not!' I am, but still, I don't like being called out, and old habits die hard.

'No one's here now. No need for charades or faking anything. Are you ready to talk to me? Be honest.'

'You're obviously feeling weird about it because you were shovelling sandbags that did not need to be moved.'

Harrison digs into his pocket before stepping forward and holding out his hand. My mother's locket sits in his palm. I gasp as I carefully pick up my most treasured piece of jewellery I thought I'd never see again.

'We need to get it cleaned up but I think it's okay.'

'How did you find it?'

'It got caught on one of the bags. It was a long shot, but I thought it might've got trapped against them with the current.'

I clasp it in my hand, step into Harrison, wrap my arms around his shoulders and whisper, 'Thank you. You have no idea what this means to me.'

'I know exactly what this means to you. I've watched you reach for this all night and look devastated when it wasn't there.'

I pull back but stay close, our bodies minutely swaying towards each other.

'Thank you for everything tonight. You took care of me in a way that no one has ever.'

'Are you regretful that we didn't figure this out earlier?'

I shake my head. 'No, it wouldn't have been the same. Tonight was perfect.' I catch my words and tap my hand to my forehead. 'Except The Shark Biscuit being destroyed and all that.'

'Not destroyed. Just ready for renovations.'

'That's Noah-level of optimism.'

Harrison laughs. 'He's growing on me.'

There's a pause in the conversation, and the silence lingers.

'What are you thinking about?' asks Harrison.

'I'm glad I didn't drive my car to work yesterday, but now I have to wait for my dad to drive me home like I'm sixteen again.'

'You want something to eat while you wait?'

'Surely you're out of food by now?'

'Never.' Harrison seems personally offended by that idea. We're tiptoeing around the elephant in the room because neither of us wants to talk about us hooking up in last night's most unexpected turn of events.

'I don't want anything to eat. I need to lie down in my bed as soon as possible.'

'Yeah, me too.' Harrison catches himself, and I think his cheeks blush slightly. 'I meant my bed. Not your bed.'

I laugh at how flustered he is; I don't remember ever seeing Harrison flustered.

'I knew what you meant. Don't stress. I'm not expecting anything. I know what it was last night and what it wasn't.'

'I wasn't trying to clarify because of that, and what does *that* mean?'

'I didn't want you worrying that I was expecting anything from you after last night.'

'You should expect something from me. Why aren't you?'

'We've gone off track. I thought you were freaking out because – you know what, it doesn't matter. We're all good. The best thing is that The Shark Biscuit is yours. I'm happy for you and Thomas.'

'I'm happy for us, too, but I'm confused about our conversation, and I'm not letting that go.'

'I can see.' There's nowhere to sit and my legs ache from exhaustion. 'I'm going to the kitchen. I need to lean against something.'

'Lead the way.' Harrison gestures for me to go first. Why does it feel like we're gearing up for one final round? Harrison versus Agnes. I'm not sure I have the strength, but I never back down. The only problem is I don't know what I'm fighting for this time.

Chapter Twenty-Nine

Every muscle in my body aches as I pull myself onto the countertop. Last night, when I sat up here, Harrison's hands roamed my body, but I try not to think about that now. I wish I could call an Uber and pause this conversation until we've had some sleep, but the roads aren't all open and most things aren't operational yet. I still seem to be trapped at The Shark Biscuit.

Harrison stands in his spot in the kitchen, his sign hanging directly above him. I wonder what the future of this place will look like once Harrison and Thomas get it back up and running.

'I assume Noah and Scout get to keep their jobs.'

'Of course.' Harrison spits it out like it's an insult to think otherwise. He wipes the counter, which is a waste of time because no food is getting cooked in this place for months.

'Do you know why I took this job in the first place?'

'I did always wonder why you chose us. I thought maybe a city restaurant would have been more up your alley.'

Harrison shakes his head before I've finished my sentence. 'No way. Never.' He takes a step closer to me but still keeps a safe distance between us. 'I like the atmosphere here. I liked that Ernie knew everyone. It felt like a family.'

In so many ways, it is a family – all the customers who come in regularly, including the Whalleys. Scout and Noah are like cousins who turn up to family gatherings only to get drunk, and you adore them for that.

'I can see that. Dad and you have built that, and now you can see that it stays that way.'

'You built it, too.'

I shrug my shoulders because if I did it was out of obligation, so it doesn't sit right to take credit for it.

'Doesn't matter, Harrison. It's all over. You call all the shots now.'

'And what will you do?'

'Apply for bookkeeper jobs first. Move into accounting roles. Hopefully stare at a computer sipping coffee while sitting on my arse all day.'

'And that will make you happy?'

'I think so. I'm not built to talk to people all day. Change will be nice either way.'

'Will you ever come back here?'

'To work?'

'No. To visit? I didn't know if it would be hard for you to be here after we take over.'

It's my turn to shake my head before Harrison finishes.

'You guys can make whatever changes you want. I just want to keep my dad.'

'I want to keep him too, though.'

'I think I'll win.'

'Me too. Just this once.' Harrison's mood is playful again as he steps closer. Whatever weirdness there was between us is slowly melting, and I'm relieved. I liked not having tension between us. 'So, you'd visit us here? Me? You'd visit me?'

I'm not sure what Harrison is asking. He's studying me with an open expression, waiting for me to reply.

'You want me to give the new staff hints on how to get under your skin?' Deflecting with a joke seemed like the easiest option.

'No one gets under my skin but you, Agnes. Haven't you figured that out by now?'

'I think I figured that out pretty early on.' I slide off the counter and step closer to Harrison, poking his shoulder with my finger. 'Push a button here, get Harrison to scowl at me.' I move my finger to his other shoulder and poke it gently. 'Push a button here and see your chopping speed go ultra-sonic.'

Harrison catches my finger before moving to hold my hand.

'You were paying attention.'

We beam at each other, and there's peace in my body. We're ending our time working together like this and not on bad terms.

'We had fun, didn't we?' I say, and the smile on Harrison's face slips.

'You're avoiding this conversation, so I'll say it first. I'm glad everything that happened last night happened.'

'Me too.'

'Okay.' Harrison observes me, but when I don't say anything, he adds, 'I want to give this a shot.'

'What a shot?'

'Us, Agnes. We could be great together.'

'Based on one night?'

'No, based on years.'

'Years of us hating each other?'

'It was never hate.'

'I agree, but it was something other than love.'

Harrison steps forward, placing his hands on my cheeks. 'Last night was the start of something. You have to have felt that.'

'I did.' I want to be honest with Harrison because last night was incredible. Unexpected and incredible. That I can't deny, but in the light of the morning, it seems impossible.

Happiness breaks out over Harrison's face and he ducks his head down to mine, but before our lips can touch, I put my hand up to stop him. I fear if he kisses me, I won't want to stop.

'But...' I whisper.

'No but. We don't need that but. That but is trying to ruin my perfect morning.'

'Perfect?'

Harrison leans in and kisses me swiftly. He pulls back and says over my lips, 'Perfect, and that was before I bought a destroyed restaurant.'

I run my fingers over Harrison's cheek and then through the short hair at his nape. I'm not sure if I'll get the chance to be this close to him again, and it makes me sadder than I've been at any point in the last twenty-four hours.

'You ready for the but?'

Harrison pushes out a giant exhale and steps back.

'Let's hear it.'

'We go on a few dates, and maybe it turns into something.'

'It's already something, but keep going.'

'Fine, it turns into something *important*.' Harrison nods because he hasn't worked out why this won't work yet. 'And then nothing changes for me. I sign up for the same thing. Again. I'd come and visit you at the restaurant.

You'll be busy. I'll wait at home for you.' I wave my hands around the kitchen. 'I'll be second to this place, again. I'll resent it and you.' He hasn't said anything, so I think the truth that this can't work is settling in for him. 'I can't do the same thing again. Repeat the same old pattern. I would love to try with you because I've never felt as cared for and protected as I was by you last night, but it's the saddest truth that it will never work between us. You want The Shark Biscuit, and I don't.'

Harrison starts shaking his head. 'This isn't right. This can't be one night, and that's it.'

'We'll stay friends—' Harrison gives me a look of sheer horror, so I stop with that line of thinking.

'Friends, Agnes. Really?'

'We could try.'

'No.'

I throw my hands up in the air because I was trying to end this on a good note.

'That was a white flag being planted by me, and you set it on fire.'

'Damn right. Fuck being friends. That's not what this is and you know it.'

Harrison turns away and paces before twisting back to me. He's not angry. There's a resigned sorrow in his whole body. His shoulders scoop over. I want to touch him so badly, but I cross my arms to stay on my side of the kitchen.

'I don't want to miss you.' Harrison's voice is low with anguish. 'I'm going to miss you. How can we not see each other every day?'

That thought makes me cry and it surprises me how instant it hits, the grief of not being in Harrison's life.

'We could if—'

'Don't say it.'

I wipe a tear and put my hands up to surrender because I'll never mention that idea of friends again.

'I'm going to miss fighting with you.'

I say through my tears, 'I don't think fighting with someone is something you should miss.'

'It is when fighting with someone is more fun than a conversation with anyone else. It makes you feel alive. We work, Agnes. Even when we're arguing, we work.'

'You understand why this won't work though, don't you? I'm getting out. I need a change from this place. I can't do this again.'

Harrison drops his chin in a resigned version of a nod, even though I know he doesn't agree.

'You love this place, Harrison. It's going to be amazing. You'll be so busy—'

'Don't soften the blow. Let me feel the full impact of this. Be honest with me.'

I reach out for Harrison but drop my arm when I see his waiting expression. He wants honesty, and he deserves that.

'Last night was amazing. That's the honest truth. But that's all we'll get. One last night.'

Harrison steps forward, kisses the side of my head and then exits through the back door without saying another word.

Chapter Thirty

The weather is picturesque, with the sun beaming down on the ocean and no traces of a once-in-a-lifetime storm a few hours ago. The effects of the storm will be visible in the streets and people's homes for months, if not years, but the weather has moved on already.

I step carefully onto the jetty, which survived the storm. A few palings are broken, but in all, it's held up well. I'm sure a few fishermen will be out this afternoon to throw in a line. Once I've reached the end, I take off my shoes, sit down and splash my toes in the cool water. I am ready for a shower.

I don't know where Harrison took off to, so I thought it best to wait for Dad down here. I didn't want to be waiting in the kitchen if Harrison returned.

Closing my eyes, I let the sun warm my face. The conversation with Harrison has left me in knots. I would have loved to run into his arms and start planning our first date, but I made the mature decision. A decision Harrison will come to thank me for when he's busy in the restaurant and doesn't have time for a relationship.

I saved us both from the heartache that would come because I know how much my dad disappeared and the hours it takes to make a small business work. At the same time, I can't wait to secretly see what he does with the restaurant and how he makes it his own.

This place will thrive. I hope I can pop in for a bug roll now and then once Harrison has forgiven me. I wonder if he'll keep The Shag Room as is or knock it down with the rest of the renovations.

I'll start applying for jobs once I know the restaurant is in Harrison's hands and Dad can rest. My mind wanders to the future of working with new people, hopefully in a friendly office, but I'm pulled away from those thoughts by the sound of someone stomping down the jetty.

Harrison.

He reaches me in seconds and puts his hand up to cover his eyes from the glare.

'Change your mind about being my friend?'

'No. Never.'

'You hurt my feelings, Harrison.'

'I haven't, and I have two things to say.'

'Okay, do you want to sit down next to me and put your feet in the water?'

Harrison throws his shoes away, plonks down beside me and places his feet in the water. I can tell he likes it, but he won't admit it.

'We should have come down here more often,' I say as I swish my feet back and forward.

'We were too busy making and serving food.'

'I know, but it's nice to finally be the ones down here relaxing rather than watching from up there.' I gesture to my regular lunch bench.

Harrison doesn't reply while he swirls his feet around in the water. It's been less than twenty minutes since we last spoke. He must've been preparing for round two, but I'm not sure what's left to discuss.

'Here's what I came down to say.' He places his hand on the worn wooden boards of the jetty and turns his torso to look at me. 'One.' He lifts his pointer finger and then points to the restaurant. 'Everything you said up there is total *bullshit*.'

'Bullshit?' I can't help the laugh that comes out because I wasn't expecting that comment. Our heartfelt goodbye to Harrison was bullshit.

'Yes, all of it.'

'Harrison—'

'Let me get to my second point.'

'The first point was insightful.'

Harrison folds his arms across his chest and turns back to gaze over the ocean. 'I understand it may not be bullshit to you, but to me it's all bullshit.'

'Is that the second point?' I throw him a cheeky smile because it's still fun to rile him up, and he catches it out of the corner of his eye.

'No, just clarifying the first. Smart-arse.'

'The second point then?'

Harrison pulls his feet out of the water and stands abruptly. 'I had an epiphany. Two, actually.' He holds out his hand and, without thinking, I take it and he pulls me to my feet.

'So that would mean you have three points?' I say, Harrison continuing to hold my hand. I try to step back, but he doesn't let me go.

'Technically, yes.'

'And you had two epiphanies just now?'

'Yes.'

I shake my head. 'You can't have an epiphany that easily. They don't happen that quickly. Or two at once.'

'Mine did.'

'What was your first great epiphany then?'

Harrison takes a moment, looks me dead in the eyes and says: 'I'm not your dad.'

I throw my arms up in the air. 'That's not remotely close to an epiphany. That's just a fact and a weird one to bring up now.'

'It's an epiphany because it's not fair that you expect me to behave the same way as your dad. I'm not him.' Harrison takes my hand again and pulls me towards him, closing the distance between us. 'Just like I'm not my parents. This is not the same situation, so we need to treat it differently.'

Harrison rubs his thumb over my knuckles as we let his epiphany sink in.

'Second epiphany?' I say.

Harrison turns over my hand and slowly links our fingers together. I know his game plan. He's slowly wearing me down, and I don't hate that it's working.

'The second one is that I have an insight into how you feel. That changes the situation.'

'What does that mean?'

'It means I know that it's an issue for you. I know what you need. I have the information to treat you properly. You and your dad never talked about it, but we can. It won't be the same.'

I've never seen Harrison's expression so open and loving. He is undeniably sincere, and it catches me off guard. I thought we'd debate a little more before I left, but he's serious about us trying.

'I know what you're saying, but what you're about to start – you'll be busy and focused here, as you should be, making this place the best it can be. There's just no room for us.'

Harrison shakes his head vehemently.

'I want balance in my life. I'm not drowning myself in work to hide from things. I'm only here crazy long hours right now because I don't have a life, and it was fun to annoy you.' Harrison leans in and lowers his voice. 'I want a life outside this job.'

'That's good. That's healthy.'

'I've been doing all this work. Getting myself ready for when the right person comes along, and it's *you*. I know it. I just know that it's all been for you.'

'Not me, it's been for *you*, which is how it should be. It's for you. To create the life you want with someone.'

Harrison is usually composed, but right at this moment, his eyes betray him, showing a profound sadness that he must keep hidden.

'It was so I knew how to care for the person I fall in love with. Treat them well because I never want to be the person who hurts the people they love.' There's a fragile quiver in Harrison's voice and it breaks my heart. Before tonight, I wouldn't have realised Harrison was speaking from experience. He clutches my hand and the desperation in his grasp is unmistakable.

'I'm still learning, but I know I'm ready. I'm ready to show you, Agnes. We at least have to try?' The anguish is visible in every line of his face. His tight eyes and furrowed brows tell me how important this is to him.

I'm in shock because I didn't let myself think that this could be a possibility until now. I didn't know how I would walk away from Harrison after tonight, which explains why I'm still here. The thought of not seeing him makes my insides panic and my future away from the restaurant a little less bright.

'You're fighting for me?' I whisper as I squeeze his hand, which is still clenching me tightly.

'For us, yes.'

I don't remember someone fighting for me like this. I thought after the conversation in the kitchen Harrison would just walk away. I didn't expect him to come back with counterpoints that would make me rethink everything.

'You think this could work? You and me? I annoy you.'

'You interest me. You ignite me.'

I take a moment and then release the words, 'I feel the same way.'

It's true because my flame with Harrison, even when we were nothing but work colleagues, burnt brighter than with any partner I've ever had. Harrison James was always under my skin.

'We know how to talk to each other. We know how to be honest with each other. You don't have to pretend with me. We know how to fight. We fight well.' Harrison gives me a cheeky half-smile, and it's hard not to lean in and kiss it.

He cups my face in his hands and tips my chin up. 'You were always in the front of my mind when you weren't even mine. I can't imagine anything easier than making you a priority, our life together a priority. I can't imagine you not being the first thing I think of every day. That's the easiest part of this.'

I lean and place my forehead against Harrison's because the need to be close to him is indescribable.

Harrison lifts his head slightly as his eyes sweep my face. 'But for this to work, you're going to have to be honest with me. Completely. Bad feelings, all of it; I need you to tell me how you're feeling. Nothing you can say scares me except if I'm in the dark. I'm not a mind reader, so don't make me guess.'

'I've had some practice at that tonight.' A smirk tugs at the corner of Harrison's mouth. 'But I was always pretty good at that part with you.' Harrison nods like I'm finally getting what he already sees clearly. 'Only you. How did I never see that?'

'You were dating idiots.' I gently smack Harrison on the shoulder as he chuckles. He sweeps me into his arms and holds me tight against his body.

'Date me, Agnes Keegan. Fall in love with me. If fighting is this much fun, imagine how good it will be loving each other.'

A shiver runs through my body and I know it's from the possibility of falling in love with Harrison. I can see it now, and the excitement of that prospect makes me giddy. I struggle to keep my joy from overspilling.

I lean in, and my lips float over Harrison's. 'If we do this, if we give this a try, will you let me cook for you?'

'Yes,' he whispers but then pulls his head back slightly. 'What are you talking? Breakfast? Something simple like eggs?'

'Dinner. Three-course meal.' Harrison leaves me hanging as he mulls over my proposal, but then a sweeping smile covers his entire face.

'Yes, I agree to those terms. I was only going for breakfast, so it meant I could stay over.'

I go to whack him on the shoulder again, but he swoops in and kisses me before I can get to him. My arms loop around his neck and I climb on my tiptoes to get my body as close as possible to Harrison. He angles his head and kisses me slowly until his hands move into my hair, and the kiss deepens.

'We're in a very public area.' I break the kiss quickly before pecking the corner of his mouth.

'You want to move to our cupboard?'

'Our cupboard?'

'It's ours now.' Harrison darts back in and continues to shower kisses over my lips while happiness and lightness bloom over my body. I have the warm sun on my back and Harrison James showing me affection that has me almost dragging him back to the cupboard. The turnaround from yesterday to today is staggering.

A wolf-whistle breaks our kiss, and we both turn to look towards the restaurant. Dad stands with his hands on his hips, but there's a twinkle in his eyes.

'Time to go home, you two.'

Harrison steps back and links our fingers together as we walk back down the jetty towards Dad.

Before we arrive, I lean on Harrison's shoulder and whisper, 'Your dinner will be ready at seven, so don't be late.'

Harrison falters before he turns his head, and our lips almost touch.

'And what time is breakfast?'

His cocky grin is adorable, and then he kisses me briefly, not expecting an answer as he takes a step, but I reach up and whisper again, 'Seven as well.' This time, I lean in and pull his face to mine. Dad can see, but I don't care. I know he loves Harrison. 'And I'm claiming it early that I sleep on the left side of the bed.'

I walk along the jetty, pulling on Harrison's hand.

'Now, wait. That's my side.'

'I look forward to you presenting your case.'

'There's no case. Agnes?'

I drop Harrison's hand as I pick up the pace down the jetty.

'Get back here. I'm a lefty!'

'We can make a roster and take turns then,' I throw over my shoulder and twist around to walk backwards so I can grin at Harrison. 'Should we take the "No Yelling" sign and place it above your bed, or is that a given?' I wink at him so he knows I am teasing.

Harrison's eyebrows jump up his forehead as he strides forward and catches up to me quickly.

'You think that's funny. You just lost left side of the bed privileges for a week for that comment.'

'You two ready to get out of here?' says Dad, ignoring our behaviour.

'Yes,' I say because, with Harrison by my side, I'm finally ready to leave The Shark Biscuit.

'I'm going to make your daughter fall in love with me, Ernie,' Harrison says matter-of-factly as he helps me up the hill to the restaurant.

I glance over my shoulder at Dad, who's beaming at us and is not at all fazed by Harrison's comment.

'Sounds like a brilliant plan,' Dad calls out, giving me a wink before he follows us.

'You think my plan is brilliant, Agnes?' Harrison whispers to me as he tightens his hold of my hand.

I rise up on my toes and kiss him before saying for the first time in my life, 'I love your plan, Harrison James.'

Chapter Thirty-One

Five years later…

I'm back at The Shark Biscuit. It's a beautiful sunny afternoon with not a storm cloud in sight. The restaurant is
closed for a private function today, so I only have to see
people I love – no customers to serve.

I stand on the renovated deck and watch the fishermen on the jetty. The palings that were damaged in the
storm still haven't been replaced. Some people still haven't
returned to their homes, so a few railings have been the
last thing on people's minds.

The deck has been extended now to feature a private
dining section with ocean views. It's booked out solidly
for months in advance with its stunning location and
exquisite food. I walk through the section and wait for
Dad.

A new ramp was installed after the storm, giving better
access to the main restaurant. I spot Dad at the bottom of
the ramp, trying to navigate his new walker.

'You need help?'

'You know the answer to that.' Dad doesn't like help,
so I wait at the top and pretend to gaze at the ocean. I
keep a watch on Dad from the corner of my eye, but he's
doing well. He shouldn't need the walker for long, but

he only had surgery for a hip fracture recently, so he's still healing.

He reaches me and I can see the sweat on his brow. I lean in and hug him tightly.

'How are you feeling?'

Dad takes in the view, and peace settles over his expression. 'I'm ready for a beer.'

'I'll get you one.'

'No, someone else can grab it.' That's true. Old habits die hard because it hasn't been my job for years.

'Let's get inside, someone is very excited to see you.'

Dad and I walk slowly through the deck and admire the fancy new shutters that manage to keep the rain out even during a storm.

'Pop's here!'

Little ears hear my voice, and Penny snaps her head up as she runs towards her grandfather. She clasps him tightly around his belly and Dad leans as much as he can into her hug.

'Happy birthday, sweetie.'

'I'm three,' says Penny with excitement. 'My cake is purple.'

'I'm so excited to see it,' says Dad, giving her another squeeze.

I bend down, pick up my daughter, and hold her on my hip, which has been moulded over the years to fit her perfectly.

'Noah's been working on the cake all morning. He's very proud.'

I'm telling Dad so he gives Noah lots of praise. He's invested his whole heart and soul into Penny's butterfly cake and he needs some words of encouragement. The icing wasn't behaving well, so there's been some cursing coming from the kitchen.

Penny wiggles down from me and runs through the restaurant and into her dad's waiting arms. Harrison scoops her up and she wraps her arms around his neck, then turns to give me a cheeky grin. She's about to ask him for ice cream, which I already said no to earlier.

I mouth, *No*, to Harrison as Penny whispers in his ear. Harrison gets the same devilish glint in his eye that he passed down to our daughter and he and I have a stand-off across the room from each other. Slowly, he drags his eyes off me and talks quietly to Penny. I can see he's backing me up, but I'm sure there's a trade-off being offered as well. He's a complete and utter pushover when it comes to that little girl.

Harrison carries Penny to the bar and retrieves a beer before joining Dad and me.

'Ernie, I saved you the best spot in the restaurant.' Harrison passes the beer to Dad. He gestures to the centre table nearby, and Dad lowers himself into a seat.

'Cheers, mate,' says Dad, as he tips his beer to Harrison.

I place the walker off to the side and then step into Harrison's outstretched arm. He pulls me close as his hand runs up my back and cups my shoulder. We stand with one of his arms holding Penny and the other holding me.

'Is it cake time?' asks Penny for the tenth time since she and I arrived.

'Soon, we have to wait for more friends to arrive first,' Harrison says before he kisses her head.

He twists his head and whispers to me, 'Does your dad need anything?'

'He'll be fine once everyone's here and he can have a chat.'

I place my hand on Harrison's chest and lean into him because it's my favourite place to nuzzle, and the three of us won't get much time together once everyone arrives.

My eyes sweep the restaurant that hasn't changed much since Harrison and Thomas took over. It has a modern feel while keeping the signature touches from the original Shark Biscuit days. The photo of Mum and Dad still hangs on the wall, and I catch Dad admiring it as he sips his beer.

Harrison and Thomas spent months renovating the place and flood-proofing the bathroom. The storage cupboard remains untouched, though. Harrison didn't want anything about it to change. He sometimes pulls me in for a kiss when I visit, although it's more challenging with a little one following us.

It's not long until the Whalleys arrive and Dot, Scott and Dad are drinking, laughing and catching up. It makes me overjoyed to hear Dad's boisterous laugh fill the restaurant.

Willy, Yael and their daughter, Isabel, arrive with a present in a giant purple box and get extra points for remembering that purple is Penny's favourite colour. Isabel is only six months older than Penny, so we always catch up for playdates. Isabel and Penny love getting into mischief together.

Thomas stomps around the restaurant, looking stressed and irritated. That's his default position most days, but I had hoped he'd relax today and enjoy his niece's birthday.

Penny spots him, and she and Isabel run over and grab a leg of his each. Thomas freezes and is sweet enough to join in with their games.

'A little help here, Agnes. Your creature has latched onto me,' says Thomas, trying to shake Penny off his leg.

She giggles because Thomas has made the game more fun for the girls.

'Did you call my daughter a creature?' Harrison peels Penny off Thomas's leg and holds her against his chest.

'Yes, but she's a cute creature,' says Thomas with a bop on Penny's nose. Isabel is still attached to his leg, so Willy comes over to save his daughter.

'Cake time, Dad?' Penny asks, her patience for waiting any longer wearing thin. Mine is, too.

'We'll have to ask the boss,' says Harrison, then turns them to look in my direction.

'I'm the boss?' It's the first I've heard of this new job title, but if we get to eat cake sooner, I'll take the job.

Harrison grins as he says, 'You don't want to be the boss? Okay, I'll do it.'

'Mum's the boss,' says Penny with a finality in her tone, making Harrison and me both laugh. I think she might be the boss now.

'Doesn't matter who's the boss, I think we agree, it's cake time,' I say.

Penny beams as she claps her hands together. I take our daughter from Harrison and set her up at the table next to Dad.

Everyone gathers around as the kitchen door flies open and Noah proudly walks through the restaurant holding a giant, three-layered butterfly-shaped cake. The frosting is various shades of purple, with pink rosettes around the sides. The butterfly has a face made with piping and chocolate drops. Dot lets out a gasp of delight when she sees the cake, and Noah blushes.

Penny's body positively vibrates as Noah places the cake before her. I quickly rush over and hug him.

'It's beautiful. Thank you,' I say because he saved me several levels of stress, offering to bake Penny's cake.

'It's my honour,' he says with reverence, and I just realise how much pressure he put on himself to cook a cake for his boss's daughter. Harrison isn't just a boss to Noah, though. Noah is a part of this family and The Shark Biscuit story.

Harrison shakes Noah's hand before he leans over to light the candles.

The front door bursts open and Scout rushes through, pulling a large suitcase behind her.

'I made it!' she shouts over the restaurant.

'I didn't think you were coming back yet?' I say as I dash over to hug her. I've missed her like crazy.

Scout pulls back and says, 'And miss a party at The Shark Biscuit? No way.'

I guide her to the table and we gather to sing Happy Birthday to Penny.

Thomas emerges from the kitchen just in time for the song, but the second he sees Scout, the colour drains from his face. I would have given him a heads-up that his ex was here, but I didn't have any warning myself.

He eyes her carefully and stands at the opposite end of the table. Scout seems to be avoiding his gaze blazing down on her. I've never known Scout to hide away from anyone, but she's making a champion effort to appear oblivious that Thomas is in the same room as her. Penny blows out her candles and squeezes her eyes tightly as she makes her wish.

Across the room, I catch Harrison's eye and mouth, *I love you*. His eyes soften, and then mouths, *That's nice*.

It makes me laugh, and Harrison tries to hide his chuckle while he helps pass around slices of cake.

298

I glance around the group and, while it's only a tiny gathering, it's all we need. I love this restaurant. I've come to love it in a way that I always wished I loved it. It feels like home as it always should have, and I love that with Harrison running it, The Shark Biscuit stayed in the family after all.

–

Penny is asleep on Dad's lap while he continues to catch up with everyone, so I take the opportunity to duck away quietly. I slip off my shoes and dip my feet into the cool water as I rest against a stump on the jetty. It's my favourite place to relax. I can watch the ocean and see The Shark Biscuit at the same time.

Over the years, this jetty has become a place that holds my most beloved memories. The first was when Harrison and I decided to give our relationship a go – one of the best decisions of my life.

Almost two years later, I asked Harrison to meet me down here after work and revealed I was pregnant – unexpectedly pregnant, but overjoyed. I remember the shocked look on Harrison's face when I told him our news and how tight he hugged me as he whispered his love for me and our unborn baby into my ear. He cooked me every weird food craving throughout my pregnancy, including an unlimited supply of bug rolls.

The following year, we gathered here on a still afternoon to exchange our wedding vows. Only Dad, Thomas, Scout and Noah were invited to our intimate ceremony, and it was perfect. Penny slept in her uncle Thomas's arms until Harrison took her back, and she rested on his shoulder while we exchanged rings, the sun setting in the distance. A few fishermen clapped for us, which I loved and Harrison hated.

We did everything in the wrong order. Enemies. Friends for a few hours, which Harrison will never admit. Then lovers, then parents and then a married couple.

'At least I always know where to find my wife when she goes missing.' Harrison's voice drags me from my thoughts, and he joins me in cooling his feet in the water.

'Penny's still sleeping?'

Harrison takes my hand, kisses it briefly and then rests it on his thigh as he links our fingers.

'Nope. Scout's playing with her.'

'Does Scout need help?'

'Shouldn't you ask if Penny needs help?'

'Should we get back then?' I take my feet out, but Harrison gently holds my legs in place.

'In a minute. It's nice having a moment alone with you.'

I rest my head on his shoulder and Harrison's arm wraps around me as we mindlessly study the ocean.

After a few peaceful minutes, I say, 'Are Scout and Thomas going to be okay?'

'What do you mean by okay?'

'Okay, being in the same space?'

'I hope so. Thomas needs to pull his finger out and talk to her.'

The on–off nature of Thomas and Scout's relationship has given us all dizzy spells over the years, but when Scout left to travel throughout Australia, I thought they were done for good. From the pain in Thomas's eyes all afternoon, I'm guessing they're not done, or at least not to him.

'He still loves her?' I ask.

'I'd say so. You've seen his moods since she left.'

'I thought that was just because he has to work with you every day?'

Harrison nuzzles his nose into my hair and kisses the side of my head. It's still fun to tease him.

'I have some news,' says Harrison as he removes his arm and leans his elbows back on the jetty.

'News?'

'Noah wants to join the business. He's saved up some cash and wants to buy in.'

I sit with the idea for a moment before saying, 'I love that idea.'

'I do, too. It will give me more time at home.'

Juggling parenthood and our careers has been challenging, but we manage it. I work from home doing accounting three days a week, so it's flexible, and my introverted body loves it. It also allows me to help the boys with the books for The Shark Biscuit. They never let me leave entirely. I can still pull Harrison up if they overspend or have too much wastage.

Harrison helps me to my feet and leans in to kiss me softly.

He turns to walk back to the restaurant, but I tug on his hand.

'I have some news, too.' I was going to wait until we were home tonight and Penny was asleep, but it seems the jetty will be the setting for another memorable moment in our lives.

I wrap my arms around Harrison's neck and whisper over his lips, 'How would you feel about another baby?'

Harrison's fingers tighten on my hips as he pulls his head back a few inches to stare down at me with his signature Harrison quizzical look.

'That's not news, that's a question, but it makes me think you've been hiding a secret from me today.' A smile pulls at his lips because he can't help being excited about what he knows I'm about to say.

'I only did the test this morning.'

'That was at least seven hours ago. You've kept it a secret all day.'

'Well, you still haven't told me the secret ingredient in your mayonnaise. And we've been together for five years, so you're worse.'

Harrison throws back his head and laughs. He cups my face, kisses me on the lips, and peppers kisses towards my ear.

'There was never a secret ingredient. I just liked your attention while you tried to guess.'

'What?!' I try to pull out of his embrace, but he holds me firmly before I give in. I wrap my arms around him and kiss him until we hear wolf whistles from the deck of the restaurant.

Harrison pulls back and shoos away the hollers, which we know are coming from Scout and Noah.

'Are we having another baby, Agnes?' Harrison speaks softly and it makes me teary how excited I am and I know Harrison will be with our news.

'In seven months we will be. You happy?'

'This was all part of my plan. You know that.'

'Of course. It's been a brilliant plan, Harrison.'

I lean in and kiss him before Harrison whispers, 'I love you,' and I whisper back, 'That's nice.'

Acknowledgements

I've always loved contained stories – limited locations and tight time frames where you lock your characters together and see what happens. In 2022, my hometown, Brisbane, was hit with a 'rain bomb', a term I'd never heard and was described as a 'running river in the sky'. We received the same amount of rain in three days that London would typically receive over an entire year. This weather event and my love of seafood all formed the inspiration for *One Last Night*.

Thanks to some special people, The Shark Biscuit feels very real to me and I wish I could take each of you there to eat one of Harrison's bug rolls and have a cocktail made by Scout.

As always, thank you to my fabulous agent Megan, Annie, Rachel and the awesome team at Watson, Little.

To the hard-working team at Canelo: Emily, Thanhmai, Deirbhile, Nicola, Kate and Alicia, thank you for getting my books out into the world. Emily, thank you for your insightful edits, understanding Agnes, loving Harrison and getting them to shine.

To the Aussie team at Hardie Grant, thank you for all your brilliant work on my side of the world; it's much appreciated. Thank you to Emily Courdelle for another beautiful cover, copy editor Chere Tricot and proofreader Vicki Vrint.

I feel so fortunate to have found an amazing group of beta readers whose feedback is invaluable. To Stephanie, Bailee, Shika and Jen, thank you for your constructive comments on this story and for being so supportive that I feel safe sending you early drafts of my work.

Thank you to Mum and Michael for not blinking an eye when I turned up one night and asked you to design a seafood restaurant with me. Mum, thank you for being the first person to read my stories and helping The Shark Biscuit come to life.

Thank you to my family and friends for your love and for celebrating this time with me.

To the book and writing community – the biggest thank you! You are a fantastic bunch of people, and I'm so glad I found you. Thank you for your messages, reviews, support and friendship. If I could hug you all, I would, or I could ask Willy to dance for you.

Thank you to Steve, Poppy and Lyla for forgiving me when my mind drifts off to writing land, and filling our home with laughter and love.